Une éblouissante fantaisie en couleurs!
LE MAGICIEN D'OZ
JUDY GARLAND · FRANK MORGAN
BERT LAHR · RAY BOLGER
JACK HALEY · BILLIE BURKE · MARGARET HAMILTON
CHARLEY GRAPEWIN et les MUNCHKINS
Réalisation de VICTOR FLEMING
Metro Goldwyn Mayer

C.I.A.
Judy GARLAND
Frank MORGAN
Regia: VICTOR FLEMING
il MAGO di OZ
in TECHNICOLOR
PRODOTTO DA MERVYN LE ROY
ARTERO - ROMA

The WIZARD of OZ™
AN ILLUSTRATED
COMPANION TO THE
TIMELESS MOVIE CLASSIC

Wizard

The WIZARD of Oz™
AN ILLUSTRATED COMPANION TO THE TIMELESS MOVIE CLASSIC
John Fricke and Jonathan Shirshekan
Foreword by M-G-M "Munchkin" Margaret Pellegrini
FALL RIVER PRESS

This 2009 edition published by Fall River Press by arrangement with becker & mayer!

The Wizard of Oz: An Illustrated Companion is produced by becker&mayer!, Bellevue, WA.
www.beckermayer.com

Design: Todd Bates
Editorial: Amy Wideman and Kristin Mehus-Roe
Image Coordination: Chris Campbell
Production Coordination: Diane Ross

Fall River Press
122 Fifth Avenue
New York, NY 10011

ISBN: 978-1-4351-1704-4

Printed and bound in China

10 9 8 7 6 5 4 3 2 1

For laughter, for love, for life: for Kellen.
— John Fricke

To my parents, for bestowing upon me
the brain, heart, and courage to succeed
and for elucidating the sanctity of home.
— Jonathan Shirshekan

ENDPAPER ART: Across the years and across the miles with M-G-M's *The Wizard of Oz*. Front endpapers, left page: 1939 three-sheet poster; 1939 window card (top); 1949 reissue title lobby card (bottom). Right page: *Le Magicien d'Oz* (France, 1946); *Il Mago di Oz* (Italy, 1947; courtesy The Willard Carroll Collection). Rear endpapers, left page: 1988 home video cover art; 1970 one-sheet reissue poster. Right page: 1939 title lobby card (top); front-of-house scene still (bottom; Great Britain, 1940); 1989 fiftieth anniversary home video cover art.

CONTENTS

6 . . . Foreword: There's No Place Like Oz

8 . . . It's Always Best to Start at the Beginning: L. Frank Baum and the Road to Oz

26 . . . Follow the Yellow Brick Road: Pre-Production

54 . . . Special Section: When the Moon Comes Over the Munchkins—Or, Taking the Bus to Oz

60 . . . Over the Rainbow: How *Oz* Came to the Screen

114 . . . You're Off to See the Wizard: The Promotional Campaign

144 . . . Special Section: The Oddities of Oz

150 . . . The Merry Old Land of *Oz*: Best-Loved Motion Picture of All Time

160 . . . We Thank You Very Sweetly: Acknowledgments and Image Credits

THERE'S NO PLACE LIKE OZ

I've never forgotten that day. Now, more than seventy years later, I guess it's safe to say I never will.

I was fifteen, back home in Sheffield, Alabama, when I got a letter from a Hollywood agent, Thelma Weiss. She asked if I'd come be in *The Wizard of Oz*.

Wow!

My dad took that letter to the owner of the hotel where he worked, and they wrote back to her for me. They wanted something explained, about transportation and room and board and all. She sent an answer right away, and everything was okay. Before I knew it—it was November 1938, I think on a Tuesday—I was on my way.

Just before getting off the train in Los Angeles, I met another little lady, Leona Parks; we got ourselves acquainted. And there was a chauffeur and limousine waiting for the two of us, so we went right straight to M-G-M, where Leo Singer had the contract for The Munchkins. We signed through him—that's when we signed our lives away!—and got to work.

Rehearsals were held in a room like a warehouse. They gave us a script; Mr. Becker was the piano player who taught the songs. When we got those down good, Dona Massin picked out the little ones who could dance. (The ones who couldn't kinda got put in the background.) In another room, they had bleachers set up to show how the set was going to be, and we learned to go up and down without falling. Then we went to wardrobe to be measured for costumes and our little pointed-toe shoes. And hats! Mine was blue—it looked like a flowerpot. People sometimes ask how to find me in the movie, I always say: look for the blue flowerpot! (When Billy Curtis sings, "And, oh! What happened then was rich!" I'm just to his left.) I got measured for a second costume, too: a pink nightgown and bonnet with white lace trimming. In that outfit, I was put in the Sleepyhead nest—I'm second in the back. That nest was beautiful; it was pink satin. Even the eggs were lined in satin.

It took five weeks to rehearse us and make the clothes. Then we did two weeks of actual filming. We'd get there at six a.m. and go right to makeup. They had a lineup of chairs; I called them the musical chairs. In the first one, they'd put on our base. Then we'd move to another for lipstick and so on; we must have gone through ten chairs. By the end, we were made up, and our hair was done. Then we'd go to wardrobe, get dressed, and go to the set.

That's when we saw Judy Garland. It was a wonderful time for her, especially that Christmas, when M-G-M gave her a private dressing room on wheels—her own trailer. In those days, that meant you were officially a star. She was so excited. They had it veiled over, in a corner, with a big red ribbon on it. When she came to work, everyone hollered, "Merry Christmas!" They gave her a scissors, and she cut the ribbon. Then she invited us to line up and go through the trailer; when we came out, she gave each Munchkin a personally autographed picture. Mine says, "To Margaret, from your pal, Judy." I still have it. Later, she explained that she couldn't afford gifts for 124 people, but she brought in the biggest box of candy I've ever seen; I guess it was twenty-five pounds. (To me, it looked like 100 pounds!) She put it down on The Yellow Brick Road and said, "Sweets for the sweet!"

Billie Burke had her dressing room over to the side. She would bring out a chair and sit down; I'd go by there and talk. Other M-G-M stars used to come in, too. They were fascinated by so many little people. Mickey Rooney came every day at lunch to see Judy. I got to take Norma Shearer's children up the stairs, show them the Sleepyhead nest, and down and around and back over to her. I got her autograph, and Eleanor Powell's, and Victor McLaglen's; I met Lew Ayres in the commissary. But I kept saying, "I've gotta meet

ABOVE: Billie Burke, Judy Garland, and The Munchkins, December 1938. Margaret Pellegrini is just to the right of Judy's left hand; a frond almost obscures her flowerpot hat. **RIGHT:** Sauntering down the aisle, tray in hand, Margaret joins fellow villagers for a catered lunch on an M-G-M soundstage.

Clark Gable!" Finally, Dolly Kramer introduced me . . . to his double. I never met Clark; that's the story of my life!

On our last day, they picked around ten little people for touch-up shots and stills. When Billie Burke started to sing, "Come out, come out . . . ," I was down underneath, hiding in the bushes. They told us when to pop up. And they were lucky they got the shot, because right after that, I got a nosebleed! Mervyn LeRoy came straight over, picked me out of the bushes, and carried me to First Aid.

When we finished, the mother of a little girl who danced in the picture asked if I'd like to go home with them. They offered to show me around Hollywood, because I really didn't have a chance to sightsee while we were working. They wrote my dad for permission; I stayed three weeks. Then they put me on the train to Alabama. But I hadn't been home long before I got word to come and work again for Mr. Singer.

During that time, the movie had its premiere. We were playing at The Treasure Island World's Fair in San Francisco, and Mr. Singer picked Karl Slover, Nita Krebs, and me to go to the theater to make an appearance. They put up a table in the lobby, and we autographed as the audience went in. When the movie came on, we got to go in and sit down. I was all eyes. When I saw myself, I got so excited. I started bouncing up and down: "It's me! It's me! There I am!"

I stayed in show business for several more years. Then in 1943, I got married, and my family became my life. My husband was average-size, an ex-fighter, Willie Pellegrini. We had a son and daughter; now I have five grandchildren, ten great-grandchildren, and two great-great grandchildren.

But everything changed again in 1985. Tod Machin—one of the nicest, finest Oz fans—helped organize an event in Kansas with three of us Munchkins. It was our first reunion in more than forty years, but once people knew we were available, offers started coming from all over. It took me a while to realize how many people love *The Wizard of Oz*, but I found out! In 1989, I met John Fricke; we've done appearances together ever since. Eventually, we made him an honorary Munchkin, because he always sees that we're looked after. He knows the questions to ask, so audiences hear our best stories. And I love to tease him—onstage, off-stage, or anywhere. (Someday, I'll tell you about the night I slept with his head on my bosom . . .) Jonathan Shirshekan is a newer friend, and a younger friend, but he sure knows his Oz!

It's amazing now to look back at over two decades of Oz festivals and traveling and autographing. I've met so many fans, all over the United States, on the Munchkin cruises—even in Australia. Recently, I had a reunion with the girl whose family I stayed with in 1939, Priscilla Montgomery. We pretty much picked up right where we left off.

It's all because of that movie. In my lifetime, there hasn't been a greater experience than *The Wizard of Oz*. I just can't believe it—even now. I love it, and there'll never be another like it. And I'm so happy and so honored to have a part in it.

— Margaret Pellegrini

THIS PAGE: "The Royal Historian of Oz" with the first-edition cover of his masterwork and the final color plate from that book, drawn by W.W. Denslow. It depicts four of fiction's most famous characters in their encounter with Glinda, Good Witch of the South.

IT'S ALWAYS BEST TO START AT THE BEGINNING

L. Frank Baum and the Road to Oz

There are movies that can be classified as popular or critical favorites. There are movies that can be repeatedly shown, providing surprises whenever they're seen. There are movies that appeal to a cross-generational audience, stirring everyone from preschoolers to senior citizens. And there are movies that have stood the test of time, entertaining virtually all who watch them, year after year.

Then there's *The Wizard of Oz*—which fulfills all of those classifications and more.

In 1970, it was estimated that *Oz* "may well have been enjoyed by more people than any other entertainment production in history." In the intervening decades, the audience for the film has never stopped growing. It's safe to say that it's now much more than a motion picture; its characters, songs, dialogue, and settings have become so familiar that they're part of everyday American life.

There's some justice in this. When published in 1900, L. Frank Baum's *The Wonderful Wizard of Oz* was regarded as the first "American fairy tale." It told of a Kansas girl, swept away by the kind of storm germane to those prairies. In her ensuing adventures, she met a scarecrow, a creation common to every farm in her native country. She rescued a man built of tin, the simple metal used to make the cans on the pantry shelf back home. She conquered a threatening lion, who turned out to be a scaredy-cat. Best of all, she exhibited a

ABOVE: Artist W. W. Denslow (1856-1915). His illustrations for *The Wonderful Wizard of Oz* immeasurably contributed to the book's success. "The pictures surpass anything of the kind hitherto attempted," praised The Louisville *Courier-Journal*; other critics concurred.

spirit, loyalty, and faith that defined the best characteristics of America at the turn of the century.

The success of Baum's tale created a demand from thousands of children for "more about Oz!" By the time Judy Garland sang "Over the Rainbow" in 1939, there had already been earlier motion pictures that depicted Dorothy's escapades. There had been stage musicals and radio dramatizations. There was a still-expanding series of (to that date) thirty-three Oz books, "founded on and continuing the famous [Baum] stories."

All of this grew from the imagination of one man. Born May 15, 1856, in Chittenango, New York, Lyman Frank Baum is best summarized as a born writer and entertainer. It took him forty years to settle into his natural calling, but once there, the impact he made was immeasurable.

Baum's road to Oz was far from a smoothly paved yellow brick path. Early on, he led a cosseted childhood in upstate New York, indulged by his well-to-do father. As a teen, he issued a family newspaper, portions of which he wrote and which he self-printed. As a young man, he authored guides for stamp collectors and chicken breeders and dabbled in acting. He wrote script, music, and lyrics for a melodrama, *The Maid of Arran* (1882), in which he played the leading role. He served as a traveling salesman for a family company that manufactured axle grease. He then relocated to Aberdeen, South Dakota, to run a specialty store and edit a weekly paper. After a move to Chicago in 1891, he worked as a reporter and traveling salesman.

The variety of Baum's careers was matched by the fates that curtailed them. His play was successful until fire destroyed its scenery. The lubricant company fell victim to an employee's embezzlement and suicide. His store and newspaper failed in the wake of Dakota drought. And his own health forced Baum off the road after a few seasons.

By 1896, at age forty, he was a married father of four. The one constant in his life (apart from an indefatigable "never say die" attitude) was this family bond, exemplified by Baum's life-long penchant for making up fantasies to entertain children—his own or those of neighbors. The tales he fabricated night after night were fascinating to youngsters in those years before movies, radio, or television. The adults who overheard Baum were no less enthusiastic; his mother-in-law, the formidable women's rights activist Matilda Joslyn Gage, told Frank that he was a fool if he didn't write down the stories and try to sell them.

Acknowledging her dictum, Baum began his real life's mission. In 1897, he authored *Mother Goose in Prose*, expanding the back-stories of classic nursery rhymes. Two years later, he really hit his stride when a picture book of nonsense verse for children went to press as *Father Goose, His Book*. It was the best-selling juvenile of 1899, aided in its appeal by the uproarious pictures of William Wallace Denslow.

Even before the success of *Father Goose*, Baum and Denslow regarded themselves as a team and contracted to produce *The City of Oz*, a full-length children's novel that grew out of Baum's storytelling. The book would be called *The Emerald City, From Kansas to Fairyland, The City of the Great Oz, The Great Oz, The Fairyland of Oz*, and *The Land of Oz* before reaching stores in 1900 as *The Wonderful Wizard of Oz*.

While not the immediate sensation of *Father Goose, Oz* sold well and was joyously received by children, adults, and critics. Baum's creations were favorably compared with those of (among others) Lewis Carroll, Hans Christian Andersen, and The Brothers Grimm. Reviewers not only recognized him as the sole American in the crowd but endorsed his thesis, detailed in the book's introduction: "The time has come for a series of newer 'wonder tales' in which . . . are eliminated . . . all the horrible and blood-curdling incident devised by their authors to point a fearsome moral to each tale." Baum sagely continued, "The modern child seeks only entertainment," and that awareness on his part would lead him to establish an inviolate foundation for joy.

The success of *The Wonderful Wizard of Oz* spurred almost instant legends and claims. Baum was widely quoted on the source of a name for his magic land: "I have a little cabinet letter-file on my desk that is just in front of me. My gaze was caught by the gilt letters on the three drawers of the cabinet. The first was A-G; the next drawer was labeled H-N; and on the last were the letters O-Z. And 'Oz' it at once became." Though he set his opening chapter in Kansas, Baum's description of the difficulties undergone by Aunt Em and Uncle Henry was drawn from his exposure to the drought that decimated the Dakota Territory a decade earlier. And although many "Dorothys" told press and public that they were the inspiration for Baum's heroine, family historian Dr. Sally Roesch Wagner has written that the girl's namesake was quite possibly Frank and Maud's niece, Dorothy Louise Gage. The infant daughter of Maud's brother and his wife had died at five months in 1898; Maud was devastated and, having given her four sons, Frank restored to Maud her Dorothy in the role of the Oz protagonist.

In the three years after publication of *The Wonderful Wizard of Oz*, Baum wrote several well-received, popular children's fantasies: *Dot and Tot of Merryland, The Life and Adventures of Santa Claus, The Magical Monarch of Mo*, and *The Enchanted Island of Yew*. But their success was dwarfed when producer Fred Hamlin and director Julian Mitchell developed *The Wizard of Oz* into a stage extravaganza. Opening in Chicago in 1902, the show became a New York blockbuster the following year. Between its original company, second company, and other touring productions, *Oz* played throughout the United States for seven seasons, grossed almost five and a half million dollars, and was seen by approximately six million people.

The play was the theatrical phenomenon of its age, although Baum's story was largely abandoned in favor of irrelevant songs, madcap comedy, and massive spectacle. Audiences sat wide-eyed through the cyclone and poppy field sequences and that magic moment when the Scarecrow was taken apart and reassembled onstage. Dorothy, her three companions, The Wizard, and The Witch of the North all figured in the scenario, but so did Sir Dashemoff Daily, a young poet in love with the now-teenage Kansan, and Cynthia Cynch, a "lady lunatic" in love with the Tin Woodman. Pastoria II and Trixie Tryfle also made the cyclonic ride to Oz; he was a streetcar conductor and ex-king, and she was a Topeka waitress. Villainous Sir Wiley Gile supplied general intrigue, and Dorothy's cow, Imogene, handled the comic relief. Adding to the show's popular appeal,

ABOVE LEFT: Denslow's sketch of Baum appeared with the introduction of *Father Goose, His Book* (1899). **ABOVE:** Fred A. Stone is shown as first discovered onstage by Dorothy in the 1902 musical. **LEFT**: This souvenir folio for the *Oz* stage play included melody line and lyrics for three Baum/Paul Tietjens numbers written for the score as well as songs by others.

ABOVE: Baum at his summer home in Macatawa, Michigan, where the family vacationed for over a decade. **LEFT:** The 1908 *Fairylogue and Radio-Plays* dramatized episodes from several Oz books and from the non-Oz fantasy, *John Dough and the Cherub.*

ABOVE LEFT: John R. Neill (1877-1943) provided artwork for every Oz series book from 1904-42, definitively defining Oz for generations of readers. **ABOVE RIGHT:** Much as *The Wonderful Wizard of Oz* title was simplified, *The Marvelous Land of Oz* (1904) lost its adjective circa 1906. Neill's cover art created an exemplary segue between his style and that of Denslow.

two dozen young women gaily disported themselves in gingham, flower costumes, and tights as farm workers, poppies, and the Emerald City marching "patrol."

Sharing top honors were Fred A. Stone and David C. Montgomery as The Scarecrow and Tin Woodman. Their interplay had been honed in eight preceding years of vaudeville, but they came to their first top-flight showcase in *Oz*. As Baum's characters, their topical jokes and variable repertoire were so fresh and effective that they quickly became the talk of the nation, long before such celebrity could be easily and electronically bandied about.

The popularity of the show also impacted on Baum's writing plans. Virtually from its publication, *Oz* inspired children to correspond with the author. ("You wrote a nice book. I couldn't write a book like that. I think I love you.") Many asked for a sequel. With the runaway triumph and ongoing tours of the play, Baum's mail doubled and then tripled. Finally, with an eye toward another story that could be adapted for the stage, he wrote *The Further Adventures of the Scarecrow and Tin Woodman*. At the last minute, and at the urging of a Chicago bookseller, Baum reworked the title to include the word "Oz," and *The Marvelous Land of Oz* (1904) was issued to the same glee won by its predecessor. The book was illustrated by John R. Neill, as Baum and Denslow had parted professional company over disagreements about the division of royalties from the 1902 musical. Neill's Irish fancies extended to his excellent draftsmanship and expert turn of pen; he was an ideal choice to continue the Oz tradition.

Although *The Woggle-Bug* (1905)—the musical based on the second Oz book—was a failure, Baum's reading audience remained primed for anything he offered. There were excellent fantasies in *Queen Zixi of Ix* (1905), *John Dough and the Cherub* (1906), *The Sea Fairies* (1911), and *Sky Island* (1912). He adopted a series of pseudonyms and turned out other stories and booklets for children, five different series for teenagers, and three adult novels. Baum's passion for the stage continued as well; between 1903 and 1917, he contemplated some two dozen theatrical ventures, most of which never reached completion.

But increasingly, his world centered on Oz and, by demand, he continued to write Oz books. He brought Dorothy back into the stories with *Ozma of Oz* (1907), *Dorothy and the Wizard in Oz* (1908; per the title, she was joined by another favorite); and *The Road to Oz* (1909). In *The Emerald City of Oz* (1910), the Kansas child moved permanently to the title location with her aunt, uncle, and Toto in tow. Then Baum tried to conclude his Oz work, announcing that Glinda the Good had made the country invisible to all outsiders, protecting it from any possible hostile invasion. As a result, he had no way of garnering the latest news from the magic land.

Baum's audience was miserable. By this time, he was their "Royal Historian of Oz," whose writings transcribed events as they happened in a legitimate if "imagi"-nation.

ABOVE LEFT: "My Wonderful Dream Girl" was the hit ballad from *The Tik-Tok Man of Oz* (1913), and one of the few songs in the score for which Baum did not provide the lyric. **ABOVE CENTER:** French acrobat Pierre Couderc appeared onscreen as *The Patchwork Girl of Oz* (1914); the jovial Woozy was "personated" by Fred Woodward. **RIGHT:** Baum's early optimism for The Oz Film Co. is reflected in this announcement of its first production.

Over the next two years, the author attempted to win them with other fantasies. But the new books failed to match the selling power of the Oz series, and when his own financial problems became acute, Baum re-established communication with the Emerald City by wireless telegraph. (One of his young readers had provided him with that ingenious idea.) From 1913 through 1920, there was a new Oz book every year.

Oz remained predominant as well in the theatrical efforts that he actually saw through to production:

- The 1908 *Fairylogue and Radio-Plays* "starred" Baum himself, narrating a multimedia program of hand-colored silent films and lantern slides, accompanied by a live orchestra. A complex, ground-breaking entertainment, the venture cost more to produce and tour than it grossed at the box office and closed after three months. Its failure sent Baum into bankruptcy in 1911.
- Three one-reel Oz films were produced by Colonel William Selig of Chicago in 1910. His studio had been utilized in the filming of some *Radio-Plays* footage, and Baum gave Selig the movie rights to several books in compensation for his debt. All three films utilized characters and situations from the first Oz book, along with pantomimed dance moments meant to emulate the 1902 musical. Only the first, *The Wonderful Wizard of Oz*, is known to survive. Upon release, it was praised in *Moving Picture World*: "The reproduction of a story of this character is an achievement of sufficient importance to attract more than the usual degree of interest. . . . The reputation for this house for producing striking and unusual films is too well established to require further description. An excellent film, well acted and clearly photographed."
- *The Tik-Tok Man of Oz* came to the 1913 musical stage, rewritten by Baum from a 1909 script (originally *Ozma of Oz* or *The Girl from Oz*). More happily received than *The Woggle-Bug*, *Tik-Tok* toured the West Coast and Midwest, although it was never successful enough to risk a New York engagement. Charlotte Greenwood and Charlie Ruggles appeared in *Tik-Tok* at the onset of their careers, later winning great public affection as movie character actors.
- The Oz Film Manufacturing Company was launched by Baum and a consortium of Los Angeles businessmen in 1914. They hoped to "picturize" his entire oeuvre, but their first effort, *The Patchwork Girl of Oz*, was detrimentally reviewed as "children's entertainment." After producing *The Magic Cloak of Oz*, *His Majesty, the Scarecrow of Oz*, some fairy tale shorts, and two movies conceived for adults, the company shut down in 1915.

ABOVE: "Ozcot" was the name Frank Baum devised for the Hollywood home he and wife Maud built in 1910.

ABOVE: The 1921 Oz book was credited to Baum, but "enlarged and edited by Ruth Plumly Thompson" (1891–1976). This was the publishers' ploy to effect a transition between authors; *The Royal Book of Oz* was entirely Thompson's work. In addition to nineteen volumes in the official forty-book series, Thompson wrote two later Oz stories, published by The International Wizard of Oz Club in 1972 and 1976.

None of this output approached the achievement of the 1902 musical. Fortunately, apart from the *Radio-Plays*, Baum had no money in the productions, though they took their toll of his health. In 1910, he and Maud relocated to Hollywood, then a quiet suburb of Los Angeles, and he continued to write his books. For relaxation, he raised prize-winning flowers, cultivated songbirds, went on golf outings, and met with young fans. But angina, gall bladder, and appendix ailments kept Baum bedridden for the last sixteen months of his life. He passed away on May 6, 1919, just short of his sixty-third birthday. His publishers, however, had no intention of letting Oz die with its creator. Baum's final two Oz books were published posthumously and, by 1921, Ruth Plumly Thompson had been contracted as the new "Royal Historian." Bright and young, Thompson provided verve, imagination, and an annual Oz book (coupled with Neill art) for the next nineteen years.

Spurred by the vigor of her work during the 1920s, formal and informal dramatizations sprang up. Thompson wrote *Scraps in Oz* (aka *A Day in Oz*), which was produced at department stores and book fairs beginning in 1925. Between 1928 and 1937, The Junior League Plays scripted five Baum titles, including *The Wizard of Oz*, for presentation by community theaters, service organizations, and schools.

At the same time, Baum's son, Frank Joslyn Baum, pursued Hollywood concerns in an effort to bring his father's work to the silent screen. Negotiations with Metro-Goldwyn-Mayer barely reached the talking stage; instead he sold *The Wizard of Oz* to Chadwick Pictures in 1924. Their film, a heinous mélange of slapstick and pointless original plotlines, is now almost unwatchable and gains its historical footnote only because of its title and the presence of Oliver Hardy. Just prior to his screen partnership with Stan Laurel, Hardy appeared here as a farmhand who disguises himself as a Tin Man.

In 1932, Baum's son leased film rights to the Ethel Meglin Kiddies performing group; their two-reel *Land of Oz* quickly disappeared. Animator Ted Eshbaugh contracted with him for an Oz cartoon in 1933, but complications with the Technicolor Corporation limited its distribution. Meanwhile, Baum's widow Maud had better luck when she placed radio rights with NBC and Jell-O. During the 1933-34 season, thousands of children from the East Coast to the Rockies were introduced to Baum's characters via a twenty-six week network hookup. Oz programs were performed "live" from New York every Monday, Wednesday, and Friday afternoon; the scripts were adapted from *The Wizard of Oz*, as well as (however loosely in places) *The Land of Oz*, *Ozma of Oz*, *Dorothy and the Wizard in Oz*, *The Road to Oz*, and *The Emerald City of Oz*.

Such omnipresence, along with the annual publication of a new book, meant that Oz remained paramount in many Hollywood minds. The fact that movies had learned

LEFT: A 1925 *Wizard of Oz* still shows Larry Semon and Dorothy Dwan; the latter played her namesake in the film. **BELOW:** Semon was the force behind this version. His clowning was internationally appreciated, but he overextended his activities and health and died at thirty-nine in 1928. **RIGHT:** Nancy Kelly, Bill Adams, and Jack Smart posed in Oz garb never seen by 1933-34 radio audiences. (Not shown: Agnes Moorehead—later mainstay of TV's *Bewitched*—who voiced witches, the evil Queen of the Scoodlers, the haughty Princess Langwidere, and a cow.)

to talk and sing since the 1925 film was an additional boon. In 1933, M-G-M again considered *The Wizard of Oz* as both a potential feature and cartoon series, but the ideas were rejected. It's also possible that Baum's son backed away from an M-G-M deal, as he'd won interest in *The Wizard of Oz* from producer Samuel Goldwyn. After months of negotiation, Goldwyn paid $40,000 for screen rights to *Oz* and announced the picture in late summer 1933 as a Technicolor vehicle for Eddie Cantor. Cantor, a Broadway star since 1917, was a recent movie favorite, showcased in Goldwyn's *Whoopee, Palmy Days, The Kid from Spain,* and *Roman Scandals.* To support Cantor as the Scarecrow, the producer publicized the idea of casting other top box office names and pursued theatrical wunderkind Moss Hart as scenarist. Hart thought the project eminently worthy but stipulated that it should be a musical and agreed to participate if Goldwyn could convince legendary songwriter Irving Berlin to write the score. Hart and Berlin had just enjoyed New York success with their collaboration on *As Thousands Cheer* (1933). But in December 1933, Berlin declined the *Oz* offer, so Goldwyn tabled the picture and cast Cantor in *Kid Millions.* Over the next two years, the producer occasionally reconsidered *Oz*; in early 1936, Marcia Mae Jones received praise for her work in Goldwyn's *These Three*, and her name was put forward as a potential screen Dorothy.

But by that time, another performer seemed not only logical but ideal. Shirley Temple's interest in Oz was sometimes mentioned in feature stories about that preeminent star. Several journalists suggested the diminutive charmer as the perfect Dorothy, if someone would just make the film. In hopes of getting the project beyond gossip, Ruth Thompson suggested that the Oz book publishers gift Temple with some of the series for publicity purposes.

Meanwhile, Goldwyn retained the *Oz* film rights, while Temple was contracted to Twentieth Century Fox. It wasn't until late 1937 that Hollywood again exhibited any active passion for *The Wizard of Oz*, and it finally took a coalescence of several forces to realize the motion picture the world would come to know. Not at all coincidentally, each of those forces shared—in individual ways—the same communicative power for entertainment as L. Frank Baum himself.

LEFT: The Oz books for 1910 and 1909. Whatever the title, locale, or protagonists, Neill often crafted stunning cover art to highlight characters and settings best loved by Oz fans.

"We had four boys, and my husband used to tell them stories when they were young. He could rattle on and on with no effort. People say he took his characters from real life, but that's not true. He made every bit of it up out of his head. He had one of the most vivid imaginations I've ever known. There was nothing he couldn't do. A publisher once said that if he ever wanted to revise the Bible, he would get Frank to do it!"

— Mrs. L. Frank (Maud Gage) Baum

ABOVE: Maud Gage Baum and her four sons in 1900, the year *The Wonderful Wizard of Oz* was published. From left: Robert (fourteen), Harry (ten), Kenneth (nine), and Frank Joslyn (sixteen).

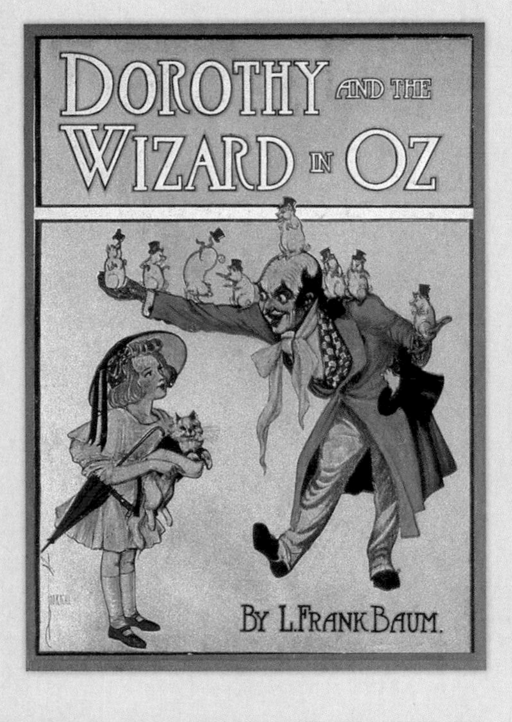

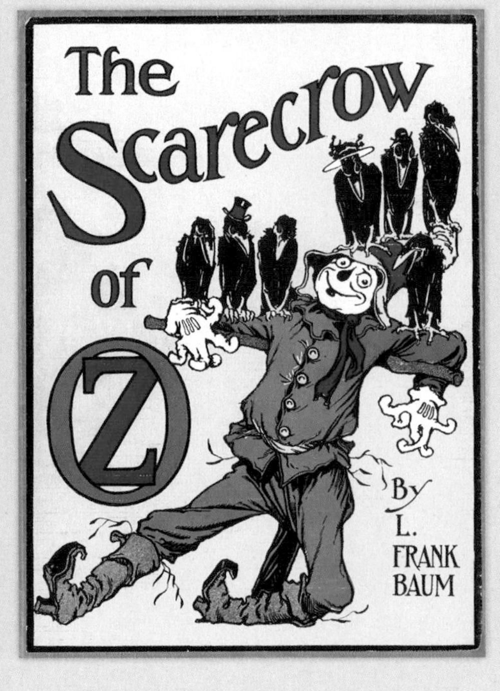

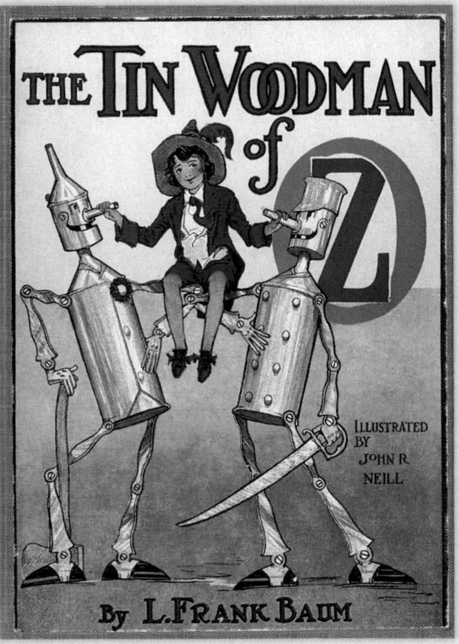

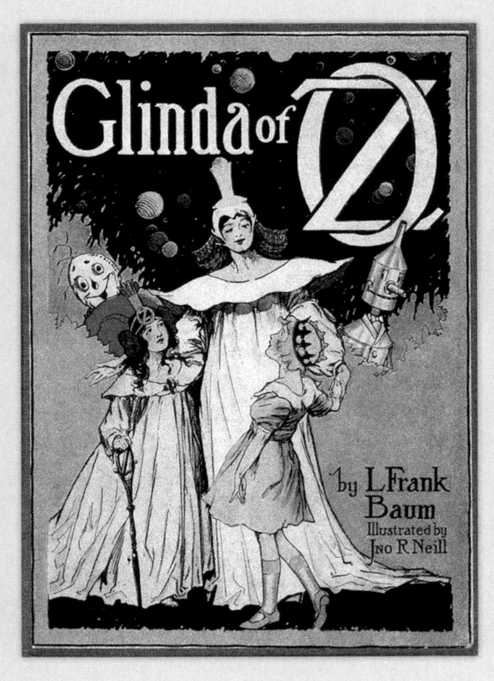

FAR LEFT: The Oz books for 1908, 1915, (below) 1918, and 1920. Baum built several later stories around new adventures of familiar faces. **NEAR LEFT:** Thompson continued the tradition with *The Cowardly Lion of Oz* (1923).

BELOW: Baum and his ever-loyal constituents, California (1908).

"L. Frank Baum is dead, and the children, if they knew it, would mourn. . . . [they] have suffered a loss they do not know. Years from now, though they cannot clamor for the newest Oz book, the crowding generations will plead for the old ones."

— The New York Times, *May 11, 1919*

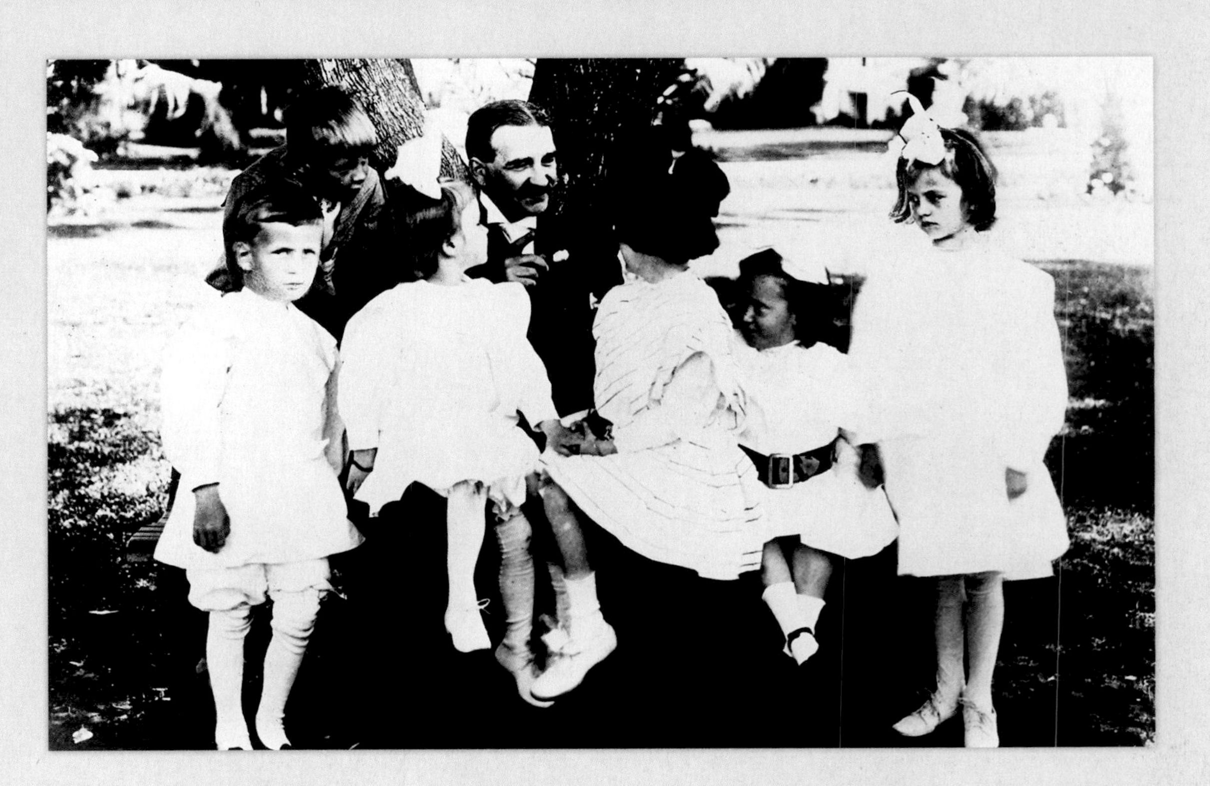

ABOVE: Vaudevillians David C. Montgomery and Fred A. Stone came to fame via Oz. Their subsequent triumphs included *The Red Mill, The Old Town, The Lady of the Slipper*, and *Chin Chin*. After Montgomery's death in 1917, Stone continued in *Jack O'Lantern* (where, in one performance, he dazzled a young audience member named Ray Bolger), *Tip Top, Stepping Stones, Criss-Cross, Three Cheers*, and *Ripples*. Stone is best remembered today for the 1935 film, *Alice Adams,* in which he played Katharine Hepburn's father. **RIGHT:** In 1904, Baum gratefully dedicated the second Oz book to the team who'd made such a success of the stage *Wizard*; Neill sketched them "in character."

"On June 16, 1902, *The Wizard of Oz* opened in Chicago at the Grand Opera House and, from opening night, it was a tremendous hit. It was clean as a whistle. There were lots of people who declared that stage entertainment without sophistication was doomed to failure in New York, but we proved them wrong. We opened the new Majestic Theatre on Columbus Circle in January 1903; we filled the house for a year and later came back to the Academy of Music and [other New York theaters]. Dave Montgomery and I played *The Wizard* for four years, and other companies carried it on for two more years, with several road shows traveling all over the country. The Scarecrow was a strenuous part. The width of the average stage is 32 feet, and somebody once figured that during the run of the show, I danced from New York to San Francisco."

— Fred Stone

To those excellent good fellows and eminent comedians David C. Montgomery and Fred A Stone whose clever personations of the Tin Woodman and the Scarecrow have delighted thousands of children throughout the land, this book is gratefully dedicated by The Author

> "In the early years of the [twentieth] century, any VIP visiting New York was always given the same preferred treatment: During the day, he saw the Statue of Liberty and Grant's Tomb, then dinner at Rector's or Delmonico's, and in the evening, *The Wizard of Oz*, starring David C. Montgomery and Fred Stone. . . . Although it had little resemblance to Baum's fairy tale, somehow enough of the book's charm clung to it to make the elaborate production probably the best-loved play in the history of the American theater. Even today, people who can remember having seen *The Wizard* speak of it with a nostalgic affection never accorded any other play."
>
> — *author/historian Daniel Mannix, 1968*

TOP RIGHT: The stage version of *The Wizard* was an unprecedented success, but Baum's later musicals failed to match its popularity. **ABOVE LEFT:** *The Woggle-Bug* (1905) closed in five weeks, playing only Milwaukee and Chicago. **INSET:** The button was an offshoot of a 1904 campaign for the second Oz book, in which that "very big bug" debuted. ("What Did the Woggle-Bug Say?" was a Baum-authored song and tied in with the newspaper serial, "Queer Visitors from the Marvelous Land of Oz.") **ABOVE CENTER:** The Woggle-Bug gained such familiarity that he inspired a non-Baum spinoff in the "March Humoresque." **RIGHT:** *The Tik-Tok Man of Oz* (1913) was happily received in Los Angeles, San Francisco, and on most of its tour. But Chicago critics were only mildly enthusiastic, unfavorably comparing the show to the rapturously remembered *Wizard*.

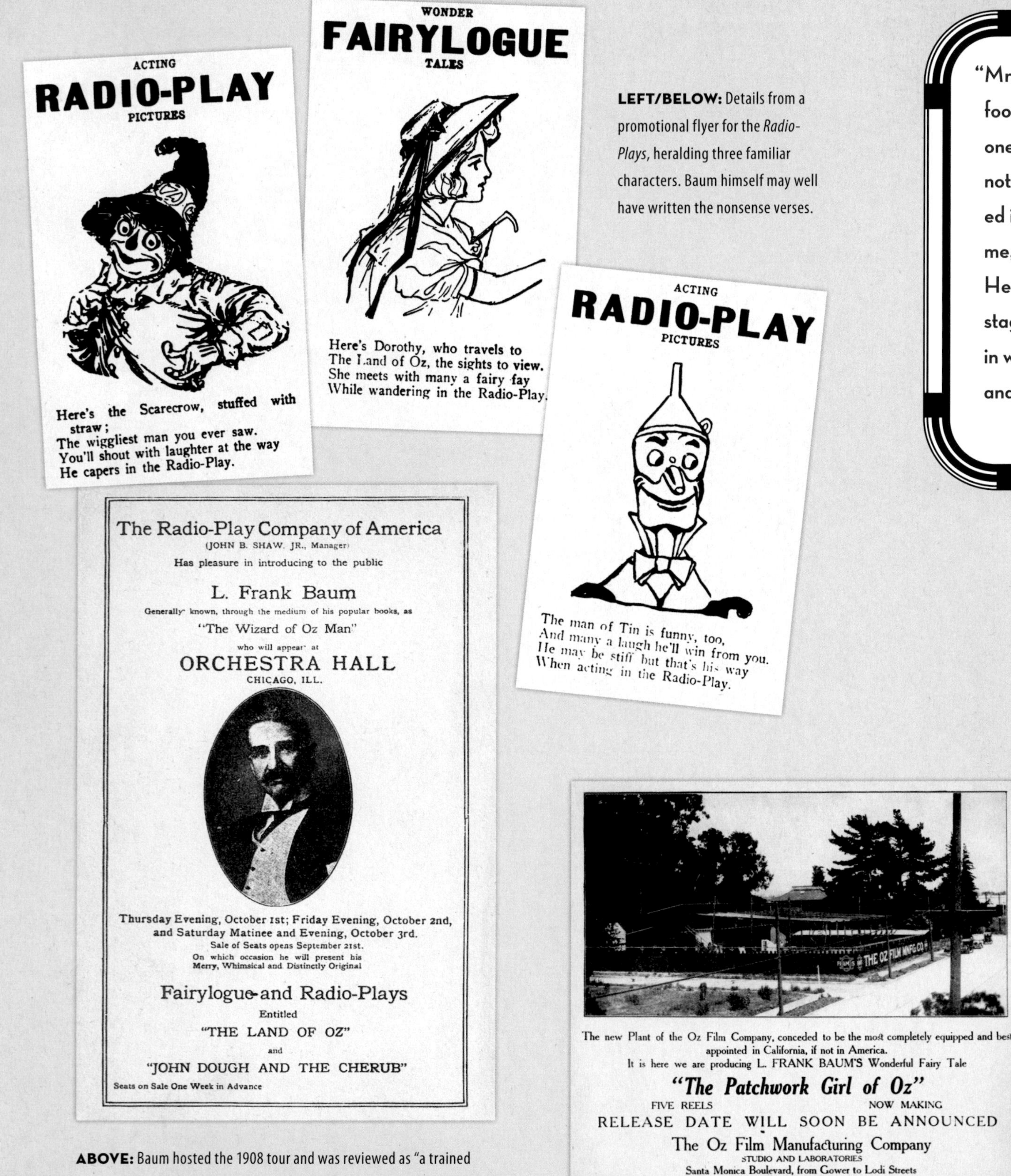

The Radio-Play Company of America
(JOHN B. SHAW, JR., Manager)
Has pleasure in introducing to the public
L. Frank Baum
Generally known, through the medium of his popular books, as
"The Wizard of Oz Man"
who will appear at
ORCHESTRA HALL
CHICAGO, ILL.

Thursday Evening, October 1st; Friday Evening, October 2nd, and Saturday Matinee and Evening, October 3rd.
Sale of Seats opens September 21st.
On which occasion he will present his
Merry, Whimsical and Distinctly Original
Fairylogue and Radio-Plays
Entitled
"THE LAND OF OZ"
and
"JOHN DOUGH AND THE CHERUB"
Seats on Sale One Week in Advance

The new Plant of the Oz Film Company, conceded to be the most completely equipped and best appointed in California, if not in America.
It is here we are producing L. FRANK BAUM'S Wonderful Fairy Tale
"The Patchwork Girl of Oz"
FIVE REELS NOW MAKING
RELEASE DATE WILL SOON BE ANNOUNCED
The Oz Film Manufacturing Company
STUDIO AND LABORATORIES
Santa Monica Boulevard, from Gower to Lodi Streets
Los Angeles, California

LEFT/BELOW: Details from a promotional flyer for the *Radio-Plays,* heralding three familiar characters. Baum himself may well have written the nonsense verses.

"Mr. Otis Turner directed [the 1908 *Fairylogue and Radio-Plays* footage], but Mr. Baum superintended everything. He went from one set to another to give directions—always in a calm voice . . . not aggressive, very calm. When he gave an order, they respected it. I thought a great deal of Frank Baum, and I think he liked me, too. He never talked down to me; he talked to me as an adult. He had a wonderful rapport with the audience; when he came on stage, you could feel that magnetic rapport. He was dressed all in white . . . very genteel, but without being cold. He had warmth and graciousness. I think he loved people very much."

— Romola Remus [Dunlap], the first motion-picture "Dorothy Gale," 1984

ABOVE: Baum hosted the 1908 tour and was reviewed as "a trained public speaker of abilities unusual in a writer. . . . his ability to hold a large audience's attention during two hours of tenuous entertainment was amply demonstrated."

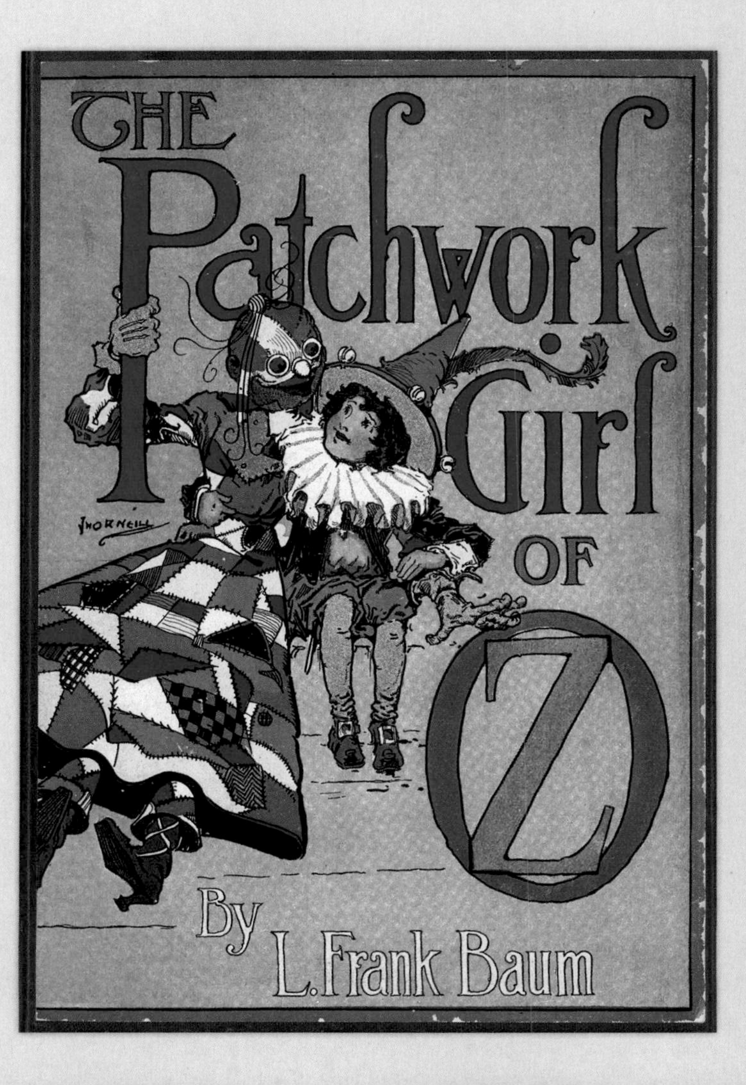

RIGHT: The 1913 Oz book served as The Oz Film Manufacturing Company's first dramatization. **ABOVE:** The announcement of its production proudly accompanied a photograph of their new studio (1914).

"*The Patchwork Girl of Oz* is a real extravaganza (the first in motion picture) and appeals strongly to the adult who tires of a steady diet of dramas or slapstick comedies. The Oz Co. has made a debut which places it in a decidedly strategic position on the motion picture map" (*The New York Morning Telegraph*). "Novelties in photography [of *His Majesty, the Scarecrow of Oz*] are plentiful. Director J. Farrell McDonald and his cinematographer have created scenes which seem like a miracle. The most impossible things are done on earth, under water, and in the air" (*Photoplayers Weekly*).

— Contemporary reviews of two silent Oz films produced and written by L. Frank Baum, 1914

ABOVE: Promotion for *The Patchwork Girl* includes copy written in Baum's own hand.
ABOVE RIGHT: Pierre Coderc as Scraps, the film's title character.

ABOVE: The Guardian of the Gate (right) greets The Patchwork Girl on her return to the Emerald City with Dr. Pipt (Raymond Russell). To appeal to adult cinema audiences, Baum added a love interest to his children's story; it didn't help.

LEFT: *His Majesty, the Scarecrow of Oz* (1914) incorporated storylines from earlier and future Oz books. Seen here: Old Mombi the Witch (Mai Wells), The Tin Woodman (Pierre Coderc), Button Bright (Mildred Harris), The Scarecrow (Frank Moore), and Dorothy (Violet MacMillan). After *The Patchwork Girl* failed, The Oz Co. changed the title of *His Majesty, the Scarecrow* to *The New Wizard of Oz* to capitalize on memories of the 1902 stage musical; that didn't work, either.

ABOVE: A lobby card for the 1925 silent screen *Wizard* shows G. Howe Black as Kansas farmhand Snowball, Oliver Hardy as The Tin Woodman, Charlie Murray as The Wizard, and Larry Semon as The Scarecrow. Josef Swickard as evil Prime Minister Kruel dictates their capture by the army of Oz. **RIGHT:** The front jacket panel of a 1925 "tie-in" edition of the first Oz book. Some of its interior Denslow art was supplanted by stills of the film cast; ironically, their cinematic adventures had virtually nothing to do with Baum's plot.

"Several New York critics were disappointed that the [1925 *Wizard*] film bore so little resemblance to Baum's original story. Calling the film 'a good picture,' Mildred Spain of the *Daily News* nevertheless found it difficult to 'take so kindly to a story that only suggests the beloved original.' And the *Evening Post* wrote that 'we rather expected a fantasy as fascinating as the book and, of course, we did not find it,' although, as the newspaper further noted, 'probably the slapstick is above average slapstick.'"

— *Mark Swartz, Oz Before the Rainbow, 2000*

ABOVE: Oliver Hardy, Dorothy Dwan, and Larry Semon pose as their Ozian counterparts in the 1925 *Wizard*. In real life, this Dorothy and Scarecrow were married after the picture was finished and just prior to its premiere.

It's the Nine Little Pigs Now!

NANCY KELLY, 12-year-old star of the "Wizard of Oz" programs on WTMJ and N. B. C., is shown with the nine Oz piglets who won fame nearly 40 years before the big bad wolf and Walt Disney put porkers in the news. Nancy's role as "Dorothy" of Kansas is the biggest child part on radio. The program may be heard each Monday, Wednesday and Friday at 4:45 p. m.

ABOVE/INSET: Nancy Kelly voiced Dorothy and General Jinjur in Jell-O's 1933-34 radio series. She won greater fame as the mother in *The Bad Seed* on Broadway (1954) and on screen (1956).

ABOVE: Toto and Kelly are joined by Jack Smart, who (per publicity) "roars for the Lion." The radio series encompassed seventy-seven fifteen-minute segments, emceed by Ben Grauer and with Frank Novak's four-piece band for random accompaniment and dramatic underscoring.

ABOVE: Kelly commiserates with Tin Man Parker Fennelly. He came to later radio prominence as "Titus Moody" ("Howdy, bub!") on Fred Allen's "Allen's Alley" and served as Pepperidge Farm spokesman in many fondly remembered TV commercials. **BELOW:** Land of Oz favorite Jack Pumpkinhead is used here to hock Jell-O.

"Here's a new deal for the children. Gangsters are on the out and out. Those juvenile crime dramas have an invincible competitor. *The Wizard of Oz* is making his debut. Tune in every Monday, Wednesday, and Friday at 5:45 p.m. over the NBC-WEAF network. . . . Now these magic stories of The Land of Oz, dramatized for the first time on the air, are quickening the pulse of childhood with wholesome enthusiasm, giving the oldsters a thrill, too, for, like *Alice in Wonderland*, the *Wizard*'s appeal is universal."

— NBC press release for "Jell-O Presents The Wizard of Oz," September 25, 1933

Pick
your favorite
...ask mother
to try it!

ABOVE: M-G-M considered filming *The Wizard of Oz* with Laurel & Hardy, but Samuel Goldwyn won the screen rights to the book in 1933. (Stan and Ollie did *Babes in Toyland* for Metro instead.)

ABOVE: Goldwyn conceived *Oz* as a vehicle for prize star, Eddie Cantor, even though the part of The Scarecrow was still fervently associated with Fred Stone in theatergoers' memories.

ABOVE: Goldwyn hoped to cast W. C. Fields in the title role—an idea endorsed by M-G-M in 1938 when they were looking for their own Wizard. But as Jack Haley, Metro's Tin Man, later summed up the concept, "Whoever thought of that idea was being ridiculous. 'Ah yes, Dorothy. My little chickadee!' I don't think Fields would have had any feeling for the role."

ABOVE: For Dorothy, Goldwyn initially suggested casting either Mary Pickford, left ("America's Sweet-heart," whose celebrity dated back to the silent screen) or Broadway's Helen Hayes, right, whose Hollywood stardom had begun two years earlier. Pickford was then forty; Hayes was thirty-three.

ABOVE: Eleven-year-old Marcia Mae Jones was rumored as a potential Dorothy for Goldwyn's *Oz* in early 1936.

THIS PAGE: Kenneth McLellan hoped to make cartoon shorts of the post-*Wizard* Oz books and established a contract with Maud Baum for those rights. By 1938, he realized that animation had become the provenance of Walt Disney, and he opted instead for a series of short, stop-action marionette productions. They were never realized, but test photographs survive of his Scarecrow design.

"[Kenneth] McLellan is developing the animation of Oz marionettes, and the results thus far have been most satisfactory. Several large companies in the East are anxious to manufacture dolls and toys based upon the marionettes, and I feel that such dolls and toys would be more readily accepted than those sold in connection with a standard production. I believe that you will agree with me that . . . Mr. McLellan's interpretation of the Scarecrow . . . has charm."

— Mrs. L. Frank Baum, *in a letter to the licensing concerns at M-G-M, September 12, 1938*

FOLLOW THE YELLOW BRICK ROAD

Pre-Production

In a kind of spontaneous predestination, *The Wizard of Oz* had its genesis at Metro-Goldwyn-Mayer in autumn 1937. But it took the alignment of five different entertainment entities to make it happen.

There was M-G-M itself, the Tiffany of the business and the only studio that would have invested the time and money to create *Oz*. There was lyricist Arthur Freed, under contract to Metro and aching to diversify into production. There was Mervyn LeRoy, then concluding his stint as (mostly) a Warner Bros. director and planning a move to M-G-M as an executive producer. There was fifteen-year-old Frances Ethel Gumm, recently renamed Judy Garland and a thirteen-year veteran of stage, radio, recording, and film experience. And there was Walt Disney, whose studio was preparing the first full-length animated musical comedy fairy tale, *Snow White and the Seven Dwarfs*.

According to Hollywood legend, Freed and LeRoy approached M-G-M chieftain Louis B. Mayer at roughly the same moment with the same idea. LeRoy later reminisced, "As a boy, I read and loved Baum's books. That wasn't unusual; children of my era and children of all the eras yet to come loved *The Wizard of Oz* and all the others. It had long been an idle dream of mine to take those fantastic, enchanting creatures and turn them into a movie. The dream remained a dream until I found myself at M-G-M." Meanwhile, Freed specifically asked that Mayer allow him to mount *Oz* as a vehicle for Garland, whose talent had been the talk of the industry since 1934.

Discussions between the men progressed into early winter. Then Disney's feature opened in December and won instant, unprecedented success. The triumph of such entertainment was confirmation of the public appetite Frank Baum tried to cultivate decades before. But it took *Snow White* to convince movie moguls there was a market for family films and fantasy in musical form. So, Mayer—officially M-G-M's vice president in charge of production—gave his conditional blessing for Freed and LeRoy

OPPOSITE PAGE: The M-G-M art department developed numerous ideas for *Wizard of Oz* sets, most of them never realized. This early concept for the Emerald City promenade includes buggy, cabby and the potential Horse of a Different Color.

THURSDAY, FEBRUARY 24, 1938

Judy Garland to Play Dorothy in Metro's 'Wizard of Oz' Film

METRO-GOLDWYN-MAYER CORPORATION
STUDIOS
CULVER CITY
CALIFORNIA

INTER-OFFICE COMMUNICATION

To Mr. I. H. Prinzmetal

Subject "WIZARD OF OZ"

From Geo. W. Cohen   Date 5-27-38

I am enclosing herewith four copies of the proposed agreement between yourselves and Samuel Goldwyn Inc., Ltd., covering the assignment of the latter's right, title and interest in "Wizard of Oz". The enclosed assignment has been modified to accord with the suggestion made by Mr. Decker in his wire of May 23rd. If and when you are ready to close for this property, will you please execute all four copies of the enclosed contract and send them to me with your check for $75,000.00. I will deliver the latter to Samuel Goldwyn Inc., Ltd., if and when Samuel Goldwyn Inc.,Ltd., has executed two copies of the same and has handed them to me for delivery to you. Should you prefer any other method of closing, please let me know, or contact Mr. Espy directly.

Geo. W. Cohen.

LEFT: When M-G-M announced *Oz*, its star was on a singing tour. Here, she's greeted by Miami announcer Sam Park. **BELOW:** Sam Goldwyn made a $35,000 profit on the screen rights for *Oz*. **BOTTOM:** Arthur Freed, Garland, and Norman Taurog on the set of *Little Nellie Kelly* (1940). Taurog was the first *Oz* director, lasting only through a few tests. But he and Judy happily worked together thereafter—and Freed's producing career was launched by his uncredited efforts as Mervyn LeRoy's *Oz* associate.

to pursue *Oz*. But because the project seemed formidable, he suggested that the experienced LeRoy produce the film with Freed as unbilled assistant.

LeRoy signed on at Metro in February 1938. By then, Freed had outlined cast and staff suggestions, and negotiations were underway to buy *Oz* from Samuel Goldwyn. The deal-making dragged on until June, when Goldwyn received $75,000 for film rights to the first Oz book and several other earlier dramatizations of the story. Initially, M-G-M planned to get the movie underway that spring, with release at Christmas. But preproduction challenges kept mounting. Despite Freed's groundwork, it took eight months to assemble cast and staff, achieve songs and script, plan special effects, and design and construct preliminary sets and costumes. *Oz* didn't go before the cameras until mid-October.

M-G-M actually announced LeRoy's *Oz* on February 24, long before the deal with Goldwyn was finalized. Garland then was the only performer publicly linked with the project, though there was a tenuous moment when another candidate was considered as Dorothy. In those days, M-G-M was controlled from New York by Loew's, Inc., and President Nicholas Schenck was already worried about the burgeoning *Oz* budget; he preferred to abandon the production altogether. Barring that (and with no slight meant toward Garland, whom all agreed was on the brink of stardom), he suggested that Metro arrange a loan-out agreement with Twentieth Century Fox to cast Shirley Temple. She was closer in age to Baum's Dorothy and, more importantly, her box office draw was a virtual insurance policy for the picture.

Schenck's proposal has long since spun off into a wildly inflated myth, accepted as scripture. The most widespread aspect of the anecdote states that M-G-M was prepared to swap their own Clark Gable and Jean Harlow for *In Old Chicago* (or any other project at Fox) for the use of Temple in *Oz*. But this is historically impossible, as Harlow had been dead for more than seven months by the time LeRoy arrived at M-G-M. Additionally, it's unlikely that Fox would have considered it wise to lease their greatest asset to a rival studio. Finally, Temple's own legal file at Metro doesn't begin until 1940, a year after the *Oz* premiere.

It is true that, under pressure from Schenck, Freed sent his most trusted associate over to Fox to hear Temple sing "live." Within hours, Roger Edens was back to pronounce the child's "vocal limitations . . . insurmountable." Discussion of Temple went no further. And despite years of rumor, neither Temple nor any other actress was ever mentioned in Hollywood trade papers or columns as a potential Dorothy. If Freed, LeRoy, and Edens had to fight to keep Garland in the role, the battle was a quick, closed-door, intra-corporate affair. They also knew it was essential; the scenes, songs, and sensitivity

"I feel as if I've known you all the time": Actual or potential members of the cast shared pre-*Oz* screen time with Dorothy Gale. **CLOCKWISE FROM BOTTOM CENTER:** Judy with Jack Haley, *Pigskin Parade* (1936); with Buddy Ebsen, *Broadway Melody of 1938* (1937); with Billie Burke, *Everybody Sing* (1938); with Fanny Brice, *Everybody Sing* (1938; Brice was Freed's first suggestion for the role of Glinda); and with Charley Grapewin and non-Ozian Freddie Bartholomew (*Listen, Darling*, 1938).

of Dorothy were to be sculpted to Garland's abilities. Years later, this was acknowledged by *Oz* Tin Man Jack Haley. He worked in two early Temple films and observed, "Shirley was a competent actress and a great dancer, but I think she would have been terrible as Dorothy. She wouldn't have touched you emotionally as Judy did."

The rest of the casting process endured similar upheaval. Buddy Ebsen and Ray Bolger, respectively, were slotted to play The Scarecrow and Tin Man, until Bolger argued that he'd be more effective as the man of straw. Ebsen agreed to switch, and it cost him the picture. Early designs for the Tin Man's facial makeup involved clown white paste, repeatedly dusted with aluminum powder to achieve the required silver sheen. After two weeks of inhaling the tiny particles, Ebsen collapsed, poisoned by an unsuspected allergy. Hurriedly, M-G-M replaced him with Jack Haley, on loan-out from Fox. Haley then had trouble with the revised formula: "For me, they made the aluminum into paste and painted it on instead. So I wasn't poisoned, but I did get a serious eye infection and lost a few days work because of that."

For the title role, Freed suggested M-G-M's Frank Morgan; LeRoy countered with venerated radio and Broadway comic Ed Wynn. But when Wynn read an early script, it included only the throne room and balloon scenes for The Great Oz; the appearances of Professor Marvel, the Guardian of the Gale, Emerald City cabbie, and Palace Soldier had not yet been crafted. So he declined the role as too small. M-G-M next approached W. C. Fields, purportedly willing to pay him $100,000 for the few days it would take to complete his work. They

ABOVE: Soprano Betty Jaynes missed the opportunity to duet opera vs. jazz with Dorothy when her role as Princess Betty of Oz was dropped from the script. But she and Garland did a similar routine in *Babes in Arms* (1939). **RIGHT:** Second assistant director Wallace Worsley, Jr., served as *Oz* script clerk. His long career included fifteen years at Metro and several films with Judy. He later defined her as "naturally brilliant. . . . Where other people really had to work . . . she picked it up like that."

spent weeks in discussion, but Fields finally stepped back as well. The part would be conjectured for at least five others before Morgan was assigned after all.

Some casting difficulties corresponded to ongoing script changes. At first, The Cowardly Lion was reconceptualized as a singing duke or prince, transformed into an animal by The Wicked Witch. Kenny Baker was slotted to play the dual role, both as timid beast and musical consort to Princess Betty. The latter was another original character, cast with operatic soprano Betty Jaynes. (An early *Oz* summary described Dorothy/Judy as "an orphan from Kansas who sings jazz." It was envisioned that she and the Princess would vocally compete and contrast at an Emerald City soiree.) Eventually, the Baker/Jaynes subplot was dropped, and M-G-M returned to Baum's concept; the studio supposedly considered using a trained lion with a dubbed voice to enact the part. But by late spring 1938, composer and lyricist Harold Arlen and E. Y. "Yip" Harburg had arrived at Metro to write the *Oz* songs. The duo had worked on Broadway with comedian Bert Lahr, and their enthusiasm for him underscored the LeRoy/Freed decision to slip Lahr into what proved an obvious guise.

Preliminary scripts also played havoc with the witches of Oz. In Baum's book, The Good Witch of the North is an older woman who helps Dorothy on her arrival in Munchkinland. At the end of the novel, the girl is aided by Glinda the Good, a beautiful, ageless redhead and Sorceress of the South. M-G-M decided to conflate the characters as a comic opportunity for Fanny Brice, remembered today as the comedienne immortalized by Barbra Streisand in *Funny Girl* and *Funny Lady*. When this proved unworkable, other actresses were penciled in, until it was decided that redheaded Billie Burke could encompass characteristics of both of Baum's beneficent rulers.

The Wicked Witch presented an equal problem; her scenes were first scripted as an uneasy amalgam of murderous evil and cantankerous, crotchety comedy. Then, in obvious homage to Disney's Evil Queen in *Snow White*, she was reconfigured—first as a slinky, sequined seductress and then as a hateful crone. After testing and rethinking on

LeRoy's part, Margaret Hamilton won the role: "I had played The Wicked Witch before in a Junior League production of *Oz* in Cleveland. When I tested, it seemed like old-home week. But M-G-M also considered Gale Sondergaard; they wanted her to play a glamorous witch. She was connected with glamour and beauty—and I wasn't! Then, suddenly, Mr. LeRoy decided that Gale was *too* beautiful to play The Wicked Witch. And I was hired."

Additional conflicts beset casting the pivotal roles of Aunt Em and Uncle Henry; they finally were filled by Clara Blandick and Charley Grapewin. Fortunately, primary adjuncts for The Witch were hired with little drama. Highly regarded Mitchell Lewis played the leader of her Winkie Guards, and veteran animal impersonator Pat Walshe signed on as monkey sidekick, Nikko. A younger veteran turned up via trainer Carl Spitz when female Cairn terrier Terry proved to be a perfect Toto. The brindle-colored trouper had already appeared in six films.

Getting the storyline "back to Baum" was an onerous task.

Populating Munchkinland was a problem M-G-M decided to delegate. As early as February 1938, they discussed requirements for the little people of Oz with impresario Leo Singer. He agreed to provide a nucleus of performers from his own troupe, "The Singer Midgets," and to search for the rest. By November, he'd contracted or arranged for approximately one hundred twenty hypopituitary dwarves—perfectly scaled-down miniature people—to convene in Culver City to begin rehearsals.

The casting process wore on from February through September. At the same time, thirteen writers or consultants churned out draft after draft of *Oz* treatments, scenes, and scripts. Only Noel Langley, Florence Ryerson, and Edgar Allan Woolf received credit for their work, although invaluable counsel was provided by Freed and Edens, and some actual writing was contributed by Harburg. Getting the storyline "back to Baum" was an onerous task, as many extraneous characters and situations had been crammed into the plot. Happily discarded were the aforementioned Princess Betty and Grand Duke Alan, whose names evolved from script to script as Sylvia and Florizel, Kenelm, or Kenelin. They were to be featured in Kansas as well, playing Mrs. Gulch's niece, Sylvia, and her beau Kenny. In turn, Gulch was to have a son, Walter, and the actor in that role would reappear in Oz as Bulbo, offspring of The Witch. (Another subplot detailed his mother's plans to conquer the capital and make Bulbo king.) Meanwhile, Lizzie Smithers, a Kansas "hired girl," would also work in The Emerald City, assisting The Wizard.

TOP/BOTTOM/LEFT: With *Oz*, M-G-M's Adrian graduated from garb for Garbo, sheaths for Shearer, and crinolines for Crawford to design scores of individual "coztumes" for the little people who played The Munchkins. **ABOVE:** Adrian's ideas colorfully came to life, as demonstrated by some of the cast during a Technicolor test.

THIS SPREAD: Few of these concepts for effects and sets were realized, but the art department's creativity is everywhere apparent. **LEFT:** En route to Munchkinland, the Kansas farmhouse is cosseted by cloud children. **BELOW:** The Witch's Tower Room contains crystal ball, winged monkey, hanging bat, and skull-and-serpent wall decorations. (Her resemblance to The Witch of Disney's *Snow White* hag is doubtless—if tongue-in-cheek—intentional.) **OPPOSITE PAGE:** Two views of a diminutive Dorothy and Toto in The Emerald City Throne Room display an astounding range of décor: massive men in wall hangings, the incomplete legend "Nokus Pocus Es . . . ," the Giant Head of the Great Oz, a sarcophagus, a huge image of a charlatan holding a wand and white rabbit, and (below and beneath him to his left), "the [tiny] man behind the curtain." **OPPOSITE PAGE, CENTER:** Notice of Arlen and Harburg's initial submission hit the trade papers on May 26, 1938.

As such characters were presented and purged, scenes were developed and dropped. In one sequence, The Witch was to entice Dorothy to certain death on a translucent rainbow bridge. But the girl walked to safety, thanks to the magic of the ruby slippers. In an abandoned finale for the film, crowds of angry Emerald Citizans were to turn on the Wizard, Dorothy, and her friends. They were to escape from the mob in The Wizard's balloon, but an errant woodpecker was created to destroy it in flight, so that Glinda and The Munchkin Fire Department (!) could come to the rescue.

Some originality was retained to benefit M-G-M's approach. The idea that Dorothy's adventure be presented as a psychological delirium was unique to the Metro script; in Baum's book, the trip to Oz actually happened. Much as farmhands in the 1925 *Wizard* were later seen as Ozians, Langley expanded upon that approach in 1938, adding Mrs. Gulch/The Wicked Witch to the mix. (When the subplot about her son was dropped, Almira Gulch returned to spinster status.) From the 1902 musical, Langley appropriated the conceit that The Good Witch send a snowstorm to rout the poppies. In the Oz book, Dorothy is carried from the flowers by The Scarecrow and Tin Man, while The Lion is rescued on a

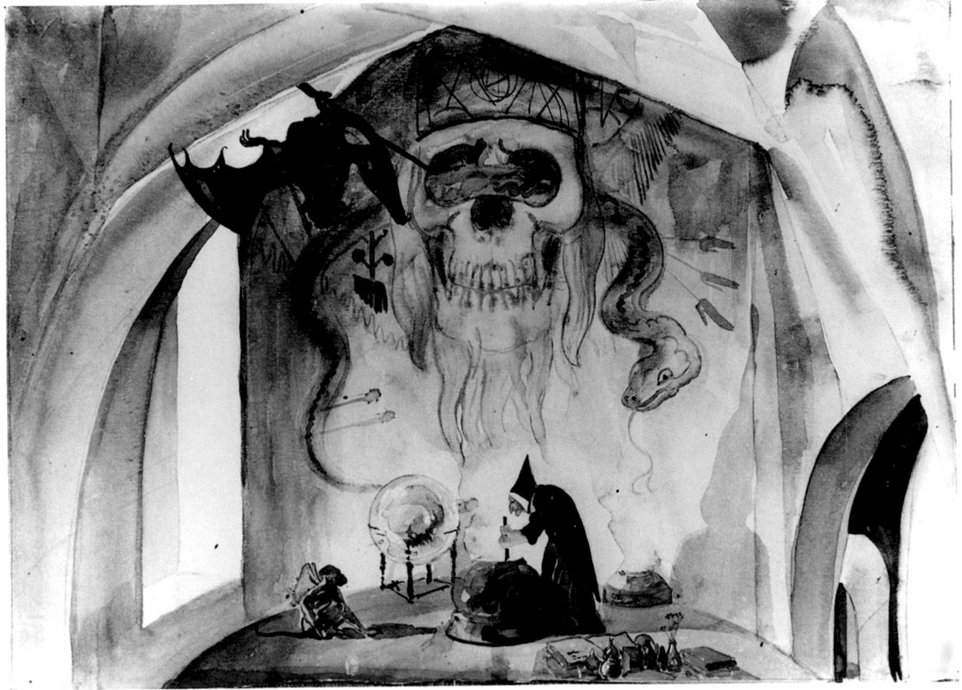

cart pulled by hundreds of mice. Not surprisingly, this concept was deemed cinematically unfeasible. Finally, it's now not certain whether the idea was his, or if he acted under advisement from others. But during Langley's stint on the script, Dorothy's footwear changed from Baum's silver shoes to the more Technicolor-friendly ruby slippers.

Freed's musical acumen was especially beneficial during preproduction. He wanted *Oz* to boast an integrated score, each song advancing the storyline or helping define the characters. Among his suggestions for the job were Jerome Kern, Ira Gershwin, and Dorothy Fields; in succeeding months, the teams of Mack Gordon/Harry Revel and Al Dubin/Nacio Herb Brown were rumored to have the assignment. But Metro ultimately opted for Arlen and Harburg, whose fanciful numbers had brightened a half dozen stage shows and movies. In barely three months, the duo crafted six songs and the "Munchkinland Musical Sequence," all specifically designed to tell the saga of *Oz*.

Others behind-the-scenes began work as well. Gilbert Adrian was then Hollywood's preeminent costumer, best known for his high fashions for M-G-M leading ladies. A lifelong Oz fan, he reveled in designing the disparate garb of Munchkins, Winkies, and Emerald City residents, and he welcomed the pleasure of conceptualizing screen-worthy wardrobe for the principal cast, true to the Denslow and Neill art. A. Arnold "Buddy" Gillespie and his special effects team found their greatest challenge to that date in fulfilling Baum's imagination. In an era long before computer-generated magic, it fell to Gillespie to melt a Wicked Witch, sweep the Kansas plains with a tornado, transport a farmhouse through the air, and manipulate scores of flying monkeys (whether actors or rubber miniatures). Cedric Gibbons, William Horning, Jack Martin Smith and their staff had to design and build Oz as nothing else in existence—from the green glass shimmer of the capital to the vista of deadly flowers; from the lilliputian village of Munchkins to The Haunted Forest and lair of The Witch. Finally, all sets, effects, and costumes had to be coordinated with the temperamental "eye" of the comparatively new three-strip Technicolor camera. Harold Rosson photographed *Oz*, and he and his crew were confronted by the daily hazards of intense lighting and the trial-and-error required by a process in its infancy.

'Jitterbug' For Judy

Yip Harburg and Harold Arlen have completed the first song, "Jitterbug," for MGM's "The Wizard of Oz." Judy Garland will sing the number in the Mervyn LeRoy production.

To guide the *Oz* actors through their scenes and scenery, LeRoy first selected Norman Taurog, who was especially known for his masterful direction of child stars. But after some preliminary test work in summer 1938, Taurog was removed from the picture and sent to oversee Mickey Rooney's performance in *The Adventures of Huckleberry Finn*. Richard Thorpe succeeded him, to be replaced in turn by George Cukor, who then swiftly handed over the *Oz* directorial reins to Victor Fleming. All three men would have an impact on the still-evolving script, the makeup and costume concepts for several of the film's key players, and the general outcome of the film.

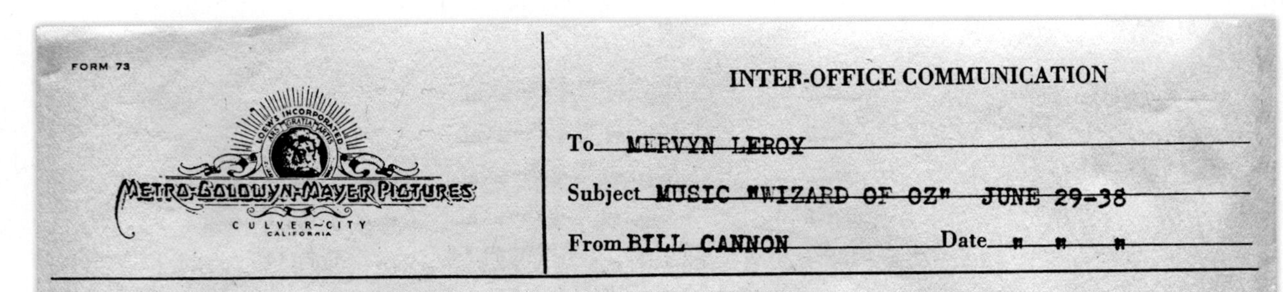

FORM 73

METRO-GOLDWYN-MAYER PICTURES
CULVER-CITY CALIFORNIA

INTER-OFFICE COMMUNICATION

To MERVYN LEROY
Subject MUSIC "WIZARD OF OZ" JUNE 29-38
From BILL CANNON Date " " "

SC...# 2..."HARMONICA TUNE" EXT FARM YARD
SC...# 7..."OVER THE RAINBOW" " " " DOROTHY SINGS(SONG I:43)
SC...# I7..."ACCORDIAN SELECTION" MARVEL'S CAMP "DRAWF PLAYS"
SC...# 5I... REPRISE"OVER THE RAINBOW" MUNCHKINLAND DOROTHY SINGS(2 LINES)
SC...# 58..."DING DONG THE WITCH IS DEAD" MUNCHKINLAND ENSEMBLE (5:30)
SC...# 7I...RERRISE"DING DONG THE WITCH IS DEAD" MUNCHKINLAND (:40)
SC...# 75... " " " " " " " " " " " (:50)
SC...# 84..."IF I ONLY HAD A BRAIN" SONG AND DANCE(CROSSROADS) (SONG I:I0)
SC...# 86..." MARCHING SONG------------------------(" ") (:40)
SC...# 87..." " " ------------------------ (APPLE TREES) (:30)
SC...#I00..."IF I ONLY HAD A HEART" SONG AND DANCE(TINWOODMAN) (I:I0)
SC...#I02..."MARCHING SONG"------------------------(TINWOODMAN'S HOUSE) (:30)
SC...#I03..."MARCHING SONG" VOICES JOIN IN RHYTHMN DARK FOREST (:45)
SC...#III..."IF I ONLY HAD THE NERVE" DARK FOREST---------(SONG :50)
SC...#II6..."MARCHING SONG"----POPPY FIELD-----------------(:30)
SC...#I20..."MARCHING SONG" HUMMING WHILE WALKING---------POPPY FIELD (:30)
SC...#I37..."THE HORSE OF A DIFFERENT COLOR"------CITY SQUARE
SC...#I52..."KING OF THE FOREST"------COURT YARD OF THE PALACE (Lion SONG)
SC...#26I..."JITTER BUG"----HAUNTED FOREST-------(SONG I:45)
SC...#276..."REPRISE"OVER THE RAINBOW"----WITCH'S ROOM (SONG I:45)
SC...#280..."DEATH TO THE WIZARD OF OZ" WITCHS COURTYARD AND DRAWBRIDGE
SC...#376..."REPRISE"THE WICKED WITCH IS DEAD"--WITCH'S NO#2 ROOM
SC...#369..."REPRISE"THE WICKED WITCH IS DEAD" CITY SQUARE ENSEMBLE
SC...#378..."WIZARD'S SONG" WIZARD'S THRONE ROOM (WIZARD SINGS)
SC...#405..."REPRISE"OVER THE RAINBOW" EXT FARM FADE OUT

THIS FIGURES OUT ROUGHLY TO ABOUT-----34 minutes and I0 seconds
or -----3060 feet of film

ABOVE: Composer Harold Arlen and lyricist E. Y. "Yip" Harburg, in contemporary photos. The principal cast of singers was fairly well in place when they were contracted, so they knew the scope of talent and vocal range with which they'd be working. The songwriters were especially fortunate in Garland's assignment; in Harburg's estimation, "Judy's voice was the greatest in the first part of our century. It went right through the bone and flesh and into the heart. She had an emotional quality that very, very few voices ever had."

LEFT: By summer 1938, M-G-M was deep into *Oz* preproduction. Though script revisions went on around them, Harburg and Arlen turned out songs for sequences in early drafts. Bill Cannon, assistant to producer Mervyn LeRoy, composed this memo to summarize progress made on the score as of June 29. His listing serves as proof that *Oz* was then very much a work in progress; there are references to numbers that were dropped before being written and to reprises that were abandoned.

Over the years, rumor has cited Shirley Temple (top left), Deanna Durbin (above), or Bonita Granville (left) as M-G-M's possible Dorothy of 1938. But only Temple was actively considered; further, Durbin was Universal's prize and unlikely for a loan-out, and Granville was a fine actress but not a musical performer. (When Temple was briefly under contract to M-G-M in 1940-41, there was gossip that she might star in an *Oz* sequel, but by then, her box office clout had waned.)

"I had been writing [lyrics] for Judy, and I was interested in her. I bought *Oz* for the studio with only one person in mind for Dorothy, [and] it was finally decided, by all, that *Oz* should be used to establish a good box office reputation for Judy."

— *Arthur Freed*

ABOVE: While on the road for M-G-M in early 1938, Judy Garland did this photo session in addition to interviews, broadcasts, homework, and four daily performances. She would turn sixteen on June 10, which made her much older than the seven-year-old of Baum's book; the *Oz* shooting script put Dorothy's age at twelve. Garland biographer Christopher Finch later summed up her effectiveness: "For [a fantasy film] to be a commercial success, it must appeal to adults as well as children. In *Oz*, Judy is an adolescent with a grown-up's singing voice acting the part of a child. She is close enough to childhood to be completely convincing, but she is role-playing enough to draw adults into the action, too."

BELOW: Although LeRoy always claimed Judy was his "perfect Dorothy," he and the wardrobe, makeup, and hair departments initially did all they could to transform her. From left: In early *Oz* tests, she evokes Alice in Wonderland, one of the Von Trapp Family Singers, and Marcia Brady. **FAR LEFT:** Dorothy and Toto as pictured by John R. Neill.

FAR LEFT: When *Oz* filming first began under director Richard Thorpe, Garland's appearance gave every indication she'd been cast as "Lolita Gale of Kansas." **LEFT:** In addition to the blonde wig shown here, Judy was also tested with red hairpieces.

ABOVE/RIGHT: In George Cukor's few days on the set, he managed to effect changes for Judy that materially improved her appearance and approach to the role. Even then, however, the hairdressers at first seemed to be referencing Pippi Longstocking, Heidi, or Laura Ingalls.

BELOW: "Dorothy Two Shoes" tests different ruby slippers. On her left foot: a standard pump overlaid with glass bugle beads—one of the pair in which she filmed for two weeks under Thorpe. On her right foot: a low-heel "Arabian" slipper with curled toe, embellished by glass stones and sequins. Neither design made it into the finished film, but they point to Adrian's flair for the extravagant.

"Judy didn't need the 'Andy Hardy' film series to further her career. She established herself entirely on her own with that classic performance as Dorothy, the little girl who was one part charm and three parts wonder. Judy established herself on her own because she had a curious quality. The word is talent. She couldn't wiggle like Lana Turner, swim like Esther Williams, purr like Donna Reed, or (maybe) hit as high a note as Kathryn Grayson. All Judy could do was entertain. She could make any audience laugh or cry, or, if she were so inclined, get them to stand up and throw silver dollars."

— Mickey Rooney

ABOVE: Garland's appearance coalesced Baum's written word and Judy's own everyday beauty. Her jumper, like the dress in the book, was royal blue-and-white gingham. (Beneath it, she wore a special corset, de-emphasizing her bust and giving her a younger silhouette.) Her final hairstyle wove extensions into her own hair; her natural dark chestnut color was dyed auburn for the Technicolor cameras.

ABOVE: In 1938, Ray Bolger was thirty-four and a veteran of both vaudeville and Broadway. *Oz* would be his fifth picture.

"Arthur Freed approached me one day with a twinkle in his eye: 'Guess who is going to play The Scarecrow in *Oz*?' It was wonderful news. The big draw for me was that the movie was going to be produced in color, and I was to have maybe the most important role in my life as an actor. I rushed to the rehearsal hall and began plotting my Scarecrow dances and wobbles. That's where I was when Ray Bolger walked in with his agent. That's when those icy fingers started running down my spine. Ray's agent grinned into my stricken face, 'Ray's going to play The Scarecrow. . . ' So Arthur blurted out, 'You're going to play The Tin Woodman!' I became determined to make the role of The Tin Woodman a winner."

— Buddy Ebsen

RIGHT: Buddy Ebsen was signed by M-G-M after early Broadway success; he was thirty when cast in *Oz*. In seven earlier films, his dancing partners included Shirley Temple, Eleanor Powell, George Murphy, and kid sister Vilma Ebsen.

RIGHT: An early makeup test for Bolger emulated the appearance of Fred Stone in the 1902 stage musical. **LEFT:** Neill's drawing of The Scarecrow, "the most popular man in Oz," according to Baum's description.

NEAR RIGHT: Depending on your generation, The Scarecrow here resembles Edna Mae Oliver, Boy George, or Marilyn Manson. **CENTER:** Without the burlap texture, Bolger's facial makeup is vaguely lacking. **FAR RIGHT:** When filming began, The Scarecrow looked like The Mummy of Oz.

LEFT: As adjusted under Cukor's guidance, Bolger's final makeup consisted of a mottled, thin rubber mask, glued over most of his face and painted to simulate burlap. The process took two hours every morning. **RIGHT:** Bolger's dancing sobriquet as "Rubber Legs" is everywhere apparent.

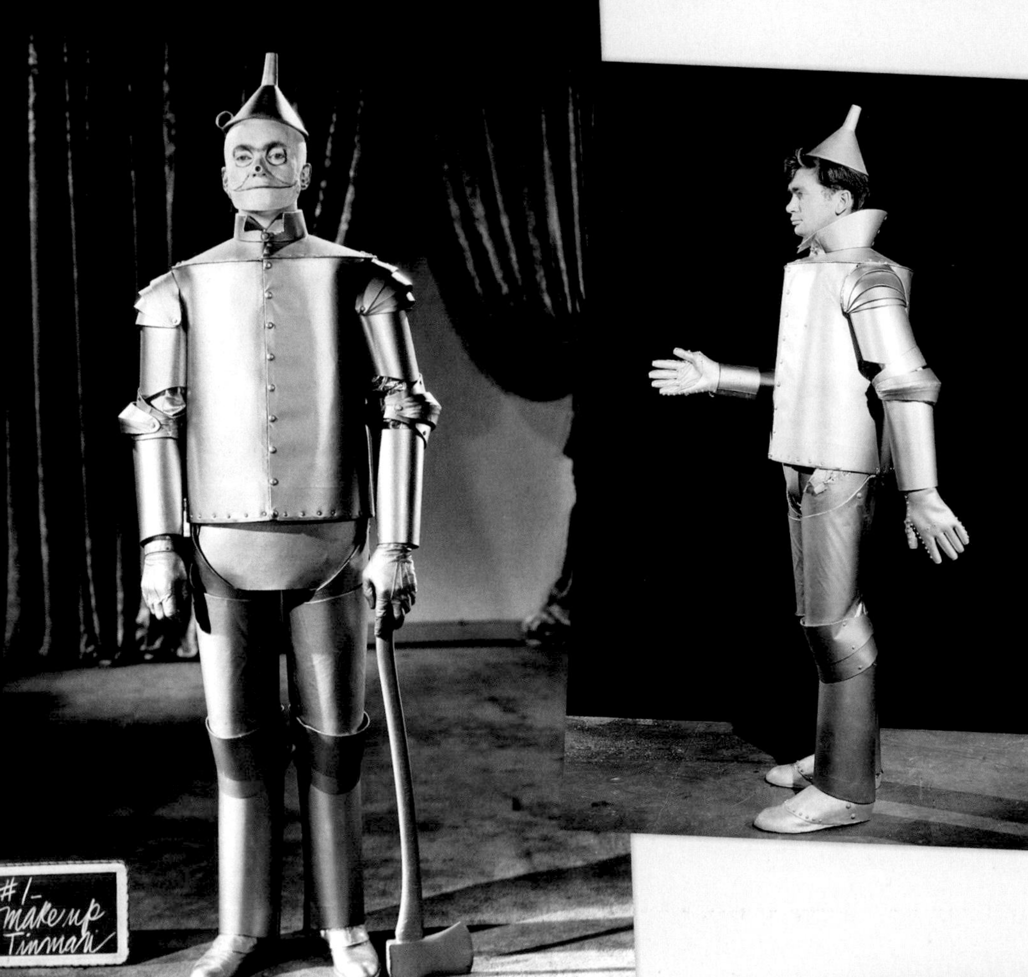

FAR LEFT: In Neill's drawings, the famous Oz characters proved adaptable to many poses. **CENTER:** Early on, Ebsen tried out a makeup similar to that worn onstage by David Montgomery in 1902. **NEAR LEFT:** When columnist Hedda Hopper visited the set, she asked, "What are you going to do as the Tin Man?" Ebsen's succinct reply: "Suffer, mostly!" His lack of makeup here reflects a conscious (if far from final) effort on the part of M-G-M to avoid the problem that beset Paramount's *Alice in Wonderland* (1933). Most of their all-star cast was unrecognizable beneath character masks.

LEFT: Hours after this scene was filmed, Richard Thorpe was fired as *Oz* director, and aluminum poisoning sent Ebsen to the hospital. (The Tin Man is shown here with The Lion, The Mummy, and Lolita.)

"A consortium of brains from the wardrobe and prop departments, assuming that tin meant tin, made me a suit out of stove-pipe. There is very little stretch in stove-pipe. The second model of the Tin Man suit was an improvement. It was essentially the same construction, but it was created of stiff cardboard, covered with a silvery metallic-looking paper. Improved—but still no joy. It was almost impossible to sit down; to dance was an ordeal of pain."

— Buddy Ebsen

"Jack Dawn (Metro's head makeup man) affixed a rubber jaw and rubber funnel to Buddy's head, covered his face with white clown makeup, and sprayed him with aluminum dust. It looked perfect, halfway between human and metallic. [But] one morning, a couple weeks after we began shooting, he woke up and couldn't breathe. His wife rushed him to the hospital, where they had to put him in an iron lung. Naturally, in her panic, she hadn't thought to call the studio. All I knew was that my Tin Man wasn't there! Dawn had learned a lesson the hard way; Ebsen had been a guinea pig and had lost a great part because of it."

— Mervyn LeRoy

LEFT: Ebsen's replacement was thirty-nine-year old Jack Haley, who had several dozen Broadway and film credits. At the time of *Oz*, he was also the star of his own network radio show.

ABOVE: "People ask me, 'It must have been fun, making that picture?' Fun!? Like hell it was fun! It was a lot of hard work!" Haley's honest emotion about the pressures of *Oz* is evident in this Technicolor test.

RIGHT: Popular radio vocalist Kenny Baker was briefly cast in a dual role: The Cowardly Lion/The Grand Duke Alan. The latter was scripted to sing operatic duets with Princess Betty [Jaynes]; it was only after a transformation by The Wicked Witch that Baker would appear as a lion. (He is shown here during a 1939 production of *The Mikado*.)

LEFT: Bert Lahr brought decades of stage experience (vaudeville, burlesque, and Broadway) to the M-G-M soundstages when, at forty-three, he fulfilled the role he seemed born to play.

ABOVE: *"Does he know this is an audition?"* When Betty and Alan were written out of the early scripts, M-G-M contemplated using a real lion to portray Baum's coward. Rumor had it the famous Leo—whose roaring countenance opened every Metro film offering—would be given the part.

"The producers accepted Bert because they thought he was funny. I didn't. I wanted him because the role was one of the things that *Oz* stands for, the search for some basic human necessity. At the heart of this seeking after courage is fear. Call it anxiety now; call it neurosis. We're in a world we don't understand. When the Lion admits he lacks courage, everybody's heart is out to him. He must be somebody who embodies all this pathos, sweetness, and yet puts on this comic bravura. Bert had that quality to such a wonderful degree. It was in his face, it was in his talk, it was in himself. To me, that kind of comedy is on a higher plane, approaching a more humanitarian, universal statement about Man. It is not a temporary gag. A lyricist is lucky to have a Bert Lahr in his lifetime, who incorporates humor and humanity in his performance."

— E. Y. "Yip" Harburg

LEFT: This is not a happy actor. Lahr's costume weighed more than fifty pounds and consisted of two lion pelts lined with padding. Between takes, he was peeled out of wardrobe, so that he and the clothing could be blown dry with primitive cooling devices.

No other actor in *Oz* received the kind of critical praise won by Lahr. *The Boston Transcript* chortled, "There should be an Academy Award, even if a special award has to be created, for . . . Bert Lahr." "Were it the season for acting prizes," suggested *The New York Mirror*, "Mr. Lahr would get them all."

ABOVE/TOP: Long before Lahr's Lion "got a permanent, just for the occasion," Neill's Lion boasted the same sort of hairdo, complete with crowning bow.

In addition to W. C. Fields (who had been Goldwyn's choice five years earlier), M-G-M's potential Wizards included: Ed Wynn, now best remembered as "Uncle Albert" in Disney's *Mary Poppins*; Wallace Beery, so eager to play the part that some early self-publicity prematurely credited him with the role; Hugh Herbert, forever a fluttery, silly soul on screen; Victor Moore, the perennial "milquetoast" of Broadway and Hollywood; Robert Benchley, journalist and film personality in a variety of comedy shorts; and Charles Winninger, "Captain Andy" of the original *Show Boat* and "Barney Kurtz," former vaudeville partner of Fred Mertz on TV's *I Love Lucy*.

ABOVE: Forty-eight-year-old Frank Morgan imbued both The Wizard and Professor Marvel with the same bumbling characteristics he brought to many screen appearances. Movie audiences anticipated such familiar qualities and felt suitably fulfilled when they got them. **ABOVE LEFT:** Baum's Wizard, as drawn by Neill, after his return to Oz.

ABOVE: An early Technicolor test shows Morgan in ultimately rejected makeup as the small, bald Wizard of Denslow's drawings (see page 107). Although originally planned as "The Wizard's Song," the actor's throne-room presentations instead were made via superlative Langley and Harburg dialogue, in which Morgan offers Dorothy's companions proof that they already possessed the qualities they'd long been seeking.

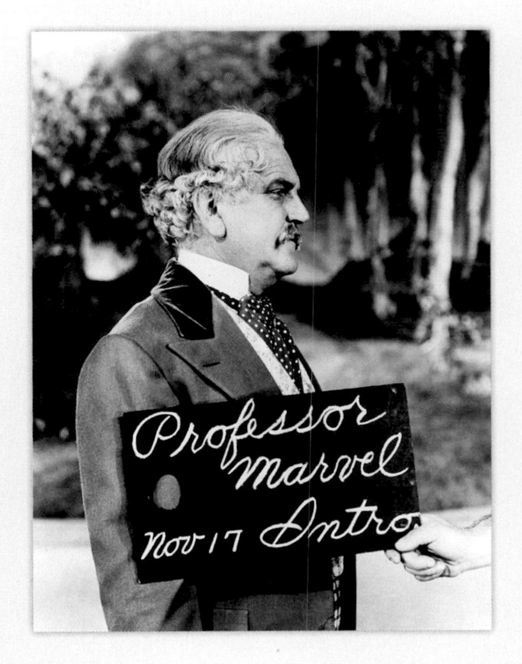

ABOVE: This wig and makeup for Professor Marvel were photographed on the orchard/Tin Man cottage set three months before the *Oz* Unit began work on the Kansas sequences. Morgan wears the costume he'd been provided for the Wizard's Technicolor test a day earlier. **LEFT:** Morgan models a possible ensemble and visage for The Emerald City palace soldier.

ABOVE: The blustery Guardian of the Gate *("Who rang that bell?!")* was given several styles of wig and mustache before a decision was reached as to his ultimate appearance.

RIGHT: Eager to play The Wizard, Frank Morgan even did a screen test for the role. Scenarist Noel Langley later described it as "one of the funniest things I ever saw."

ABOVE: Arthur Freed's first suggestion for the role was "Funny Girl" Fanny Brice, whose comedy and mock elegance matched the occasionally burlesqued concepts of preliminary *Oz* scripts. **LEFT:** Baum's Oz book's Good Witch of the North was a genteel older woman. His Glinda, depicted here by Neill, was a different—and much younger—redheaded sorceress.

ABOVE: Scenarist Langley proposed the casting of British comedienne Beatrice Lillie, known for her regal, tongue-in-cheek appearances on stage and film.

ABOVE: When the role became more that of a traditional good fairy, M-G-M starlet Helen Gilbert was a rumored candidate.

ABOVE: Thirty years prior to *Oz*, Billie Burke's onstage redheaded radiance made her one of Broadway's most glamorous leading ladies. She was fifty-four and under contract to M-G-M when they cast her as The Good Witch of the North.

ABOVE: Glinda's gown was one of the few "second-hand" *Oz* costumes, created by Adrian for Jeanette MacDonald and *San Francisco* (1936). For Burke, the dress was amended with butterfly and star appliqués. Such embellishments would frequently flare into the camera, reflecting light from the massive arcs required for color cinematography. (The same problem occurred with Dorothy's ruby slippers.)

ABOVE: Crusty Edna Mae Oliver was penciled-in to play The Wicked Witch during early preproduction. At fifty-five, her acting persona was ideal for the combination of comedy and malevolence scripted for the character.

ABOVE: But rewrites and an obsession with The Evil Queen of Disney's *Snow White* materially altered the role. The new concept—a slinky Witch of the West—was cast with thirty-nine-year old Gale Sondergaard, who had successfully worked with LeRoy in *Anthony Adverse* (1936).

ABOVE: Ten days later, Sondergaard retested as a typical hag, but she had no desire to appear this way and was released from *Oz*.

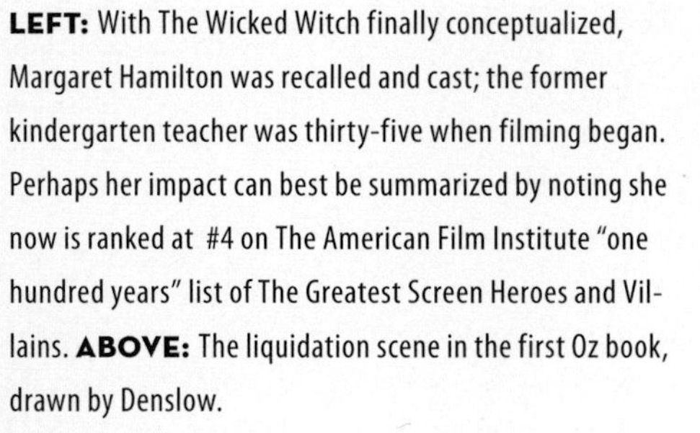

LEFT: With The Wicked Witch finally conceptualized, Margaret Hamilton was recalled and cast; the former kindergarten teacher was thirty-five when filming began. Perhaps her impact can best be summarized by noting she now is ranked at #4 on The American Film Institute "one hundred years" list of The Greatest Screen Heroes and Villains. **ABOVE:** The liquidation scene in the first Oz book, drawn by Denslow.

"Mervyn LeRoy had a sudden thought to make a glamorous witch instead of an ugly witch. We actually did the costumes—a high, pointed hat of sequins, a very glamorous sequined gown. It was absolutely gorgeous. And then, I suppose Mervyn got to remembering that this was a classic by now, and the children who read it (and grownups, too) were going to say, 'That isn't the way it was written.' And everybody agreed that you could not do that to *The Wizard of Oz*. And Mervyn said to me, 'I don't want you to be an ugly witch.' So we dropped the whole thing."

— Gale Sondergaard

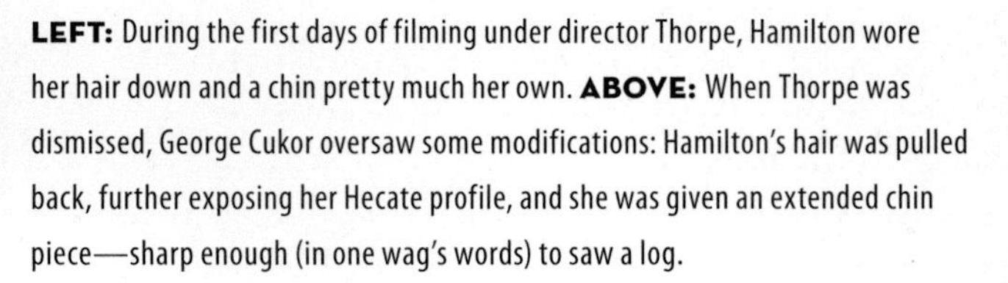

LEFT: During the first days of filming under director Thorpe, Hamilton wore her hair down and a chin pretty much her own. **ABOVE:** When Thorpe was dismissed, George Cukor oversaw some modifications: Hamilton's hair was pulled back, further exposing her Hecate profile, and she was given an extended chin piece—sharp enough (in one wag's words) to saw a log.

ABOVE: According to M-G-M publicity, Oz fans were rabid that the movie characters "follow the original illustrations by Denslow." In this instance, Metro certainly seems to have paid attention.

ABOVE: Terry made her film debut as "Rags," Shirley Temple's companion in *Bright Eyes* (1934). The Cairn terrier had been left with trainer Carl Spitz in hopes he could cure her innate shyness. Spitz worked wonders, but the dog's owner refused to pay for the achievement, so Spitz inherited Terry and eventually put her to work.

TOP: Judy and Terry became inseparable companions during their six months in *Oz*. **INSET:** In this test frame, Terry is shown just prior to creating Emerald City havoc during the balloon sequence.

NEAR RIGHT: Eighty-year-old May Robson was first choice for Aunt Em, but the revered actress rejected the role as unchallenging. **CENTER:** Janet Beecher, at fifty-four, was perhaps too elegant for a farmwoman, although she was considered as well. **FAR RIGHT:** Sarah Padden actually screen-tested for the part in January 1939; the British-born player was fifty-seven and had been doing bits in movies since 1926. **BELOW CENTER:** Artwork by Neill from the sixth Oz book: Dorothy welcomes Aunt Em and Uncle Henry to the Emerald City.

ABOVE: Clara Blandick was almost fifty-nine when named to play Auntie Em. A stage veteran, she made her movie debut in 1911 and, over forty years, worked in more than 120 films.

ABOVE: Harlan Briggs (left) was cast as Uncle Henry, but the fifty-nine-year-old lost the role when first-choice Charley Grapewin (right) became available. Grapewin had been announced for the part in late 1938 but opted for retirement instead. By February 1939, he'd changed his mind and returned to M-G-M for *Oz*. Then seventy, he went on to make another twenty-five films over the next dozen years.

LEFT: Perhaps wishing to capitalize on the fantasy of *Oz* in their promotion, M-G-M released only three stills taken during the Kansas scenes. This finale grouping is one of them and shows, from left to right, Morgan, Garland, Grapewin, Bolger, Haley, Lahr, and Blandick.

ABOVE: Denslow's "Winkie slaves" were more easily dismayed than the M-G-M "Winkie Guards," enchanted servitors to The Wicked Witch. **RIGHT:** A Technicolor test underscores the studio decision that The Winkies should resemble their mistress, at least where coloring and noses were concerned.

RIGHT: Pat Walshe is never called by his character name in the dialogue that survived script and film editing. But he's deservingly credited in the cast list at the end of *Oz* for his sly portrayal of Nikko, "familiar" companion to The Wicked Witch.

LEFT: Mitchell Lewis was fifty-eight when he uttered the classic phrase, "She's dead! You've killed her!" The highly regarded veteran enjoyed a four-decade screen career, appearing in over 200 films.

ABOVE: Walshe's makeup was so innovative for its time that a similar design approach was utilized in the *Planet of the Apes* film series nearly thirty years later. **RIGHT:** Denslow's mischievous winged monkey. According to Baum, the simians had to obey the dictates (good or evil) of anyone who possessed the magic Golden Cap.

LEFT/BELOW: The Winged Monkeys have terrified every generation since 1939. They might have caused additional horror if some rejected costume and makeup ideas had been implemented. The bat wings were probably abandoned as too unwieldy, while the monkey with the double set of teeth is either clowning or unwittingly foreshadowing FX film aliens of the future.

LEFT: A Technicolor test frame reveals that, between takes, these three winged compatriots were a bit more cavalier in their attitude than when otherwise performing in The Haunted Forest.

RIGHT: Notes prepared by comic Sid Silvers, who was assigned to work with director Thorpe and provide additional gags for the final script. The pages shown include basically extrinsic suggestions for interplay between Professor Marvel and his cowardly adjunct, ironically named Goliath. (This was a role intended for Bert Lahr; the part of a third farmhand had not yet been incorporated.)

From:
Sid Silvers
10/19/38

NOTES ON "WIZARD OF OZ"

PAGE 7.

Instead of Uncle Henry backing against the fence and getting the paint on his rear, I think the gag should be saved for when Uncle Henry drops his hold on the gate and it swings closed and gives Miss Gulch a smart little spank and on the DISSOLVE as she turns we see a design of white slats printed on her rear.

BOTTOM OF PAGE 14.

Instead of Dorothy leaving her bag behind, she should take it into the wagon with her. And instead of staying on Goliath rummaging in the bag we should cut into the wagon immediately and play the scene as follows.

Professor Marvel
(as he is donning his head-dress and robe)
The same genuine authentic magical crystal used by the priests of Isis and Asiris in the time of the Pharohs of Egypt.
(he bends over a crystal which is between two lighted candles)

Professor Marvel (to Dorothy)
Do you know the Pharohs of Egypt?

Dorothy (mystified)
No.

Professor Marvel
Wonderful people. If you're ever in Egypt drop in on them.
(getting back to his spiel)
In this crystal I can see past, present and future.
(as he talks his leg reaches over to where Dorothy has laid her bag and he starts edging it toward himself)
--Let me delve into the past.
(coming out of trance for second - to Dorothy)
Did you ever delve into the past?

Dorothy
(still mystified and in awe)
No.

CONTINUED:

CONTINUED (2) 2

Professor Marvel
You ought to try it sometime - it's wonderful.
(getting in the mood again)- staring and pointing into crystal)
There's Richard the Third. He's in a predicament. He's calling for something. I hear him now, "My Kingdom for a horse! My Kingdom for a horse!"

As the Professor says this he bends down and picks up Dorothy's bag without her seeing him. Goliath sticks his head in through the rear curtain.

Professor Marvel
MY KINGDOM FOR A HORSE!

Goliath (whispering to him)
War Admiral just lost.

Professor Marvel (weakly)
Ah -- My Kingdom for a horse.
(he slips Goliath Dorthy's bag and nods to him meaningly - to Dorothy)
Where were we?

Dorothy
With Richard the Third.

Professor Marvel
(again bending over the crystal)
Ah, the scene changes -
(pointing into crystal)
- and Queen Elizabeth enters. Something is wrong. She's in a quandry -- No, she's in the Palace -- Well, I mean she's in the Palace in a quandry -- Shall she help Columbus and pawn her precious jewels and stones -- Shall she -- She shall -- And as we say in Latin "Hockus precious stoneus." Ah, but where is Columbus. He has not arrived yet. Where is Columbus? WHERE IS COLUMBUS?

As Professor Marvel says the last "Where is Columbus" Goliath again sticks his head through the rear curtain.

Goliath (whispering)
In Ohio.

Professor Marvel gives him a look of disgust. Goliath slips him something.

INSERT: The object in the Professor's hand. It is a picture of the farm with Dorothy and Aunt Em at the gate.

CONTINUED:

"The public itself demanded production of *Oz*. After *Snow White*, letters began pouring into the different studios, asking for dramatizations of various childhood classics. Of all storybook characters, Baum's [were] the most in demand. Even after M-G-M announced the picture, the letters did not cease . . . it sometimes seemed as every man and woman in America between the ages of twenty and sixty had definite ideas about the casting or playing. Mervyn LeRoy promised a faithful reproduction, but we continued to be attacked on all sides by enthusiasts who insisted that certain pet scenes and characters must on no account be slighted or left out. All [these scenes] had to be planned down to the last detail, yet they seem to have grown spontaneously in the mind of some happy child. When shooting began, the same joyous mood prevailed. Judy would sneak the other pupils [from the studio school] onto the set. If these children were satisfied, Victor Fleming chuckled. There, he said, was the audience he was aiming at: "People may be sixty when they come into the theater, but by the Great Horn Spoon, they'll be exactly six while they're looking at the picture!""

— Florence Ryerson and Edgar Allan Woolf, Oz Scenarists

PROD. 1060 WIZARD OF OZ — PRE-RECORDINGS — SCORER Herbert Stothart

SONG NUMBER	TITLE	COMPOSER	LYRICS	COPYRIGHT & DATE		MPPA	PUBLISHED
3511	Jitter Bug	Arlen	Harburg	168650	5-28-38	5-28-38	
rev	(sequence)			171654	7-18-38		
				179010	8-12-38		
3254	Ding Dong the Witch Is Dead	Arlen	Harburg	175157	8-24-38		
3525	If I Only Had a Heart	Arlen	Harburg	171656	7-18-38		
3537	Over the Rainbow	Arlen	Harburg	171647	7-18-38		
rev				175159	7-18-38		
3544	If I Only Had a Brain	Arlen	Harburg	171652	7-18-38		
	(additional verse)			179783	10-1-38		

NUMBER	TITLE	COMPOSER/ARR.	ORCH.	TAKE NO.	PERFORMED BY	DATE	TIME
01 rev	If I Only Had a Brain (Song & Dance)	Arlen	Cutter	2002-13/15/16/19; 2012-2/5/8; 2017-3/5/7/8/10/11;	Bolger; Garland; orch	9-30-38	1:19 3:07
	" New Endings	Stothart	"	2501 to 2503 (see log) 2575-1; 2576-1; 2583-6 to 11;			
02	If I Only Had the Nerve	Arlen	Cutter	2003 to 2004 (see log) 2032-1	B Lahr; B Ebsen; Bolger; Garland;orch	"	:44
03	Wonderful Wizard Of Oz	"	"	2005 to 2010; 2025 to 2028 (see log) 2095-3; 2102-1; 2109 to 2111; 2113 to 2117; 2119 to 2122 (see log)			
					B Lahr; B Ebsen; Bolger; Garland;orch	"	2:30
	Off To See the Wizard			2588 to 2590 (see log)	Piano; harp	7-9-39	:01
04	If I Only Had a Heart (Song & Dance)	Arlen	Cutter	2011-7/8/9; 2013-2/3/4/7; 2031-3/4/6/10/13/21/22;	B Ebsen; A Caselotti; orch J Haley; orch	9-30-38 10-8-38	3:00 1:19
05	Jitterbug	Arlen-Harburg	Salinger	2014 to 2016 (see log)	Garland; Ebsen; Bolger; Lahr; orch	10-6-38	3:29
06	Over the Rainbow	Arlen	Cutter	2019-1/2/4/6/7/8 2029-2	Garland; orch	10-7-38	2:13
07	If I Were King Of the Forest & (Recitative)	Arlen-Stothart	"	2020 to 2024 (see log) 2028-1/2; 2030-6/8/9; 2557-1/2/3	Garland; Ebsen; Lahr; Bolger; orch	10-11-38 5-8-39	3:43 1:02
08	Munchkin Musical Sequence	Arlen	Arnaud	2040-2041; 2057 to 2090; 2092-2093 (see log)	B Burke; Garland; B Bletcher; L Bridges; chorus; orch	12-14-38	9:14
	Coroner Sequence Leaving Munchkinland	Stothart	Cutter	2505-1 to 8; 2578-7/10 2580-1/3		7-9-39	1:27
	Glinka's Last Appearance			2582-1/2		7-9-39	:29
09 c	Tin Man	Stothart	Cutter	2096-4; 2097-3 2552-1/2; 2553-7/8	Haley; orch	5-8-39	:14
010	Yellow Brick Road	Arlen	Cutter	2098 to 2101; 2103 to 2106 (see log) see also #6			
	Marimba Notes			2018-1/2/3		10-1-38	:19

LEFT: The first page of the music department conductor's log provides a summary of vocal pre-recordings made (mostly) prior to the onset of filming. The multiplicity of takes and dates indicates the care and concern that M-G-M put into this specific project.

BELOW: This form had to be filed for all intended M-G-M musical numbers. Ironically, the year is mistyped; at this early date in *1938* preproduction, Buddy Ebsen was still in the cast, and the title of the film's "marching song" was "The Wonderful Wizard of Oz." It had not yet evolved into the catchier "We're Off to See the Wizard."

LOEW'S INCORPORATED

Copy to:
Publishers
Home Office
Publicity & Adv.
Music Dept.

TENTATIVE

PRODUCTION MUSIC — MUSIC DEPARTMENT

Production #1060 — Date OCTOBER 5, 1939

Title of Number: WONDER UL WIZARD OF OZ

Title of Picture: WIZARD OF OZ

Music by: Harold Arlen

Star or Stars:

Words by: E. Y. Harburg

Featured Artists: Judy Garland, Buddy Ebsen, Ray Bolger, Bert Lahr

Words and Music by:

Director: Richard Thorpe

Style of Number: Fox Trot____, Waltz____

First Shown at:

Waltz with F. T. Version____, Ballad____

Town____

Comedy Vocal Routine

Theatre____

Remarks: A - Sung by Judy, Ebson, Bolger & Lahr in a clever vocal routine as they go to visit the "Wizard".

Signed: George G. Schneider — OFFICE OF NAT W. FINSTON, Department Head.

RIGHT: An *Oz* publicity photo shows Judy in the process of either prerecording or post-synching some aspect of the movie soundtrack.

ABOVE: To Oz?! The adventure begins for some of the little people of the cast. Jerry Maren is the diminutive eighteen-year-old, front and center, wearing a sweater rather than a jacket. **RIGHT:** M-G-M's historical pose is augmented by Denslow artwork of the Munchkins as he first portrayed them in 1900.

WHEN THE MOON COMES OVER THE MUNCHKINS . . .

OR: TAKING THE BUS TO OZ

As with most legendary motion pictures, *The Wizard of Oz* and its back story have endured any number of outrageous legends over the decades, and much "gozzip" has sprung from good storytelling or personal axe-grinding rather than factual reporting. Additionally, some relatively insignificant situations have been oddly distorted or perhaps confused or conflated with events related to other films.

Several of the most remarkable *Oz* fables (or at least rabid exaggerations) are founded in the historic Times-Square-to-Culver-City bus trek undertaken in November 1938 by some of the film's prospective Munchkin cast members. Prior reports of that trip have painted wildly imaginative accounts of the number of people involved, or of the troupe's departure from New York. Perhaps the most colorful recollections were provided by M-G-M casting director Billy Grady during a mid-1960s interview with John Lahr for the latter's superlative book about his father Bert, *Notes On A Cowardly Lion* (Alfred A. Knopf, 1969). The biographer can be forgiven for taking Grady at his word at the time, although the picture painted by the Metro executive is now known to be untrue.

Looking back to 1938, Grady assured Lahr that impresario Leo Singer had nothing to do with the acquisition of any of the film's "little people." He claimed instead that "350 midgets" were delivered to the studio by "midget monologist" Major Doyle. According to Grady, Doyle "despised Singer, not only because he would give him no work, but because the five-foot-five manager was known to exploit his clientele." Although Grady remembered almost having completed a deal with Singer, he told Lahr he "called [him] off" and signed with Doyle instead. The Major promised Grady "one hundred and seventy-five midgets out of New York," with the rest to be gathered on the West Coast.

ABOVE: On several levels, this photograph is a genuine time capsule. In addition to its Ozzy associations, it depicts one of the great M-G-M "flagship" movie palaces of New York City in 1938. Loew's State Theatre was on the east side of Seventh Avenue, between 45th and 46th Streets, in the heart of Times Square.

> **"We got to Times Square to meet the bus, and my eyes were going all over the place. 'Hey, I wonder if he plays baseball? I wonder if he likes girls?' I was wondering if they liked the same things that I do. I was curious, you know? Because after all those years without ever seeing another little person, it was different, you know?"**
>
> — *Jerry Maren, "Lollipop Guild" Munchkin*

According to Grady, Singer supposedly "raised hell" about losing the contract, and Doyle was so delighted with his coup that—to further aggravate Singer—he loaded up three buses at the Times Square Hotel rendezvous point and directed the drivers uptown to Singer's apartment home, instead of proceeding out of town through the

"We weren't thinking in terms of classics. We were just doing work, earning a living and liking what we were doing, trying for a hit song or two. It was a chance to express ourselves in terms we'd never been offered before. I loved the idea of having the freedom to do lyrics that were not just songs but scenes . . . in complete verse, such as Munchkinland. All of that had to be thought out by us and brought in to the director so he could see what we were getting at. Things like the three Lullaby girls, and the three tough kids who represented The Lollipop Guild. And The Coroner, who came to aver that The Witch was dead, sincerely dead. All of that was thought up by us, it wasn't in the book."

— E. Y. "Yip" Harburg

Holland Tunnel. When the buses parked out front on Central Park West and 68th Street, the Major "went to the [building] doorman: 'Phone upstairs and tell Leo Singer to look out the window.' It took about ten minutes. Then Singer looked [down] from the fifth floor. . . . And there were all these midgets in those buses in front of his house with their bare behinds sticking out the window."

That spectacle—later termed "Major Doyle's Revenge"—makes for an unforgettable mental image but remains only a highly original tale. Leo Singer alone held the contract for The Munchkins, and all but a handful of the 124 little people who participated in the film worked through him. (Major Doyle was one of the few who indeed arranged an independent agreement with M-G-M for the project.)

As can be seen in the accompanying Metro paperwork, a number of the diminutive actors acquired by Singer traveled by train or automobile. But there was also one cross-country, banner-bearing bus simultaneously conveying a whole mass of Munchkins to the West Coast, and its departure was too good a promotional ploy for the publicity-prone movie studio to ignore. As a result, a number of little people in the New York/New Jersey/Connecticut area, as well as several from more distant East Coast origins, were directed to gather in the heart of Manhattan. The "Lollipop Guild" kid-in-the-middle, Jerry Maren (then Jerry Marenghi) was not only on the Munchkin bus, but today strongly concurs that the saga of "Major Doyle's Revenge" is pure fabrication insofar as that day, that trip, and the cast of *Oz* is concerned. And studio records conclusively show that the perpetrator of the anecdote, Billy Grady himself, was not even in New York at that time (as he told John Lahr) but actually working at M-G-M in California when the Munchkins assembled and the bus left Manhattan.

In a more minor embellishment, Aljean Harmetz offers in *The Making of The Wizard of Oz* (Knopf, 1977) that "sixty" midgets, "nearly half of" those planned for the film cast, came out to Hollywood on the chartered bus. In truth, only twenty-eight made the trip from New York; they left the city on Saturday morning, November 5, picked up two more little people in Pittsburgh, and pulled into Culver City on the evening of Thursday, November 10.

At that time, I. I. "Al" Altman worked for Loew's, Inc., the Manhattan-based parent company of M-G-M. Once the bus was underway, he wired Billy Grady in California that the corporate publicity machinery was in full swing, and that "exploitation men" had been "notified . . . at all points where bus stops." In a subsequent letter, Altman offered Grady further details of the travel arrangements, noting that the single bus required for the trip had been chartered by Loew's from the All American Bus Company, Inc.:

> It was necessary to advance them $2,666.00. This was made up as follows:
>
> - 7,000 miles @ 35 cents per mile (round trip from N.Y. to Los Angeles): $2,450.00
> - Estimated three-week lay-over in L.A. of driver and up-keep at $3.00 per day: $63.00
> - Estimated three-week lay-over in L.A. Cost of garage @ $1 per night: $21.00
> - Estimated additional two days travel each way, meals at $1.00 per person per day for 33 people: $132.00. This item was brought about by the fact that the bus is taking two additional days in order to allow the midgets to stop over at hotels nights. It is because of this provision that they agreed to travel by bus, thus saving us a very substantial sum per person.

Altman added, "We also advanced the All American Bus Lines, Inc., $200.00 covering an estimated average cost of $1.00 per person to put up the midgets for five nights. While this amounts to $165.00, the bus company asked for $200.00 in order to cover themselves."

In retrospect, it's interesting that Loew's and M-G-M felt that the Munchkin sequence of the film could be cast, costumed, rehearsed, and photographed in three weeks. The Munchkins actually worked for almost two months, finishing their ten-minute sequence on New Year's Eve 1938. But even if the bus trip that delivered some thirty "little people" to the portals of Munchkinland wasn't nearly as picturesque or highly populated as legend would have it, it remains a fascinating glimpse of the promotional workings of a major studio during Hollywood's Golden Era—and an example of how cost-conscious even M-G-M could sometimes be.

OPPOSITE: This paperwork summarizes the Munchkin "shipment" organized in New York, along with travel arrangements for other cast members who were en route to California to take part in *Oz*.

METRO-GOLDWYN-MAYER PICTURES

ARS GRATIA ARTIS

DISTRIBUTED BY
LOEW'S INCORPORATED
LOEW BUILDING -- 1540 BROADWAY
NEW YORK

November 11, 1938

Mr. Billy Grady
M-G-M Studios
Culver City, Calif.

Dear Billy:

Here is a complete list and detailed comments concerning the 73 midgets which the New York office has taken care of, in connection with "The Wizard of Oz". This supplements my recent letter to you giving detailed expenditures.

With best wishes,

Sincerely,

I. I. ALTMAN

IIA:hl
Enc.

No Agreement or Order will be binding on this Corporation unless in Writing and Signed by an Officer

em 11-16-38

Mr. [illegible]man: Here is the complete st[illegible] regarding midgets: Nov. 10, 1938

The following left by special chartered bus on Saturday morning Nov. 5th:

1. Robert Kanter
2. Charles Silvern
3. Frank Cucksey
4. John Ballas
5. Leo Mattina
6. Margaret Nickloy
7. Freda Betsky
8. Mike Rodgers
9. Ike Rodgers
10. Addie Frank
11. Frank Packard
12. Walter Paul
13. Jerry Marenghi (Money advanced by Singer to travel from Roxbury, Mass to NY. We must furnish return fare to Roxbury) from N.Y.
14. Prince Leon
15. Gus Wayne
16. Elsie Schultz
17. Elizabeth Coultier
18. Hazel Rice
19. Mitzi Koestner
20. Emma Koestner
21. Billy Koestner
22. Jimmy Rosen
23. Frank Kikel
24. Jack Glicken
25. Margaret Hoy
26. Helen Hoy
27. Mathew Raia
28. Eddie Kozicki

M. S. Rodgers, adult, parent of Mike and Ike Rodgers. Insisted upon travelling.
Mrs. M.S. Rodgers. NOTE: Mr. Rodgers says he will pay for MRS. Rodgers transportation to and from the coast. Charge Singer $60.00, which Singer should collect from Rodgers, plus any hotel accomodations and extra meals.

29. Charles Ludwig, picked up at Pittsburg.
30. Elmer Spangler, picked up at Pittsubrg.

* *

31. Joseph J. Koziel, train accomodations arranged from Spring Valley, Ill. to coast and return. He has return ticket.
32. Franklin Obaugh, train accomodations arranged from Arkadelphia, Arkansas to coast and return. He has return ticket.
33. Gladys Wolff, train accomodations arranged from St. Louis to coast and return. She has return ticket.
34. Boer Brothers, train accomodations arranged for two from St. Louis to coast
35. " " and return. They have return tickets.
36. Miss Ruth Smith, train accomodations from Marshelltown, Iowa to coast and return. She has return ticket.
37. Arnold Vierling, train tickets from Seymour, Indiana to coast and return. He has return ticket.
38. Harry Klima, train tickets from Beaumont, Texas to coast and return, He has return ticket.
39. Carl Stephen, train ticket from Beaumont, Texas to coast and return. He has return ticket.
40. Gladys Allison, train ticket from St. Louis to coast and return. She has return ticket.
41 Mr. and Mrs. Prince Denis, San Antonio, Texas. Driving in ~~by~~ their own car to
42. coast and return. Expenses incurred to be reimbursed by MGM in lieu of train tickets.

EM 11-16-38

Mr. Altman, cont:

43. David Brothers, Columbia, S. C. Train tickets arranged from Columbia, S.C. to
44. " " coast and return. ALSO, fifteen ($15.00) dollars advanced to them from New York production office for travelling expenses, to be deducted from their salary. They have return tickets. Charged to coast.

45. Anna Leslie, train ticket arranged from Minneapolis to coast and return. She has return ticket.
46. Three Royals train tickets arranged from Chicago, Ill. to L.A. and return.
47. " " They have return tickets (or Singer has them)
48. " "
49. Elmer. St. Aubin, train ticket arranged from Chicago, Ill. to L.A. and return to Chicago. He (or Singer) has return tickets)
50. Maynard Raabe, train ticket PAID FOR by Singer. Contact him to inquire if return fare has been arranged. We are to reimburse Singer for this one ticket.
51. Grace Harvey Williams Co. Driving in their own trailer from Minneapolis, Minn. to the coast and return. We paid one railroad fare from NY to Minneapolis for Grace Williams to enable her to meet others in her company. Singer advanced them $250.00 for traveling expenses.
52. " " "
53. " " "
54. " " "
55. " " "
56. " " "
57. " " " Don't know whether these '12' include any adults, or whether they are all midgets.
58. " " "
59. " " "
60. " " "
61. " " "
62. " " "
63. Daisy Doll Co. By car from Sarasota, Fla, and return. Singer advanced them approximately 200.00 (exact amount asked for, for round trip was 390.00). Additional money will have to be advanced before they return.
64. " "
65. " "
66. " "
67. Jean LaBarbara One round trip ticket from Philadelphia, Penna to coast and return mailed her registered mail. She is to leave Sat night, Nov. 12. She has return ticket.
68. Mr. Tanner*** Left by train from New York. Round trip ticket furnished, either he or Singer has return ticket.
69. Miss Tanner*** Round trip ticket from New York to L.A. furnished. Either he or Singer has return ticket.
70. Margie Raia*** Round trip ticket furnished from L.A. to coast (½ fare) Either she or Singer has return ticket.
71. Nicky Page *** Round trip ticket furnished. Either he or Singer has return ticket. From N.Y. to L.A.
72. Victor Wetter*** Round trip ticket furnished from N.Y. to L.A. and return. Either he or Singer has ticket return.

*** There was a mix-up with tickets at Penn station before leaving. Two boys didn't show. up. Finally one made proper train without a ticket, and other went out on later train. Ncessary adjustments were made by me with ticket receiver at N.Y. Penn station, and all difficulties ironed out. Duplicate train tickets were issued and wired ahead enroute % conductor on board.

73. Murray Woods - leaving N.Y. by train Nov. 11th - round trip to L.A.

Benn Jacobson

"What I remember most about the makeup was the skullcaps—the rubber skullcaps which they put on, and then they would glue them down tight; there was another wig that came on top of that. And, man! When you'd sweat on the top of your head, it would run right down your neck. And then they'd put make-up on that!"

— *Nels Nelson, Munchkin Townsman*

ABOVE/RIGHT: Signed Adrian watercolors for Munchkin wardrobe, "Commander of the Navy" and "Commander of Army," summer 1938. The former was also signed off as "okay" by producer LeRoy and includes attached fabric samples. **FAR RIGHT:** This form letter was signed by the majority of Munchkin players. In it, each guarantees to "look solely to Leo Singer for all compensation" for services related to *Oz*.

Culver City, California
October 1, 1938.

Loew's Incorporated,
Culver City,
California

Gentlemen:

I hereby warrant to you that I have entered into a contract of employment with Leo Singer, whereby I have agreed to render my exclusive services for you in connection with the production of your photoplay "WIZARD OF OZ". I agree that in rendering such services I will carry out such instructions as you may give me, and will perform all services which may be required by you conscientiously and to the full limit of my ability and as, when and wherever you may request. I further agree to observe all of your studio rules and regulations.

I agree that I will look solely to Leo Singer for all compensation for the services which I am to render for you, and will not look to you or seek to hold you liable or responsible for the payment of any such compensation.

I hereby confirm the grant to you contained in the agreement between you and Leo Singer dated October 1, 1938, of all rights of every kind and character in and to all of my acts, poses, plays and appearances and in and to all recordations of my voice and all instrumental, musical and other sound effects produced by me, and in and to all of the results and proceeds of my services for you, and the right to use my name and likeness and reproductions of my voice and sound effects produced by me in connection with the advertising and exploitation thereof. I agree that you may use such photographs and recordings in said photoplay "WIZARD OF OZ" or in any other photoplay or photoplays and otherwise as you may desire.

All notices served upon Leo Singer in connection with the aforesaid agreement shall for all purposes be deemed to be notice to me of the matters contained in such notice.

Very truly yours,

Thos. J. Cottonaro

53

IHP:em

LEFT: Nona Cooper and Nita Krebs were in the core group of the famed "Singer Midgets" troupe and thus among the first to test costumes and make-up. This still was taken in August 1938, three months before the entire Munchkin ensemble was due at M-G-M. Cooper wears the wardrobe she disports on screen; Krebs's dress was significantly altered before filming began.

RIGHT: Murray Wood, coroner Meinhardt Raabe , mayor Charles Becker, and Billy Curtis. Such photographs were made and referenced to ensure each actor was given the appropriate wardrobe, wig, and/or facial appliances every day of filming. The little people described the process as an assembly line or game of musical chairs. They went from station to station, receiving a different makeup application each step along the way.

ABOVE: In this sea of Munchkins, impresario Singer is positioned between director Victor Fleming and first assistant Al Shenberg. Approximately half the troupe of Ozzy little people can be seen here. A controversial man, Singer was much respected by the majority of those who worked in his own troupe; they lovingly called him "Poppa."

OVER THE RAINBOW

How *Oz* Came to the Screen

At least six times between April and September 1938, M-G-M set a start date for *The Wizard of Oz*, and each came and went as preproduction problems grew. By October, director Norman Taurog had left the project; when filming finally started on the 13th, Richard Thorpe was—literally and figuratively—calling the shots. Rumor had it that the *Oz* Unit first would seek and photograph whichever California barnyard most resembled Kansas. Alternately, a trade paper reported that all the musical numbers would be completed before other footage was taken. (Perhaps that misinformation grew from the fact that most Judy Garland, Ray Bolger, Buddy Ebsen, and Bert Lahr *Oz* vocals were prerecorded between September 30 and October 11.)

In the end, Thorpe began on Stage 26 on Metro's Culver City lot, filming Dorothy's meeting with The Scarecrow at the cornfield crossroads. The duo also performed "If I Only Had a Brain" under the guidance of choreographer Bobby Connolly. Bolger's initial approach to his character seems to have been very gentle; his prerecording for the song was husky, almost whispered in some places and sung legato in others.

By October 17, the expeditious Thorpe had moved on to The Witch's Castle. Over eight days, he filmed the escape of Toto; the imprisonment of Dorothy; her rescue by The Scarecrow, Tin Man, and Lion (disguised as Winkie Guards); the capture and chase by The Winkies; and scenes with The Witch, Nikko, and another monkey. Stills of these sequences show staging and visual concepts that would not appear in the finished film:

- Rather than being followed and chased by The Winkies, Toto instead escaped through their ranks to leap across the castle drawbridge.
- Thorpe kept Bolger, Ebsen, and Lahr in their Guard disguises well after they broke through The Tower Room door to free Dorothy.
- A wrought-iron (not wooden) chandelier came crashing down on The Winkies when The Tin Man cut the rope that held it aloft.
- Alternate hair, makeup, or costume designs were in place for Garland ("Lolita"), Bolger ("The Mummy"), and Margaret Hamilton.

Additionally, Dorothy performed a reprise of "Over the Rainbow" while locked up and awaiting execution in The Tower Room. Garland sang this "live," as it was too difficult a rendition to prerecord and lip-synch. Breaking down into sobs as scripted, the girl progressed through three takes before the performance was deemed satisfactory. She was accompanied by an off-screen piano, which would be supplanted on the soundtrack by full orchestra when *Oz* was in final edit.

OPPOSITE PAGE: "Look! Emerald City is closer and prettier than ever!" This detail from an *Oz* matte painting represents journey's end for Dorothy and her friends as they viewed it from the poppy field. Many of the extraordinary background vistas seen in the film were created by melding film footage with crayon drawings such as this one. The combination was called a "Newcombe shot," after creator Warren Newcombe.

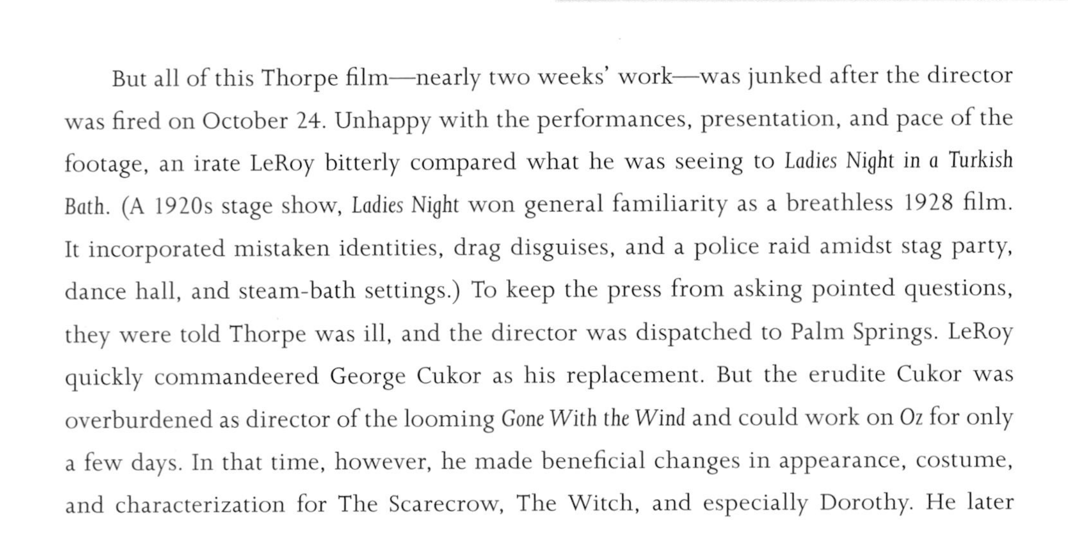

LEFT: Directed by Richard Thorpe in October 1938, this scene shows alternate staging for the capture sequence in the foyer of The Witch's Castle. Victor Fleming oversaw the later, different retake, which included Jack Haley (not Buddy Ebsen) as The Tin Man. **BELOW:** On one of his first days "in Oz," Haley is escorted to The Yellow Brick Road. No one had yet realized The Tin Man was wearing the wrong costume. **RIGHT:** Fleming adjusts the pitching arm of an orchard Ozian, November 1938.

But all of this Thorpe film—nearly two weeks' work—was junked after the director was fired on October 24. Unhappy with the performances, presentation, and pace of the footage, an irate LeRoy bitterly compared what he was seeing to *Ladies Night in a Turkish Bath*. (A 1920s stage show, *Ladies Night* won general familiarity as a breathless 1928 film. It incorporated mistaken identities, drag disguises, and a police raid amidst stag party, dance hall, and steam-bath settings.) To keep the press from asking pointed questions, they were told Thorpe was ill, and the director was dispatched to Palm Springs. LeRoy quickly commandeered George Cukor as his replacement. But the erudite Cukor was overburdened as director of the looming *Gone With the Wind* and could work on *Oz* for only a few days. In that time, however, he made beneficial changes in appearance, costume, and characterization for The Scarecrow, The Witch, and especially Dorothy. He later reflected that Garland "looked doll-like; the makeup too heavy, [and] I think she was wearing a wig. I suggested that they make her look as human and natural as possible. I told Judy the joke of it was that she *was* Dorothy from Kansas. She should really look like that and remain that way. Then her meetings with these strange people and her strange adventures would be more telling."

At this time, Ebsen was rushed to the hospital, seriously ill with aluminum poisoning after days of inhaling makeup particles. LeRoy was forced to find a substitute Tin Man, and Jack Haley was borrowed from Twentieth Century Fox to take the role.

Oz clearly needed help, and as Cukor left and Haley arrived, Metro brought in Victor Fleming. A no-nonsense man's man, Fleming had a reputation for working miracles when M-G-M product was in trouble. He also was a new father and had recently expressed the desire to achieve something in his work that would delight his daughters; he found it in *Oz*. After script conferences with writing associate John Lee Mahin, Fleming began the film again on November 4. He'd already ordered changes to the cornfield setting, and Judy and Ray went through their paces one more time as The Scarecrow lip-synched to his soft and sweet prerecording of "If I Only Had a Brain."

Moving ahead quickly, the director photographed in sequence on the orchard and cottage sets. Haley rerecorded "If I Only Had a Heart" and completed three days of filming before anyone recognized a major continuity error. The actor was wearing an adjusted version of Ebsen's costume, buckram covered with silver leather. But all the scenes shot by Ebsen took place later in the story, after Dorothy and her companions had been "renovated" in The Emerald City. Thus, Ebsen's "tin" was shiny and bright; in the Tin Man's first scenes, he was supposed to have been "standing over there, rusting, for the longest time." Haley's costume and makeup had to be redone and sixty thousand dollars of footage scrapped.

It was probably at this moment that Loew's, Inc., made another effort to scuttle *Oz*. Nicholas Schenck had first tried to keep the production from getting off the ground in February. He was all for canceling it again with the Thorpe/Ebsen snafus of October. On a subsequent, special trip of inquiry from New York to California, he thundered, "I'm not getting any answers! I want to know what's going on with Merv's picture!" But Louis B. Mayer managed to placate the money-conscious Schenck, and LeRoy declared, "Mr. Schenck, I wish I had three million dollars. I'd buy this picture from you. It's going to be worth more than that someday."

So, with a freshly tarnished Tin Man, filming continued. Elsewhere in the orchard/cottage sequence, Hamilton made her first appearances in the Cukor-mandated Witch makeup. Her skin shone in radioactive green; her chin was sharpened and elongated so that it almost equaled her extended nose. Yet one constant remained: "The Witch's laugh was a thing that came to me spontaneously. And as it went along, it got better. The important thing to remember was not to keep it level, the same thing all the time. You start high and come down low!"

When the Unit progressed into The Lion's Forest, Bert Lahr joined the troupe. Despite his off-camera agonies about almost everything, Lahr's performance was a brightener. The laughter-prone Garland repeatedly broke up at him, but her joy was contagious, and the cast of "old pros" around her was universally admiring. Haley observed: "Judy was such a doll, a lovely person. She was as lighthearted as anyone I've ever met, and she was in seventh heaven making the picture. A lovely, happy, young girl, and it was a great pleasure working with her." Billie Burke later offered, "From the moment Judy walked on the soundstage, there was no question she was a star. I think she knew it, too, but [when the work was a strain, there was] never a complaint, never a murmur." If her costars admired, they also—as Garland once gratefully reflected—"kidded the life out of me."

ABOVE: Newly tarnished but still heartless, The Tin Man is invited to join the group heading west to The Emerald City.

Meanwhile, Judy developed a self-admitted crush on her director, who would come to her aid when she became the brunt of Ozian teasing. "If you want to know a perfectly wonderful man," she enthused at the time, "you should meet Victor Fleming. He's perfectly

Script: Wally Worsley PRODUCTION #1060
"THE WIZARD OF OZ"
(Technicolor)

Tests: Job #204
Preliminary #1564
Start: 10/12/38
Close: 2/27/39
Retakes Start: 2/28/39 | 6-30-39
Retakes Close: 3-10-39 | 6-30-39
Delivered: 7/4/39
Prod. # Assigned: July 12, 1938

Producer: Mervyn LeRoy
Director: Victor Fleming
Unit Mgr: Keith Weeks
Art Dir.: Wm Horning - Mal Brown
Asst Dir: Al Shenberg
Dance Dir: Bobby Connelly
Cutter: Blanche Sewell
Camera: Hal Rosson
Prop - Harry Edwards
Mixer - Gavin Burns
Grip - Pop Arnold
Gaffer - A. W. Brown

Direction:
Thorpe: 10/12/38 to 10/24/38
Cukor: Did not shoot
Fleming: 11/3/38 to 2/18/39
Vidor: 2/20/39 to

SETS:
060-01 - Ext. Kansas Farmhouse 29
060-02 - Int. Witch's Castle Room #2
060-03 - ~~Ext. Forest & Apple Trees~~ VOID
060-04 - Int. Witch's Castle 4
060-05 - Ext. Munchkinland & Dorothy's House - 27
060-06 - Ext. Emerald City 27
060-07 - Int. Throne Room 28
060-08 - Ext. Cottonwoods and Spring 27
060-09 - Ext. Apple Orchard & Tin Woodsman's House 26
060-10 - Ext. Cross Roads 26 - 25
060-11 - Ext. Lion Forest 25
060-12 - Ext. Jitter Trees 26 - 25
060-13 - Ext. Poppy Field 28
060-14 - ~~Ext. Hillside~~ - VOID
060-15 - Int. Farmhouse 28
060-16 - Int. Stairhall Witch's Castle 28
060-17 - Ext. Castle Gates 28 - 26
060-18 - Ext. Battlements & Witch's Castle 27
060-19 - Int. Witch's Tower Room (See #76) 4 - 28
060-20 - Ext. Rock at Gates 27
060-21 - Ext. Top of Rocks 26
060-22 - Int. Palace Corridor 28
060-23 - Test Set for Costumes
060-24 - Int. Wash & Brush Up Company 28
060-25 - Ext. Hilltop (Long Shot - Newcombe) 26
060-26 - Publicity Shot - Book Cover
060-27 - Montage Song - (Yellow Brick Road) - 28
060-28 - Ext. Witch's Castle
060-29 - Int. Wagon 29
060-30 - Ext. Flying Monkeys Over Forest
060-31 - Smoke Ring Effects Shot 14
060-32 - Int. Witches Spell-~~XXXX~~Chamber
060-33 -
060-34 -
060-35 -
060-36 -
060-37 -

CAST:

Dorothy	Judy Garland
Tin Man	Jack Haley
Scarecrow	Ray Bolger
Lion	Bert Lahr
Witch	Margaret Hamilton
Wizard	Frank Morgan
Glinda	Billie Burke
Uncle Henry	Charles Grapewin
Nikko	Mitchel Lewis

060-38 -
060-39 -
060-40 -

060-60 - MAIN TITLE
060-61 - Ext. Good Witch In Sky (Process)
060-62 - Int. Miniature Horse Inside Tornado - Process
060-63 - Ext. Farm House Falling into Camera - Miniature
060-64 - Ext. Farm Tornado Leaving - Process
060-65 - Ext. Farm - Tornado Leaving - Background
060-66 - Process of Bicycle
060-67 - Ext. Approach to Farm - Process
060-68 - Ext. Farm Front Door - Process
060-69 - Ext. Emerald City Bubble (Matte) - Miniature
060-70 - Int. Miniature Cyclone - Miniature
060-71 - Ext. Miniature Cyclone - Miniature
060-72 - ~~Ext. Hotel---(Miniature)~~ - VOID
060-73 - Ext. Long Shot Tornado - Miniature Same as set #060-
060-74 - Ext. Flying Monkey Backgrounds - Miniature
060-75 - Int. Dorothy's Bedroom - Process
060-76 - Int. Witch's Tower - Process
060-77 - Ext. Flying Monkeys Approaching Forest - Miniature
060-78 - Ext. Cartoon Monkey Backgrounds
060-79 - Double Print set for Int. Tornado - Backgrounds
060-80 - Ext. Kitchen Door and Cyclone Cellar - Process
060-81 - Ext. Balloon Basket - Process
060-82 - Ext. Miniature Farm and Tornado - Process
060-83 - Crystal Ball - Process
060-84 - Ball of Fire
060-85 - Tinman Bee Shot
060-86 - Ext. Bubble (Matte) - Miniature
060-87 - Ext. Witch Skywriting - Miniature
060-88 - Ext. Witch's Tower - Miniature
060-89 - Ext. Jitter Forest - Miniature -
060-90 - Inserts -

THIS PAGE: This extraordinary reference list provides data on production dates; cast and staff; and the identification number, location, and/or type of settings (full-scale, miniature, process) required for the film. It's not infallible; Bobby Connolly and Mitchell Lewis's names are misspelled, and the role played by the latter was that of The Captain of The Winkie Guard.

marvelous. He has the nicest low voice and the kindest eyes. He shows me all of the courtesies he would to [M-G-M glamour goddess] Hedy Lamarr."

Stage 29 was next readied for *Oz*, and (according to Metro publicity) twenty men worked for a week to embed forty thousand artificial flowers into its terrain for the poppy sequence. By this point, the full complement of Munchkin actors had arrived elsewhere on the lot to practice their songs and staging, attend wardrobe fittings, and undergo make-up tests. Between obligations, some of the troupe explored, and fifteen-year-old Margaret Pellegrini wandered down an alleyway and was suitably dazzled when she "opened the door to another sound stage, and I saw this big, huge room. It was like a warehouse—but it was *all poppy fields!*" Munchkin Betty Tanner was equally impressed. Fifty-five years later, she would exclaim, "Oh, that was *beautiful*! That set was just absolutely *beautiful*!"

ABOVE LEFT: The quintessential example of movie magic in the making is exemplified by this extraordinary view of Dorothy and The Lion as they're observed, followed, tracked, photographed, and immortalized on their run across The Poppy Field soundstage. **ABOVE RIGHT:** Between takes, Judy enjoys a rare moment of repose.

By early December, Fleming had finished in the flowers and moved back to The Witch's Castle to retake the October scenes done by Thorpe. He also filmed the sequence in which The Witch torched The Scarecrow ("Just light him as if he were a cigarette, Miss Hamilton" was Fleming's offhand directive), followed by her subsequent liquidation. Hamilton later described the methods employed by the special effects crew to implement her meltdown: "I was wetted down before I stepped on a platform in the floor of the stage. And there was dry ice attached to the inside of my black cloak, and my costume was fastened to the floor. I screamed, 'I'm melting! Melting! What a world! What a world! Who would have thought a good little girl like you could destroy my beautiful wickedness? Ohhhh, look out. I'm going. Ohhhhhhhhh!' When the elevator, or platform, brought me down, the dry ice gave off vapors, and the updraft of air puffed out my skirt. And once I was through the floor, nothing was left on the stage but my hat and a little material."

The male principals of *Oz* then enjoyed a deserved vacation for the rest of December. But Judy and Toto segued directly into practice for the Munchkinland segment. By the last two weeks of December, Leo Singer's aggregation of 124 little people was primed to swiftly progress through filming on their village set. Choreographer Connolly and his assistants, Dona Massin and Arthur "Cowboy" Appell, were gently militant in their drill, plotting

ABOVE: The storm trooper Winkies rehearse during Thorpe's tenure. **RIGHT:** A December 1938 rehearsal on the battlement of The Witch's Castle shows principals and technicians; Judy's hair styling for the sequence is incomplete. **BELOW:** Two blasé winged monkeys ignore a test of the miniature rubberized flying brotherhood behind them. (At lower left of frame: "The Lilly," a six-by-nine-inch white card held up to the camera at the conclusion of each Technicolor shot. When film was processed, the white of the Lilly was a primitive means of determining if hues had been accurately captured and lighting had been correct.)

different performance patterns for the soldiers, the dancing or background townspeople, and those dozen Munchkins with specific roles and lip-synched lines.

Among the wildest anecdotes about *Oz* are the sagas about madly partying Munchkins. But those actors began their makeup process at six a.m., six days a week, and then worked until after dark. Few had the inclination for rowdy evenings. Still, the legends persist, founded and perpetrated by Garland in a strictly-for-laughs version of Munchkin misbehavior related on a Jack Paar television special in 1967. A year later, such accounts were expanded by Lahr's memories, as quoted in his son's biography. LeRoy's autobiography provided further elaboration in 1974, as did subsequent interviews with *Oz* staff, crew, and contemporary M-G-M employees. In truth, a small percentage of the 124 little people were responsible for the reputation the rest have had to defend. A few were drinkers; there was an occasional hotel fracas. An estranged husband pulled a knife on his ex-wife, dragged her by the hair across a dining room, and finally had to be sent home when he brought two guns to the set "to protect her."

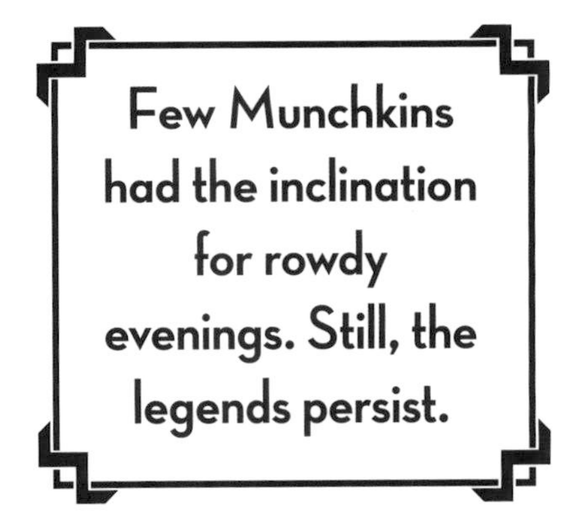

But most Munchkin memories were pleasant. Between takes, the diminutive Ozians visited with Garland, Hamilton, and Billie Burke, the latter making her debut in the picture during their sequence. When rehearsals and filming for the little people coincided with Thanksgiving and Christmas, there were few complaints. Jerry Maren spoke for the group when he reflected, "It was a job, you know? I was lucky to have a job in the Depression—and lucky to be in the movies." If they appreciated the work, however, the Munchkins were less delighted about their wages. Budgeted to receive one hundred dollars per person per week during filming, the little people never saw anything close to that amount. According to his contract, Singer collected the salaries from M-G-M but paid out less than half of it to his employees. With great good humor and a little edge, Pellegrini points out today, "Toto made more money than we did. He had a better agent."

By January 1939, the Munchkins had moved on to non-*Oz* pursuits, and the crew adjourned to The Haunted Forest for a production number with the principal cast. Contrary to other accounts, "The Jitterbug" did not take five weeks to film. But the time spent in preparing and photographing the upbeat routine added ninety thousand dollars to the budget. In addition to rehearsing a dance with Garland, Bolger, Haley, and Lahr, Bobby Connolly required several days to set the rhythmic movements of the

ABOVE: The Munchkins go into their dance. The sequence includes some of Harburg's best wordplay as Dorothy is repeatedly told, "You'll be hist'—" (i.e., hissed) before the phrase is completed as "You'll be hist-ory." A similar verbal gag ensues a moment later when she's informed—in best 1930s slang—that she "will be a bust! be a bust! be a bust . . . in the Hall of Fame!" **LEFT:** A test frame shows the massed Munchkinland cast. As they filmed such scenes, director Fleming and cameraman Harold Rosson liked to keep moving on a giant boom. When audiences watched the finished picture, they thus were provided with variety and dimensionality in both view and depth perception.

LEFT: A rare view of the set that got away: a Haunted Forest grove of Jitter Trees, unseen by any but the early sneak preview audience who viewed *Oz* before "The Jitterbug" number was deleted.

tree branches that also participated in the staging. The choreographer finally devised a means of "tapping out the correct musical time on the controls by which technicians signaled the trees." Thus the men encased in the rubber tree trunks got their orders by audio signal, "much as an aviator 'flies blind' with his radio." Despite the effort, "The Jitterbug" was dropped from *Oz* after its first sneak preview. There's been much conjecture about the edit ever since; the film of the number no longer survives, but there are random home movies taken during a dress rehearsal plus the original prerecording. From these, it's easy to ascertain that the jazzy song is inessential and would have been a jarring mood-breaker at a point in the story when dramatic tension had been masterfully built and sustained.

Conversely, the same tension was well served elsewhere in the sequence. The attack of The Winged Monkeys has provided a potent emotional strain for most young viewers for seven decades. But there were technical frictions in its creation as well. Haley explained, "It took a long time to get the monkeys to land just right. Some of them were made of rubber, and some were really people dressed up in costumes. The stuntmen were made to fly by wires. And all of those scenes where they were flying were difficult to coordinate. If it didn't work, or if one of the wires broke, the scene would have to be redone. It took several takes to get it just right." Bolger recalled an offshoot of such filming: "After the first take, Vic yelled, 'Take 'em up again!' That meant twenty-five dollars more; they were told they'd get twenty-five dollars per flight. Then they went up a third time. Another twenty-five dollars. A fourth time. We could hear them saying to each other, 'They'll never pay us all this money. Never!' Finally, to make sure Metro did fork over the cash, the [monkeys] struck the picture. Stopped it cold for a few hours."

The most expansive and populated segments of the film were achieved between mid-January and mid-February in The Emerald City. After testing costumes two months earlier and prerecording "The Merry Old Land of Oz" in December, Frank Morgan finally joined the company and was gainfully employed for the rest of the shoot. Fleming first photographed the arrival of Dorothy and friends at the city entrance; "Who rang that bell?!" was Morgan's accusatory query. Once the doors were opened, he appeared in his second incarnation, performing a Cockney introduction to the "Horse of a Different Color" and a musical introduction to the town. After the "Renovation Sequence," Morgan turned up again as the Palace Soldier before morphing into two incarnations of The Wizard. "I am Oz, the Great and Powerful," intoned his Great Head, until the small and meek "man behind the curtain" was revealed. "I'm a very good man; I'm just a very bad Wizard," he admitted, before granting the requests of Dorothy's companions and announcing his plans to take her back to Kansas himself.

During these weeks, the throne room and balloon sequences shared camera time with Lahr's bravura "If I Were King of the Forest." Surviving prerecordings offer proof that Dorothy, The Scarecrow, and Tin Man had to work hard to maintain solemnity in the face of his determined delivery. Eventually, portions of the routine were trimmed to shorten the film (and, perhaps, to prevent the song from becoming too much of a showstopper), but the combination of Lahr, Arlen, and Harburg remains some sort of musical comedy miracle.

Two other trims were made in Emerald City scenes. The quartet's walk down the corridor for their initial audience with The Wizard was filmed as an ominous procession, with booming echoes of the voice of Oz hastening their every step. More to be regretted was the deletion of the "triumphal return," wherein the principals were escorted through the streets by three hundred green-clad extras. The accompanying chorale arrangement of "Ding-Dong! The Witch is Dead" also incorporated bits of "We're Off to See the Wizard" and "The Merry Old Land of Oz." The sequence supposedly cost one hundred thousand dollars to produce, but it was dropped from the film before the premiere.

As the months wore on, Fleming would joke about the "considerable headache" of the project: "It seemed inevitable to me that, when I finished [Oz], I would quit pictures for good!" Instead, in mid-February, he found himself enmeshed in a greater challenge. *Gone With the Wind* had been shooting for a month under George Cukor. But he was unhappy with both the script and the daily rushes. Additionally, *Wind* star Clark Gable felt that Cukor's direction favored his two leading ladies, Vivien Leigh and Olivia de Havilland. On February 13, producer David O. Selznick and Cukor jointly

ABOVE: Frank Morgan is shown here in the first of five Emerald City characterizations. **RIGHT:** The *Oz* stars await their initial exposure to the fabled "Horse of a Different Color." **BELOW:** Between takes, the actors and a staff member loll about in a corner of The Emerald City.

Vidor directed the full cast in their Kansas sequences before beginning two weeks of smaller Kansas scenes and Technicolor retakes.

RIGHT: Dorothy played her first scene with Aunt Em and Uncle Henry on this set of The Gale Farm in February 1939. The "old incubator" that went bad is at the left center of the picture.

announced the director would leave the project, and Selznick privately approached King Vidor to replace him. But both producer and Gable actually were determined to get Fleming for the job; he was Gable's closest friend and trusted professional associate. When Vidor expressed qualms about *Wind*, he instead was offered the chance to finish *Oz*, so that Fleming could move over to Selznick to provide support for Gable. This was agreeable to all.

Fleming stayed with *Oz* through February 17, and Vidor directed the full cast in their Kansas sequences before beginning two weeks of smaller Kansas scenes and Technicolor retakes. Among these was a new vocal performance and dance for "If I Only Had a Brain." Bolger re-recorded the song in stronger fashion; the elaborate choreography for the number was devised by Busby Berkeley, new to Metro after a long stint at Warner Bros. Ultimately Ray's song stayed, but the dance was deleted in final editing. According to Bolger, the routine came across as just "too much fantasy."

During his tenure, Vidor also filmed cyclone scenes, although Fleming had okayed preliminary tornado footage before his departure. Vidor and Judy were aided in these by stand-in Caren Marsh, who periodically had worked on *Oz* during lighting tests and rehearsals while the underage Garland attended school. Marsh has written, "I had no idea those [wind] machines could blow so hard. I could barely move to the farmyard gate. When I did reach the gate, I could hardly open it. I wondered if I could make it to the front door without being blown over." Marsh was subjected to additional onslaughts as fans were retested. "At last they had it right, and I could relax. They called for Judy. I stepped out of the scene, and she stepped in. When they called for 'Action,' the wind blew, and Judy struggled through a perfect first take. It pleased me that my job as stand-in, rehearsing over and over again, made it easier for her."

By the second week of March, principal photography was completed. But it would take another four months to edit the film, add special effects footage, and compose and record the musical underscoring. The rough cut was prepared by Blanche Sewell; after spending his days on *Gone With the Wind*, Fleming returned to work with her into the night at M-G-M. By June, the film was still overlong, but as was then the custom, *Oz* was taken to "sneak preview," so M-G-M could gauge from audience reaction what might be expendable.

About twenty minutes were deleted in all. Some excisions involved substantial film: Bolger's dance, the "triumphal return," and "The Jitterbug." Tiny scenes were dropped if it was felt the storyline could be sustained without them. Garland's reprise of "Rainbow" had been redone under Fleming, but it was eliminated as well, possibly because Dorothy's distress was too harrowing for youngsters in the audience. Certainly it was the reaction of children that forced Fleming to make the tightest possible trims in Hamilton's dialogue.

The greatest controversy concerned Garland's solo song. Studio hierarchy felt that a star shouldn't sing in a barnyard, and even music department executives missed the point of the number. Publisher Jack Robbins complained: "It sounds like a child's piano exercise. Nobody will sing it—who'll buy the sheet music?" Sam Katz, head of the music division, was more disparaging; he felt the entire score was "above the heads of children." Arlen and Harburg were distraught when they attended the second *Oz* preview and watched as Aunt Em ordered Dorothy to "Find yourself a place where you won't get into any trouble." A moment later, Miss Gulch came into view; "Over the Rainbow" was gone, which rendered meaningless its subsequent omnipresence in the underscoring. Thereafter, Arlen refused to attend advance screenings of his films: "No more previews. From now on, I'm going to write the best I can, turn 'em in, and forget 'em."

But the fight for "Rainbow" wasn't over, although it took both LeRoy and Freed to argue the song back into *Oz*. Freed was particularly declarative, and he told Mayer, "The song stays. Or I go." Mayer decided to let the public decide about "Rainbow"; *Oz*, at a final edit of one hundred and one minutes, was ready for release.

This meant it was time for the publicity department to demonstrate its prowess. In M-G-M's history, only *Ben-Hur* (1925) and *Mutiny On the Bounty* (1935) had cost more than two million dollars to produce. By the time film prints and advertising expenses were added to its budget, *Oz* would run up a tally of $2.7 million. It would have to be touted as an extraordinary event to bring in enough customers to justify that expenditure.

Fortunately—eventually—it would surpass even the hype the M-G-M press corps could create.

Form 100

PRODUCTION — METRO-GOLDWYN-MAYER STUDIOS — SUMMARY

Title: Release: The Wizard of Oz — Script — Prod. No. 1060

Producer: Mervyn LeRoy — Director: Victor Fleming — Star: 38

Unit Mgr.: Joe Cooke — Ass't Dir.: Al Shenberg — Camera: Harold Rosson, Allan Davey

Featured Players: Judy Garland, Frank Morgan, Bert Lahr, Billie Burke, RayBolger, Jack Hale, Margaret Hamilton, Charles Grapewine

Writers: Noel Langley, Florence Ryerson, Edgar Allan Woolf — Full Pages in Script: 113

Cutter: Blanche Sewell — Mixer — Art Dir.: Wm. A. Horning

Song Writers — Composers

Book, Play, Original — Author: L.Frank Baum

Start: 10/12/38 — Finish: 2/27/39 — Retakes Start — Finish

Days Scheduled: 53 — Days in Production: 86 — Days Retakes: 22

PRE COSTS		FINAL COSTS	
Book	$ 75,000.00	Book	75,000.00
Scenario	30,171.96	Scenario	82,390.99
Director	11,125.00	Director	148,547.22
Star & Cast		Star & Cast	474,700.49
Misc.		Misc.	1,988,591.60
Total	$ 116,296.96	Total	$ 2,769,230.30
Est Total Less Pre Cost	$ 1,604,858.	Original Estimate	$ 1,721,154.84
Over or Under Est Cost Less Pre Cost	65 %	Over or Under	$ 1,048,076.
Negative Shot Dev	115,798 Feet	Length First Cut	11,986 Feet
Negative Charged	129,529. Feet	Length Final Cut	9,258 Feet
Release Printed At	M.G.M.	Negative Shipped	A. 2nd Neg 8/10/39 To
" Date:	August 18, 1939		

ABOVE: This concise Production Summary of *The Wizard of Oz* paints the kind of financial picture that would have elicited an apoplectic "I told you so!" from Nick Schenck. But the film was M-G-M's prestige offering of the year—a demonstration of the kind of dedication and imagination that made that studio the most venerated of all during Hollywood's Golden Era.

LEFT: This set reference still shows workers as they apply finishing touches to the cornfield crossroads in preparation for the first day of filming, October 1938. Richard Thorpe was then directing. **BELOW:** There was no audible sigh of relief at M-G-M, but *Daily Variety* offered front-page notice on October 14 that "LeRoy Starts *Wizard* . . . yesterday at Metro . . . in first song and dance number, 'Scarecrow Song.'"

"I fell in love with Dorothy when I read the Oz books. She was my favorite person—such a wonderful child—and we all wanted to follow her. So I wanted to be The Scarecrow, so I could follow her longest down The Yellow Brick Road! And when I walked on the film set the first day, I looked over, and I saw the most beautiful child. I thought she was the most adorable creature ever put on this earth—and so right for the part. She wasn't pretty; just plump. But in a way, she was beautiful, with an unusual beauty, a special kind of beauty. And I said, 'That's Dorothy!' And I remember what a beautiful person she was inside."

— Ray Bolger

LEFT: In an early script, the Kansas girl heard the strawman's lament and observed to Toto, "Here, if you've got no brains, they stuff you and make you a Scarecrow—but back home, Uncle Henry used to say that if you had no brains, you could always go work for the Government." **BELOW:** Thorpe's scenes included Dorothy's confrontation with The Witch. The sequence later was re-filmed by Fleming—and recollected by Margaret Hamilton in the 1960s: "There were some shots that even I was appalled at!"

ABOVE: Thirty years later, Judy Garland reflected on her two weeks as a blonde Dorothy: "They thought the bridge of my nose 'dipped in' too much, so they put a piece of rubber [on it]. And I kept thinking, 'If I'm so *perfect* for this part, why are they putting rubber on my nose?!'"

LEFT: This still reflects Thorpe's staging for Toto's departure; the sequence was eventually reconfigured under Fleming, whose version appears in the finished film. **BELOW:** This set reference still displays the evil accouterment of The Wicked Witch, including hourglass, broom, mortar, and pestle.

ABOVE: The early, eventually abandoned hairstyle and makeup for Margaret Hamilton are clearly visible here as she and Garland react to Toto's escape.

"For some mysterious reason, reports on the 'rushes' were strangely nonexistent. If anybody had seen them, they weren't talking, and this included Richard Thorpe. Finally, the company was shut down. The principal actors were to report to Mervyn LeRoy the following morning. As we assembled, he acknowledged our presence with a nod, a terse greeting, and a chilly look. Then, without much preamble, he launched into a chewing-out the likes of which I have never experienced [elsewhere] in all my years in show business. It was as virulent as it was unjustified. . . . We sat there, stunned. To the best of our abilities, we were doing what we were directed to do and what the lines called for."

— Buddy Ebsen

ABOVE: A rare off-the-set candid shows Judy bonding with Pat Walshe as Nikko. The latter was distinguishable from other Winged Monkeys in that The Witch had his wings clipped in order to keep him at her side. (This was an early plot point that went unexplained in the finished *Oz* script.)

RIGHT: A Technicolor test frame shows Bert Lahr, Buddy Ebsen, and Ray Bolger in their Winkie Guard disguises. This scene, their rescue of Dorothy, and their mad dash through The Witch's Castle are the only sequences Ebsen filmed.

"I don't believe any of the footage remains of the few days I was on the picture. It's not the first time a producer has disagreed with a director (especially if the producer is a director himself), nor will it be the last."

— Richard Thorpe

LEFT: When Thorpe filmed this scene, Dorothy's companions retained their Winkie garb. When Fleming redid it, he had them shuck the heavy wardrobe several moments earlier, as they released the girl from The Tower Room.

RIGHT: The chandelier used by Thorpe (seen here before and after its descent) was moved to a different location in the castle entryway when this scene was redone by Fleming. A wooden chandelier took its place.

THIS PAGE: George Cukor's influence on the makeup and costumes of Dorothy and The Scarecrow clearly can be seen in an examination of the characters as filmed by Thorpe in October (above) and Fleming in November (right).

"One afternoon after classes at the M-G-M schoolhouse, I was playing softball with some other girls, when a man walked by, stopped *dead* in his tracks, pointed to me, and said, 'You're *Dorothy*!' 'No, I'm Judy,' I said. The man was Mervyn LeRoy, and he thought I'd be perfect as the lead character in *Oz*. So I was called in to make a screen test of my features—the features that, supposedly, were 'perfect' for the part. But first I had to pass through the makeup, hairdressing, and wardrobe departments. They decided my bosom was too big, so at first they tried to tape it down. Then a woman turned up who was called the Cellini of the corset world. She made me a corset of steel, and I was laced up in that. I looked like a male Mary Pickford by the time they got through with all the alterations! But I emerged five hours later with blonde hair, rosebud mouth, sunken cheeks, a slim corseted figure, and a straight putty nose. I looked like I could pick locks with that nose. But the makeup department thought I looked great. So did I. 'Who are you?' the producer asked. 'I'm Dorothy,' I answered. He roared with anger and told them to get me out of there and return me to my original appearance—the 'Perfect Dorothy.' That picture was a turning point in my career and my life."

— Judy Garland

BOTTOM LEFT/NEAR LEFT: Baum & Denslow meet M-G-M in this comparison between original book art and the Garland/Bolger sequence of the film. **BELOW:** The cross-roads was repaved and curbed by the time Fleming began the picture "from the top." The new Yellow Brick Road was made of Masonite and redesigned to appear as if composed of actual bricks—not the odd ovals of a month before.

RIGHT: The M-G-M apple orchard, as shown in a set reference still, had its origins in a later chapter of the first Oz book, "Attacked by the Fighting Trees."

BELOW: This is the second filmed version of "If I Only Had a Brain," as staged by Bobby Connolly. Four months later, the number would be rerecorded by Bolger and rechoreographed and refilmed by Busby Berkeley.

ABOVE: During his few days with the *Oz* Unit, Cukor cautioned Judy not to act in any "fancy-schmancy" storybook manner as Dorothy. Such instruction was a key element to her success in the role. Cukor and Garland would later team as director and star of *A Star is Born* (1954), in which a segment was built around her character's demolition by studio makeup artists. As Esther Blodgett, Judy was once again provided with a blonde wig, puttied nose, and frilly costume.

LEFT: In a relaxed moment, Judy seems to take the tree much more in stride than does Dorothy when it reprimands her during actual filming. **ABOVE:** "I'm ready for my close-up": a Technicolor test of an obstreperous Ozite.

RIGHT: Bolger and Garland would meet many times in succeeding decades. At their final encounter, Judy attended his 1968 New York supper club act at The Waldorf. When members of the audience called for her to sing "Over the Rainbow," Bolger gently reminded them, "She's already sung it—into your hearts."

FORM 72

METRO-GOLDWYN-MAYER CORPORATION
STUDIOS
CULVER-CITY
CALIFORNIA

INTER-OFFICE COMMUNICATION

To Mr. Melbourne

Subject ALUMINUM POWDER

From F. L. Hendrickson Date November 23, 1938

In connection with the Jack Haley matter, I enclose herewith two statements regarding the use of aluminum powder by Jack Dawn, one statement dated November 19, 1938 signed by Alfred A. Kosky, M. D. of the Laboratory of Clinical Pathology and statement dated November 21, 1938 from the Overton Laboratories signed by F. H. Overton.

Will you please keep these in your file for future reference.

F. L. Hendrickson

K

ABOVE, LEFT/ABOVE: The Tin Man is discovered—by Denslow and Garland. When he joined the *Oz* cast, Haley rerecorded "If I Only Had A Heart" and random solo lines for his role, but the original prerecordings of "We're Off to See the Wizard"—featuring Buddy Ebsen's voice with Garland, Bolger, and (later) Lahr—remain on the film soundtrack to this day. **LEFT:** A series of M-G-Memorandums flew back and forth attendant to The Tin Man's makeup.

THIS PAGE: These happy photographic "captures" were made during dress rehearsal of "If I Only Had a Heart" and belie the actor's discomfort in his costume. Off-camera, its bulky construction prevented Haley from even sitting down; instead, he reclined on a slant board and napped between takes. (Insomniac Lahr muttered in disgust, "Look at that Tin Man, going sound asleep on an ironing board! I can't sleep at night!" Not without affection for his long-time friend, Lahr appreciatively continued, "That son-of-a-bitch could sleep hung up on a meat hook!") Haley's dance was longer in its original version than in the edit used in the final film.

"Every day, I shuddered at the thought of climbing into The Tin Woodman outfit, which I did after a long ritual with the makeup artist. This costume required me to stand the entire day . . . I've described it as a portable torture chamber. To think they designed it for a role which involved dance is absolutely sadistic!"

— *Jack Haley*

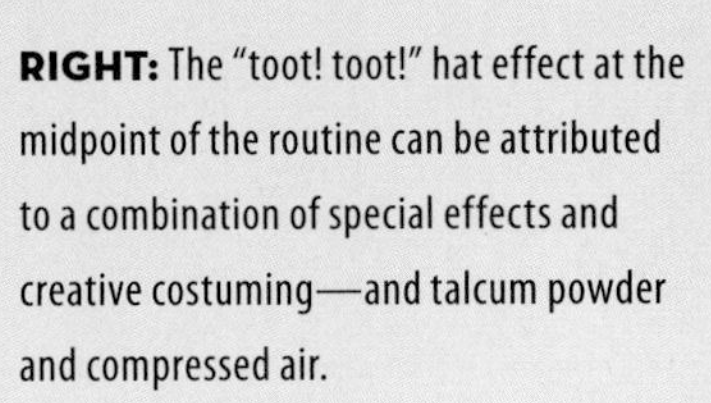

RIGHT: The "toot! toot!" hat effect at the midpoint of the routine can be attributed to a combination of special effects and creative costuming—and talcum powder and compressed air.

LEFT: The population of the cottage/orchard set also included birds from Los Angeles Zoo Park, which gave an exterior feeling to an interior soundstage. A toucan, peacock, and crane are visible during the sequence; it's the latter that has been mistaken for everything from a swaying stagehand to a stray actor, producer, publicist, technician, or Munchkin.

LEFT/ABOVE: This sequence marked Margaret Hamilton's first filming under Fleming. "Every time we started with a new director, we thought, 'Now this is where I get fired!'" But she found Fleming "delightful to work for . . . He had a good, firm hand on the production." Ironically, after terrified children were carried out of *Oz* previews in June 1939, Fleming was forced to delete as many of Hamilton's lines as possible before the film's premiere. Her rooftop "trims" included such threats and sarcasm as "Forgotten about *me*, eh? Well, I haven't forgotten about *you*!" and "As for you, my little Dorothy, I wish you *luck* with The Wizard of Oz. And a *happy* journey back to Kansas!"

> "Vic Fleming had never experienced guys like us. Some legitimate directors can't imagine anyone thinking about something else and, when he yells, 'Shoot!,' just going in and playing. We'd kid around up to the last minute and go on. You could see he got mad and red-faced. Some actors try and get into the mood. They'll put themselves in the character. I never did that. I'm not that—let's say—dedicated."
>
> — Bert Lahr

ABOVE: The trio's entrance in this sequence was originally considered a logical spot for a musical number. Instead, the storyline momentum dictated that "Lions and Tigers and Bears" remain just a chant and not a chanson. Here, Dorothy and her friends have just spotted their next companion.

RIGHT: Just one area of The Lion's Forest is represented in this reference still, but every twist and turn in The Yellow Brick Road was photographed in the event a set had to be reconstructed for future retakes.

ABOVE/RIGHT: The Technicolor test captures the actors in place but out of character; the black-and-white still immortalizes the onset of Lahr's star-turn. The sequence was capped with the quartet of "We're Off to See the Wizard," and it was assistant choreographer Dona Massin who created the variations of skip-step that distinguished each rendition of the song. She later laughed that no one had trouble "except for Bert—he was all feet!"

ABOVE: For The Lion's entrance, Lahr's athletic double performed a trampoline-style leap onto The Yellow Brick Road. **RIGHT:** But the character's bravado would soon collapse into the same pose made famous by Denslow's portrait.

"I had to work with [these] three very professional men. And they had so much makeup on . . . and each one was busy complaining about his makeup and making bets as to which was the most difficult to put on. Well, whenever we'd do that little dance up The Yellow Brick Road, I was supposed to be with them . . . and they'd shut me out. They would close in—the three of them—and I would be in back of them, dancing. And so the director, Victor Fleming (who was a darling man; he was always up on a boom) would say, 'HOLD it! You three *dirty* HAMS, let that little girl in there! Let her in there!'"

— Judy Garland

ABOVE: The Poppy Field entrance is captured in a set reference still. **BELOW:** Denslow's characters are no less overwhelmed by the flowers than would be the M-G-M actors some thirty-eight years later.

ABOVE: December 1938: The toll taken by costumes, makeup, intense lighting, the dash through The Poppy Field, and film-making in general is fairly apparent. Judy would later review her trip to *Oz*, "I enjoyed [the film] tremendously, although it was a long schedule and very hard work; it was in the comparatively early days of Technicolor, and the lights were terribly hot. We were shooting for about six months, but I loved the music, and I loved the director, and of course, I loved the story."

"Fleming had a wonderful understanding of people. He knew the makeup was wearing; after a couple hours, it was depressing to have it on. In order for us not to lose interest, to try and keep our animation, he would call us together and say, 'Fellahs, you've got to help me on this scene.' Well, I knew this guy was a big director. He didn't need actors to help him. He'd say, 'You guys are Broadway stars; what do you think we should do here?' The scene might be waking up in the poppy field, and we'd give our suggestions on how to play it . . . But I always thought he was just trying to keep our interest."

— *Jack Haley*

ABOVE: This set never appears in *Oz* and seems to be the transition between The Poppy Field and the Gates of The Emerald City. (In the film's rough-cut, there was a medium-long shot of the foursome, "tramping to the right," accompanied by the off-camera "Optimistic Voices." This was replaced in the final edit by a Newcombe scene of the travelers photographed from behind as they marched toward Emerald City.) **RIGHT:** "We're almost there, at last! at last!" Early on, Arthur Freed advised the *Oz* scenarists, "When the picture is over, besides our laughs and our novelty, we [should] have had a real assault upon our hearts." This jubilant moment follows his directive; the joy of Dorothy & Company is emotionally shared by audiences every time the film is seen.

THIS PAGE: Via concept art, set reference, Technicolor test, and production still, it's possible to travel from idea to execution for this segment of the film. The intrepid trio and Toto are off to rescue Dorothy; the drawing and set still show part of the terrain they would cover. The test frame (below) captures a technician-in-action with the stand-ins for the leading men; the three doubles actually appear in long shots at this moment in the picture. Finally, the scene still (right) offers Haley, Lahr, and Bolger—and, in the bottom left corner, the recording microphone shell.

ABOVE: In December 1938, Fleming reshot the Thorpe footage made in October on The Witch's Castle sets. The Tower Room was slightly redressed for the occasion. **LEFT:** The Baum/Denslow Wicked Witch is a brief, one-chapter threat who doesn't even realize Dorothy wears magic slippers until The Monkeys bring the girl to her castle.

ABOVE: Although their mutual admiration isn't apparent here, Judy would later rhapsodize about the friendship Hamilton extended to her: "What a wonderful woman. And what a performance she gave."

LEFT/ABOVE: In both Thorpe and Fleming footage, Dorothy tried to escape The Tower Room. Locked in and hopeless, she sang a harrowing reprise of "Over the Rainbow," which was deleted before the film premiere. **RIGHT:** This sound department memo notates Thorpe's version, confirming that the recording was done live on the set; Garland's third rendition/breakdown was deemed usable.

Production No. 1060

Date: 10-17-38

Scene	Take	Description
2029	3 C	"Over the Rainbow" "Witches Tower" - Recorded on set - Sc. 196 A shot to above P. B. Judy Garland and Piano

No H/C either end

Key No. 6 F 90665 to 6 F 90797

Signed C. P. Kahn

ABOVE/BELOW: Led by Mitchell Lewis, The Winkie Guards were cast with strong men, all over six feet tall. Each costume of coat, headdress, and armor weighed fifty pounds; one can imagine the reaction of Lahr and Haley when told that such additional wardrobe would have to be worn over the Lion and Tin Man outfits.

ABOVE: Perhaps it was the sympathetic Fleming who got Dorothy's companions out of their Winkie uniforms as quickly as possible. By the time he reshot the sequence in the foyer, the trio was back to its unencumbered best. Note the string that ties The Lion's tail into position for the purpose of a better publicity photograph.

LEFT/RIGHT: The penultimate moments of the chase scene played out on The Witch's Battlement. The set was partly constructed, but several glorious camera angles were also composited with a matte painting. M-G-M's attention to detail was so precise that the river below the castle was made to appear as if it was flowing, with light reflecting off the water.

ABOVE/RIGHT: Another threat by The Witch was cut from this sequence: "I'm going to start in on you *right here—one after the other.*" Bolger wore a chemically fireproofed costume when torched by Hamilton, but the actress remained nervous about the staging. It took five takes to satisfy Fleming; "Let's try it again," he'd say, and add, pointedly, "Miss Hamilton, *please* look as if you enjoyed it."

LEFT: To populate the vast Munchkinland set, M-G-M utilized 124 "little people" and approximately ten little girls from a local professional academy. The talented children filled in the choreographic foregrounds and cluttered up the backgrounds. **BELOW LEFT:** It's a toss-up as to who was more dazzled: The Munchkins at the chance to meet one of Metro's reigning stars—or Norma Shearer and two of the children who got a tour of the set. (Margaret Pellegrini, flowerpot hat and all, is center.) **BELOW:** Judy and the cast await their cue to "Follow the Yellow Brick Road."

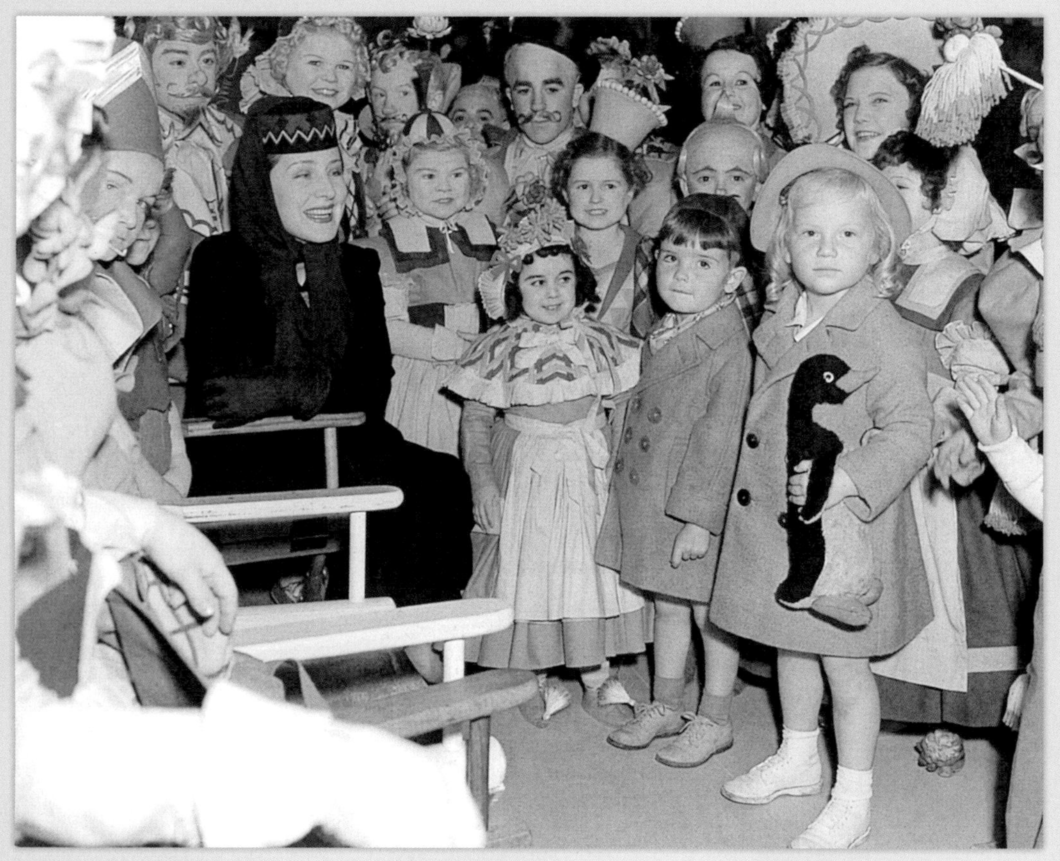

"That set! It was big and monstrous! I thought, 'My goodness, they're spending plenty of money! Holy Toledo!' I looked and looked—'Look at the houses for The Munchkins! Look at the beautiful bridge and the water!' The water was blue! And the flowers were something else. That's the only movie I ever worked where they had ten green men; they take care of the flowers and the trees and the pots and all that stuff. And there were so many people *behind* the cameras; it seemed like everybody had four assistants."

— Jerry Maren

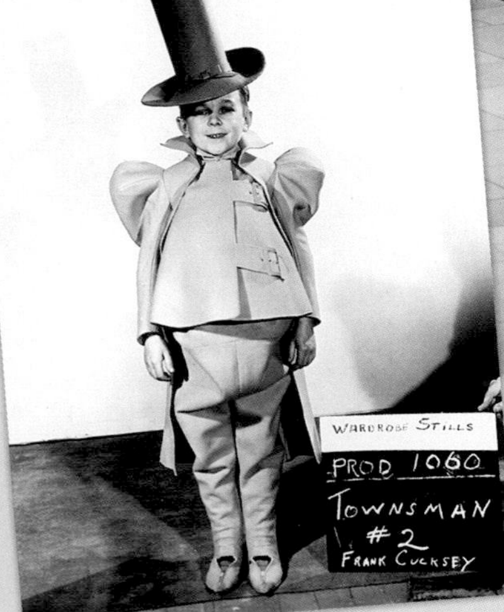

ABOVE: This set reference still features a phantom Munchkin presence at right. **RIGHT:** As can be seen in a separate wardrobe test, it's Frank Cucksey as "Townsman #2."

> "I think I could, without any trouble, recite a list of all my plays, and give most of the casts, many of the playing dates. . . . But I go blank when I try to remember the pictures. My favorite role was Glinda, the Good Fairy, directed by the great Victor Fleming. I never played such a being on stage, but this role is as close as I have come in motion pictures to the kind of parts I did in the theater. I recall Ray Bolger in that film. Day after day as the shooting went on, I waited for Ray to dance. Finally I asked him when. 'Dance?' he said, amazed. 'Dance? Why I'm a professional dancer. That's what I do. I'm a dancer. So, of course, I don't dance.' My roles in pictures have been something like that!"
>
> — Billie Burke

LEFT/RIGHT: Session vocalist Lorraine Bridges recorded "Come out, come out, wherever you are . . . " for the soundtrack, but her take went unused in the film. Thus, despite claims to the contrary over the years, Billie Burke did her own singing as Glinda. She also made an indelible impression on coworkers. Munchkin Karl Slover remembers the contrast between the off- and on-camera actress: "She came in like an old woman, with a cane. I thought, 'My gosh, she must be one hundred years old—or close to it.' But when I saw her all dressed up [and] made up, she looked like she was about thirty-five! She looked beautiful . . . I mean *beautiful*!"

BOTTOM LEFT: When Dorothy arrived from Kansas in the Oz book, she was greeted by three Munchkins and The Good Witch of the North, and later feted at a private Munchkin home (as Denslow pictures it here). **LEFT/BELOW:** With Munchkinland the first Technicolor sequence in their film, however, M-G-M opted for a massive cast, a major production number, and an awe-inspiring setting. Metro's scope is manifested in photographs of between-takes chaos (note Glinda's alternate wand) and a formally posed still.

ABOVE/RIGHT: Charley Becker's dignity and bearing made him, in Meinhardt Raabe's later estimation, "an automatic pick" for Mayor of Munchkinland. Similarly, Raabe felt he was cast as Coroner "because I had been doing a bit of public speaking, [and] I had learned to enunciate a little bit more distinctly." But in truth, all but two sentences of the Munchkin soundtrack were prerecorded by professional voice doubles. The only gentlemen who speak for themselves are thought to be Joseph Koziel and Frank Cucksey, who greet Dorothy in her carriage.

BOTTOM ROW: Once the little people arrived in California, there was a general audition for individual parts. Young Jerry Maren (center) aced the opportunity: "After the choreography test, they looked at me and said, 'He'd be perfect for the Lollipop guy, so get two other guys his size. So the fellow on my left was Harry Doll, and the fellow on my right was Jackie Gerlich. I was in the middle; I got to hand Judy Garland the lollipop." The toe dancers of The Lullaby League (left) were played by Nita Krebs, Olga Nardone, and Yvonne Moray.

ABOVE: Everything about *Oz* was kept under wraps; assistant director Worsley remembers "a cop on the door" through much of the filming. But when possible, The Munchkins posed for private, souvenir snapshots: (from left) Prince Denis, Margaret Nickloy, Hildred Olson, Ethel Denis, and Johnny Winters.

"On the first take [of my disappearance], the shot was perfect. But Mr. Fleming wanted another take for insurance . . . and a few things went wrong. The smoke started too fast. Or the smoke and the fire came too late. He became impatient and shouted, 'I want the shot *done*, and done *right now*!' And the fire started before I went down; it came too quickly. My skirt, my hat, and my broom were on fire. Two men waiting for me [under the set] were busy fussing over me. I thought their concern was funny, because I wasn't aware that anything happened. One of them quickly knocked the hat off; then they hurried me over to first aid. My right hand was badly burned; my nose and chin were burned. On top of it all, my green makeup was toxic, because it had copper in it. They used alcohol to clean it off; I will never forget that pain. I was told I'd be out for at least a month . . . and that the production would shoot around me. I was out for six weeks."

— Margaret Hamilton

ABOVE: Stand-in Betty Danko appeared as The Witch in the long shot of her entrance. **BELOW:** Thereafter, Hamilton supplied the fright: "The Witch was fun to play, because she enjoyed everything she did . . . She is also the keynote throughout the whole picture. Even though you don't see her all the time, you know she's still there. The audience feels a certain anxiety about what she may do next." Her dialogue was trimmed from this scene, too: "I'm here for vengeance!" "So it was you, was it? You killed her, didn't you?" "Didn't mean it, eh? Accident, eh? *Well, my little pretty, I can cause accidents, too*—and this is how I do it!" Only the italicized phrase remained in the picture.

TOP ROW: The conclusion of the Munchkinland sequence offers two views of the village border. The distant horizon consisted mostly of matte painting (above) and, according to Maren, the little people looked behind Judy to see only "a guy at the end of the dirty, filthy soundstage with a handkerchief: 'Look at the handkerchief and say good-bye!' They put the plate in afterwards." From the opposite point of view (top left), the town can be appreciated even unpopulated. **LEFT:** Judy, flanked by producer LeRoy on her right and director Fleming on her left, earned great affection and admiration from The Munchkins. "She was the typical all-American girl," enthuses Maren. "If I were six feet tall, I'd have wanted to marry her!"

LEFT: January 1939: The New Year was launched when the film unit moved into The Haunted Forest. Technicolor tests show Garland and Haley (with The Witches Castle sign over his shoulder) and Stafford Campbell and Bobbie Koshay (doubling for Bolger and Garland) on the same location. When the time came for Dorothy's abduction, Koshay was harnessed and "flown" by The Winged Monkeys in Judy's stead.

RIGHT: A still from the onset of the sequence was hand-tinted for promotion in Great Britain in late 1939. The gentlemen are armed with a pistol, butterfly net, giant wrench, walking stick, an oversize spray gun of "witch remover," and The Tin Man's ax. In a deleted moment, the spray gun disappeared and the net flew out of The Lion's paw. (This precipitated The Scarecrow's line, "I believe there're spooks around here.")

DATE: 12/22/38　　PRODUCTION NO. 1060

Scene & Take	Description
	Hoffman - Ruthven #1 Dunbar - Film Reproducer Rm. 4. Shepherd - E. Machine. Miles - Cell'd #3 (Cut & PB.)
Per - Stoll:	
2095 - 2 - 3	Piano and violin (Stoll) tempo track of YELLOW BRICK ROAD. Second take of take 2 Selection.
8528 - 2	Wild dialogue of Judy Garland: "Follow the yellow brick road?" Wax cut and played back.
2096 - 1	Charley Haley replacing Buddy Ebsen's singing in JITTERBUG Number. Made to film play-back 2401 St.L.
- 2	"It's giving me the jitters in the joints around my knees." and "I haven't got a heart but I've got a palpitation."
- 4	(Same as above only "Thar she blows!" on the end. No wax on takes 1 & 2.
2097 - 2	Charley Haley replacing Buddy Ebsen's singing in JITTERBUG Number. Made to film play-back 2401 St. . "Thar she blows!" Release to dimmer.

LEFT: Among other duties on December 22, 1938, the sound department recorded Haley's solo lines for the already-existing film track for "The Jitterbug," originally done by Ebsen, Garland, Bolger, and Lahr on October 6, 1938. Haley is misnamed "Charley" in the notations.

Judy: Do you remember a song in *The Wizard of Oz* called "The Jitterbug"?
Ray: Oh, golly! Where the monkeys came down?
Judy: Yeah!
Ray: Oh, sure! Hey, that was a great song.
Judy: They cut it out.
Ray: I know they did. And we had a very cute number. We had a great routine . . .

— Garland and Bolger on the CBS-TV Judy Garland Show, 1963

ABOVE: "The Jitterbug" swing song featured Garland's pert vocal, dancing by the teen and her companions, and the participatory branches of "The Jitter Trees." As described in the script, the jitterbug was a small, pink-and-blue spotted mosquito-like creature, sent by The Witch to sting the quartet and send them into a frenzied dance. In the rough cut of the film, the jitterbug was shown as it landed on The Lion's nose; thereafter, it bit Dorothy in the leg, The Tin Man on the neck, and stung The Scarecrow as well. During the ensuing routine, a tree pulled The Lion's tail, and another tree grabbed The Scarecrow, but he escaped to free Dorothy from similar capture. When The Tin Man raised an ax in defense, a branch hit him over the head.

BELOW: Although the number was dropped after the first sneak preview in June, by then, both commercial and "advance artist" sheet music was in circulation for all the major *Oz* songs. This was then the standard means of creating public interest in the score and encouraging professional entertainers to perform the material and plug the movie.

Advance Artist Copy

Please announce title of production when BROADCASTING THIS NUMBER

*Sung by Scarecrow, Tin Woodman, Cowardly Lion and Dorothy**

THE JITTERBUG

Featured in the M-G-M Picture
"THE WIZARD OF OZ"

LYRIC BY
E. Y. HARBURG

MUSIC BY
HAROLD ARLEN

Leo Feist inc.
1629 BROADWAY • NEW YORK

*Scarecrow - Ray Bolger
*Cowardly Lion - Bert Lahr
*Tin Woodman - Jack Haley
*Dorothy - Judy Garland

"It was originally decided to do the monkeys in cartoon. I was a little against this, because I thought you would be able to tell it was animation on the screen. After a number of tests and experiments, they gave up that idea, and we did it with miniature monkeys cast [out of rubber], with twenty-two hundred piano wires! The wires supported them on an overhead trolley and moved their wings up and down. It was an awful job to hide the wires. They had to be painted and lighted properly, so that they blended into whatever the background might be."

— *A. Arnold "Buddy" Gillespie*

ABOVE: The Haunted Forest scene reached its climax with the attack of The Winged Monkeys. In Baum's book, they capture Toto, Dorothy, and The Lion (as shown in Denslow's color plate), flying with them to The Witch's Castle. (In the film, Nikko is then ordered by The Witch to lock Toto in a basket—much as Miss Gulch had handled the dog in Kansas.) **RIGHT:** The scalloped photo from Fleming's scrapbook shows him standing on the set as several Monkeys fly in from above.

LEFT: Denslow's plate shows The Soldier with the Green Whiskers as he escorts the visitors to the palace. In Baum's book, everybody in The Emerald City wears green glasses so they are not blinded by the brightness and glory of the jeweled town.

RIGHT: When assigned to *Oz* in June 1938, scenarists Florence Ryerson and Edgar Allan Woolf expanded The Wizard's role into multiple parts: "This would give us a chance to use a man like Frank Morgan without having the audience feel cheated because they didn't see enough of him."

RIGHT/ABOVE: "The Merry Old Land of Oz" sequence is seen prior to filming (with doubles for the cast at ease in the carriage) and during principal photography (with Morgan captured in action). The carriage itself was among countless M-G-M property holdings and dates back to use by Abraham Lincoln. It is now part of The Judy Garland Museum collection in her hometown, Grand Rapids, Minnesota.

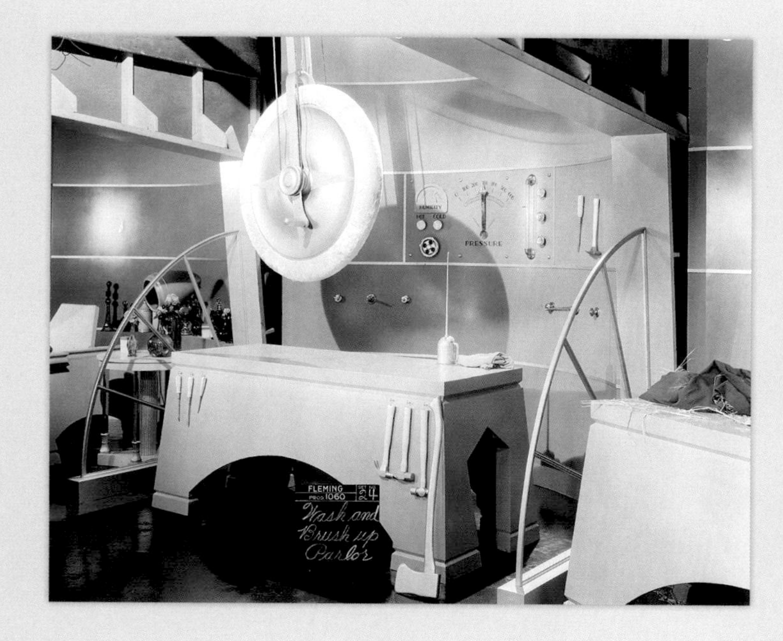

THIS PAGE: With and without the actors, here is The Emerald City Wash & Brush-Up Co., used for the "Renovation Sequence." Radio and screen vocalist Lois January (bottom right) served as primary attendant when Dorothy's hair was restyled. On the far left of The Lion's bevy (bottom left), assistant choreographer Dona Massin fills in for an absent player. Boss Bobby Connolly pressed her into service (and wardrobe) when one of the chorus didn't turn up.

ABOVE: The top of a stepladder (visible at bottom center) gives an idea of the size of the miniature set used for The Witch's departure. Barely visible in the window is the tiny puppet, about to soar out of the building.

ABOVE: The cast is intimidated by the skywriting Wicked Witch. Before final editing, her message was longer and more threatening: "Surrender Dorothy or die! W. W. W." (The Lion was scripted to look up and guilelessly note, "That bird's havin' trouble with its tail feathers!"—and then turn dumbfounded at his companions' recognition: "You guys *know* her?!")

ABOVE: "If I Were King of the Forest" originally included a deleted interior section and final chorus—the latter recorded with alternate endings. In one, Lahr circumvented a high note by graveling out a bass growl. In the other, vocalist Georgia Stark dubbed a soprano finish, to which Lahr would lip-sync. (In the final edit, he's in-pose for the eliminated end of the song; it's a completely different stance than that in the immediately preceding line, "You can say that again!")

"There was a scene where The Witch takes off from her castle and soars into the air to skywrite; the smoke comes out of the back of her broom. We shot this by pointing the camera up at the bottom of a glass-bottom tank into which we had put about half an inch of milk. We mixed sheep dip with nigrosine dye, and put it in a stylus, with which we wrote from above and backward. A tiny miniature of The Witch on her broom was attached to the end of the stylus. The mixture of sheep dip and dye being released in the milk gave a cloudy, expanding effect, just the way smoke does in the sky."

— *A. Arnold "Buddy" Gillespie*

ABOVE: In the Oz book and Denslow's illustration, only Dorothy met the giant head. To The Scarecrow, Tin Man, and Lion, The Wizard respectively appeared as a lovely lady; a five-eyed, five-armed, five-legged monster; and a great, roaring fireball. **BOTTOM ROW:** Technicolor tests, January/February 1939: The Lion and Scarecrow in The Throne Room, and the giant head of Oz as first planned in miniature. This concept was discarded in favor of the disguised face and manipulated voice of Frank Morgan, filmed and projected against smoke, flame, and throne.

ABOVE: This corridor was built up from the floor so that the camera, plinth, and track could be assembled in the adjacent gully to photograph the actors en route to The Great Oz.

LEFT: The sequence in which The Winkie Guards presented Dorothy with The Witch's broom was filmed in December 1938. It ended with the men chanting a chorus of "Ding-Dong! The Witch is Dead," which dissolved through to the "triumphal return" procession in the streets of Emerald City, filmed two months later. The entire sequence was dropped from *Oz* prior to premiere.

BELOW: *Oz* was rereleased to theaters by M-G-M in 1949. For promotion, the studio publicity department chose to display a (however incorrectly) hand-colored still from the triumphal return sequence—even though the routine had never been part of the finished film.

ABOVE: Scores of green-clad extras marched and danced to welcome Dorothy back to The Emerald City. The test frame shows the cast in position for filming; The Scarecrow clutches The Witch's broomstick. But Garland's double is momentarily in her place, and The Cowardly Lion has an unzipped sleeve and is holding a cigarette.

ABOVE: Morgan's console for this scene was as much a masterpiece of technical mumbo-jumbo as was his scripted response to the characters. **INSET RIGHT:** Denslow pictures Dorothy, et al, in their confrontation with The Great Humbug.

ABOVE: Just basket and balloon base were constructed for The Wizard's departure. The balloon itself existed only as a matte painting, and its embellished plug for "State Fair/Omaha" was a Baum factoid; his title character was born there. (Another Baum conceit: Toto's attempt to catch a cat, causing Dorothy to miss her return home with the "premier balloonist, par excellence.")

ABOVE/RIGHT: En route to save the day, Billie Burke and bubble settled on this landing. The actress cited Fleming's direction for the occasion: "Vic came up to me; I [was to] come down a flight of stairs and go up another. 'Billie,' he said, 'I want you just to float.' Float! I really felt apologetic that I must touch earth at all!"

THIS PAGE: With Fleming gone with the wind, King Vidor came in to "film" Kansas, including the barnyard and cyclone cellar scenes. Lahr, Haley, and Bolger, above, are shown in more comfortable clothes as (respectively) Zeke, Hickory Twicker, and Hunk Andrews. (Bert's farmhand role was added so much at the last minute that a surname was never crafted for him.)

"Vic was a good friend, and I spent one day with him; he took me around to all the sets that hadn't been used and went through the thing. Then he left, and I took over. It was about two and a half weeks, three weeks possibly. I remember shooting the scenes in the house during the cyclone and many of the Kansas scenes. I remember shooting the characters singing 'We're Off to See the Wizard'; I always wanted to do a musical film. Previously, in most musicals, someone stood up in front of the camera and sang directly to the camera. In directing 'Over the Rainbow,' I was able to keep the movement flowing freely, very much in the style of a silent scene. Whenever it's shown, or whenever I hear the record played, I get a tremendous kick, knowing that I was in on the beginning. But I did not want any credit, and as long as Victor was alive, I kept quiet about it."

— *King Vidor*

LEFT/ABOVE: This rare still displays the contiguous construction—indoors and out—of the Kansas front yard and parlor. Vidor enjoyed making long film "takes," and except for a required close-up of Dorothy, the parlor sequence with Clara Blandick, Garland, Hamilton, and Charley Grapewin was comprised of a single effective acting scene.

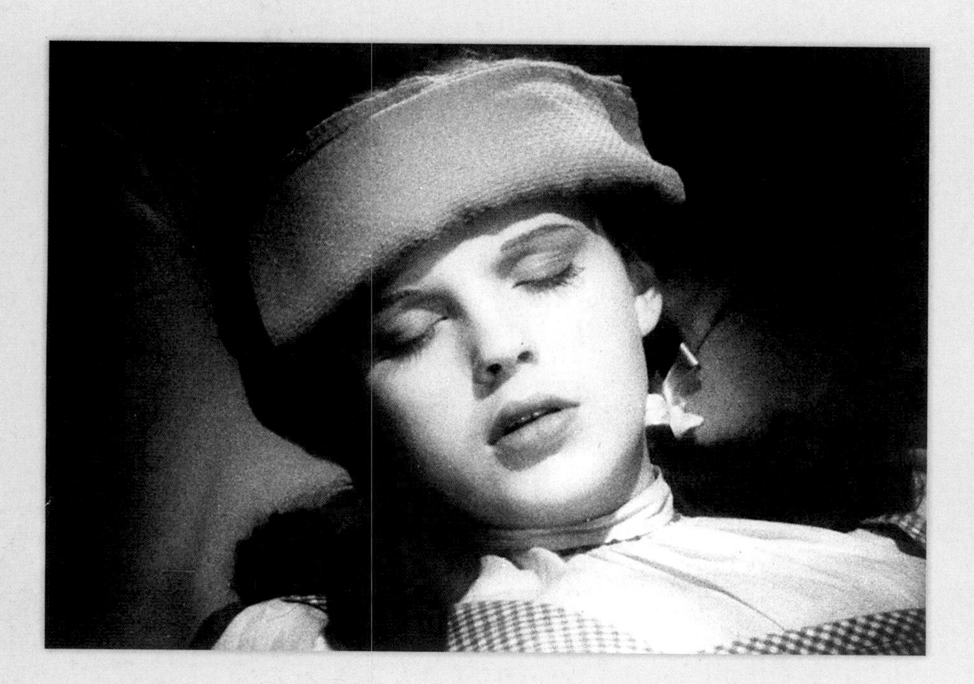

LEFT/ABOVE: In the film, Dorothy awakens in this bedroom set. Both Baum and Arthur Freed emphasized the "no place like home" aspect of the girl's desire to return to Aunt Em and Uncle Henry, although it seemed much more apparent in a 101-minute film than in a twenty-four chapter book.

"A fantasy film enabled us to create many interesting effects. The first was the tornado, inside which Dorothy, her dog, and her house are taken to The Land of Oz. We built the inside of the tornado in miniature and photographed it. Then we shot Dorothy and the dog inside the house, looking out the window at the tornado they were carried up into. We did this by projecting the tornado film onto a screen, which was the background out the window. You could see objects flying past the window, like the woman on the bicycle who later became The Witch."

— *A. Arnold "Buddy" Gillespie*

ABOVE: A frame enlargement shows the Kansas farmhouse as it dropped from the sky and tornado. **RIGHT:** The special effects work-and-cost sheets explain how the scene was created and filmed.

(4)

1060-63
Wizard of OZ
Ext. House falling into Camera

House falling into Camera was made by suspending House on horizontal shaft ---hung by wires to gantry crane. House was hung with bottom close to lens, rotated on shaft, and moved away from camera fast, As house travelled away it was raised and covered by heavy smoke cloud. This action was PRINTED reversed.

Feb. 24--Takes House travelling to Camera
Feb 25 --Correction in direction of travel of smoke
Mar. 9---House falling away agist white (Stage 30)
Mar. 10 -Correction in clouds, backing and speed.

(4)

DATE Feb. 24---25
PRODUCTION 1060
SET 63
STAGE 14
PICTURE Wizard of OZ

Estimated Construction & Special Effect.

Preparation	1600
Spcl. Camera Mounts	
Operation	1000
Elect. Operation	900
Add & Changes	
Total Approp.	3500.00
Final Cost	2831.18

TITLE OF MINIATURE Ext. House falling into Camera
Details of Min. Set Area
No. of Bldgs. or Units
Scale
Day Nite Dawn Sunset
Backing White prop sky
REMARKS

Shots of house falling into camera after it leaves tornado.

Dressing & Min. Props

One house and rigging for same. Revolving camera rig. Rigging for Smoke. Prop Sky.

CONSTRUCTION
Total Construction Cost 65.44 Total Spcl. Effects

OPERATION Construction Dept. Daily Cost

Average Crew		Foreman	Mechanics	Helpers	Labourers
	Morning	1	8	1 ptr.	1 grip
	Afternoon	1	8		1 grip
	Nite				

Total Operation Cost 1940.91

ELECTRICAL Average Load
Wind Machines & Fans
Average Daily Crew A.M. -8- P.M. -6-
Total Operating Cost 819.83

CAMERA DEPT.
Cameraman Fabian
Extra Cameras
Lens 40mm. ---24 mm.
Speed 24 and 64
Approx. No. of Feet of Film Printed

*. NOTE (OVER) (7)

DATE Jan 26- Feb 10

PRODUCTION 1060

SET 71

STAGE 14

PICTURE Wizard Of Oz

Estimated Construction & Special Effect.

Preparation	7600
Spcl. Camera Mounts	5000. *
Operation	5500
Elect.Operation	3600
Add & Changes	*
Total Approp.	21700.
Final Cost	27089.82

TITLE OF MINIATURE Ext. Kansas Farm ----Miniature

Details of Min.Set Area No.of Bldgs.or Units

Day Nite Dawn Sunset

Scale

Backing White Proj. Sky

REMARKS Shots of Kansas Farm from various angles showing tornado approaching and engulfing house.

Dressing & Min.Props --Kansas Farm built two times. Change in design. Overhead Gantry crane to carry tornado tubes. Two tornado tubes. White backing. Moving cloud frames. Moving foreground glasses for clouds. Rigging for dust.

CONSTRUCTION

Total Construction Cost 10492.87 Total Spcl.Effects

OPERATION Construction Dept.Daily Cost

Average Crew		Foreman	Mechanics	Helpers	Labourers
	Morning	1	10	1 ptr.	1 grip
	Afternoon	1	18		4 grips
	Nite				

Total Operation Cost 12423.84

ELECTRICAL Average Load

Wind Machines & Fans 2 wind machines - 6 fans

Average Daily Crew A.M. -10- P.M. 14

Total Operating Cost 4173.11

CAMERA DEPT.

Cameraman Fabian

Extra Cameras

Lens 35--40-- 50mm.

Speed 48

Approx.No.of Feet of Film Printed

1060-71
Wizard of OZ
Ext. Kansas Farm Min.

Aug.20 -Test water vortex
Nov.5 -Test cloth tube.
Jan. 26-Test of Set. Small tube.
" 27-Take long shot background
" 30-Correction in sky and dust.
" 28-Retake correction in clouds
Feb.2 -Cut 2
Feb.3 -Correction in dust control
Feb.4 -Correction in dust and length of travel
" 6 -Cut 3 BG. for front porch
" 7 -Test of long shot-cut.
" 8 -Change in set.
" 9 -Correction using small tube
"10 -Test using large tube rotating
"11 -Correction foreground clouds
"13 -Correction dust and clouds

For the Tornado used in Kansas Farm sequence a Gantry Crane travelling the length of Stage # 14 was hung from the bottom of roof trusses. The Gantry car supported a canvas cone in the shape of a Tornado which was rotated by a D.C. motor on a speed control. The motor assembly was arranged to tip sideways and was controlled from the car together with its cross travel. The approach was controlled by a motor winch on the stage floor. The base of the tornado cone was fastened to a car travelling on a predetermined track and containing arrangement for dust. This car was moved by operators below set. Set was built on platform and was 3/4 scale. Sky was projected moving clouds on white backing. This was augmented by cotton clouds on moving foreground glasses. Air was piped around set for wind effects. Wind machines were also used.

*** NOTE: SPECIAL CAMERA MOUNT ON GANTRY CRANE ($5000.00) NOT INCLUDED IN ESTIMATE. RE-DESIGN OF SET AND REBUILDING NOT INCLUDED.

THIS PAGE: The (miniature) funnel that came roaring across the (miniature) plain to envelop the (miniature) farmhouse was anything but miniature in the brain power and expense incurred to so realistically contrive a Kansas storm and setting. In 2008, The Weather Channel paid homage to 100 historically important weather events; the *Oz* tornado was one of them. In 1939, well before the extensive use and/or existence of 16mm and 8mm cameras or video equipment, it was the first approximation of a twister most people ever saw.

FORM — MUSIC NO. 1

DAILY MUSIC REPORT

PROD: WIZARD OF OZ

PROD: 1060

DATE: 10/7/38

FROM: OFFICE OF NAT W. FINSTON

The following recordings were made today:

SCENE No.	COMPOSITION	COMPOSER	TIME	DISC. NUMBER	REMARKS	LIBRARY NUMBER	CLASS.	USED IN PRODUCTION
2019	Over the Rainbow	Arlen t 1	2:06		Garland & orch.			
		2	2:13					
		4	2:11					
		6	2:12					
		7	2:01					
		8	1:57					

FORM 120

CONTRACT PAY ROLL NOTICE

Name JUDY GARLAND (FRANCES GUMM) Date 10-7-38

Dep't Stock Talent Employ. No.

Occupation Actress Soc. Sec. No.

Contract Dated 9-27-35 and letter 9-22-38

Date On Pay Rate $ Per

Change of Rate From $ $400. Per week
Effective Date 10-29-38 for 1 year 40 wks gtee

To $ $500. Per week
40 wks gtee

Date Off Pay

Approved:

mb

ABOVE: Judy first sang "Over the Rainbow" for posterity and the *Oz* soundtrack on October 7, 1938. **RIGHT:** That same day, her annual option was picked up by the studio for another year; her salary jumped to $500 per week. Given the work she did on October 7 alone, Metro was getting some kind of bargain.

ABOVE: In those days, orchestra leaders could buy ready-made musical arrangements of songs for use at dances or over the airwaves. Publishers pushed such orchestrations to make the tunes both familiar and popular as quickly as possible. But "Rainbow" didn't require much push. Beginning in mid-summer 1939, it was on the radio "Hit Parade" for months, spending seven weeks at #1: the most frequently played song in the nation.

"It's the prettiest song in the world . . . the best song ever written. It never becomes stale, because it ends with a question. That keeps it from being overly sentimental. It doesn't say everything's all right. It doesn't say everything's not all right. It just asks, 'Why, then, oh why can't I?' It's kind of like a personal prayer, especially that bit about the clouds being far behind me. 'Over the Rainbow' has become a part of my life. It is so symbolic of everybody's dream and wish; I'm sure that's why people sometimes get tears in their eyes when they hear it. I have sung it dozens of times, and it's still the song that's closest to my heart."

— Judy Garland

ABOVE: When filming wrapped in March 1939, promotion was getting underway. M-G-M logically united Judy and Mrs. L. Frank Baum for luncheon and photography; here, the widow of the "Royal Historian" shows "Dorothy" a first edition of the first Oz book.

ABOVE/RIGHT: On this set, Garland performed what would become her lifelong (and beyond) signature song. She would tell Arlen biographer Edward Jablonski, "The first song that Harold and Yip played for me was 'Rainbow.' I was terribly impressed by Harold's great genius and very much in awe of him. It seems he always treated me as an equal and not as a child. We have been great friends through the years. It's very gratifying to have a song that is more or less known as my theme song, and to have had it written by the fantastic Harold Arlen."

THIS PAGE: Two prominent promotional achievements from the original *Oz* campaign. *Screen Romances* and *Movie Life* for August 1939 would have hit newsstands just a month prior to their cover dates, which was also the month prior to the coast-to-coast debut of the film. It was all part of M-G-M's concerted effort to raise nationwide anticipation for their multi-million dollar endeavor.

YOU'RE OFF TO SEE THE WIZARD

The Promotional Campaign

Metro-Goldwyn-Mayer's promotional strategy for *The Wizard of Oz* is a testament to the publicity machinery that then existed within the studio system. Every film received a push: posters, stills, and advertising. But with a movie as expensive and unique as *Oz*, M-G-M put into play every means of hype. They allocated over a quarter-million dollars for the *Oz* campaign, and looking back at the saturation they achieved, every cent spent is visible.

Metro's goal for *Oz* is best summarized as controlled hysteria. Their approach was state of the art, and they would use that fact in exploitation as well. During this pre-television era, newspapers and magazines wielded major influence, and M-G-M cultivated all of them for articles, cover art, and ad space. They also designed lush pressbook material, providing theater owners and local media with an amalgam of every come-on device that was then *de rigueur*: lobby cards, posters, banners, buttons, journalese, and suggestions for contests and activities.

The M-G-M pitches and releases had much material from which to draw. *Oz* was touted for its actors, Munchkins, songs, sets, costumes, make-up, Technicolor, dog, staff, technical wizardry, effects, scoring, and musical comedy overtones. The publicity corps heralded sales figures of the Oz books, *The Wizard*'s earlier stage success, and the psychological ramifications that had been added to Dorothy's adventures for the film. Additionally, all such placement was monitored and well timed; M-G-M released virtually nothing until mid-summer 1939. By then, *Oz* was poised to premiere, and nothing the studio put forth was wasted.

Their control extended to music as well. *Oz* songs remained unavailable for radio play or recording until the picture was ready to be seen. When bandleader Larry Clinton issued a 78rpm single of "Over the Rainbow" and "The Jitterbug" in April 1939, Loew's legal division snapped to attention. After a strident flurry of calls and correspondence, the records were recalled. The ban on song performance held until June, when M-G-M previewed much of the score on its own network program, "Good News of 1939." Taking part were Judy Garland, Ray Bolger, Bert Lahr, Frank Morgan, Fred Stone (the 1902 stage Scarecrow), Harold Arlen, E. Y. Harburg, and Fanny

ABOVE: To provide diverse views of *Oz*, M-G-M distributed exclusive Kodachrome color art to individual newspapers and magazines. (As of 1939, fewer than a dozen feature films had employed the three-strip Technicolor process, so this indeed was a promotable aspect.) **LEFT:** Dorothy enjoyed a rehearsal reunion with The Cowardly Lion on June 29, 1939, when M-G-M's weekly radio program celebrated its final hour of the season with excerpts from the *Oz* score and stories about the making of the picture. "Good News of 1939" also featured The Scarecrow and The Wizard.

Brice, one of M-G-M's potential-but-unused Glindas and a monumental radio star as "Baby Snooks."

On July 28, Judy recorded her own Decca single of "Rainbow" and "The Jitterbug"; composer Harold Arlen chimed in as the voice of The Scarecrow on the latter track. Released in September, the disc reached number five on the *Billboard* charts, eventually achieving rank as the best selling record of 1939. Capitalizing on the perceived longevity of the score, Decca also produced a four-disc 78rpm *Oz* set, including the Garland numbers and featuring The Ken Darby Singers and The Victor Young Orchestra in six more *Oz* songs. Meanwhile, other vocalists and orchestras made successful recordings of "Rainbow" as well.

In addition to the promotability of its music, *Oz* seemed a likely prospect for more widespread marketing, and Loew's established its very first merchandising department. Their novice approach was only semi-successful; even wildly popular films then came and went so quickly that there wasn't a long-term public presence on which to build. Regardless, several dozen companies produced Oz products, all of which added to the visibility M-G-M wanted to purvey.

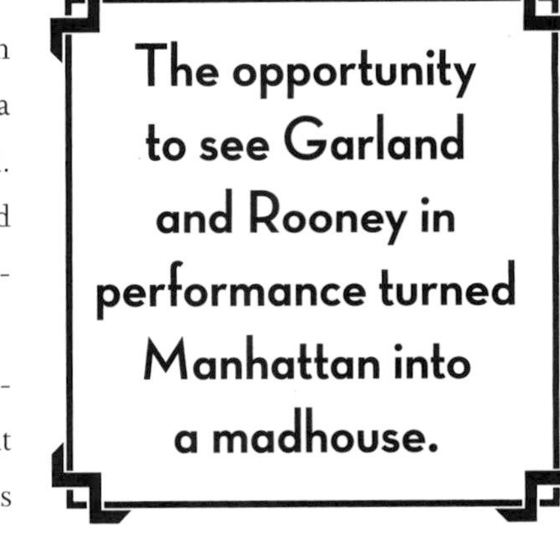

After a press screening on August 9, *Oz* received its Los Angeles premiere on the 15th at Grauman's Chinese Theatre. So masterful was M-G-M's presentation that the event itself was "reviewed" by *Daily Variety* as "another well planned and well directed entertainment." But the Hollywood hoopla was completely eclipsed when the picture opened on Broadway two days later. For the price of admission, New York audiences at The Capitol Theatre saw *Oz*, short subjects, and trailers. Then the curtains parted again to reveal the twenty-one-piece Georgie Stoll Orchestra and The Martins vocal group; their imaginative rendition of "We're Off to See the Wizard" opened the show. But the theater shook with "a reception that was as spontaneous as it was loud" when Garland and Mickey Rooney, "live and in person," took the stage. Five times a day—seven on weekends—the duo entertained the filled-to-capacity, 5,000-seat house in a twenty-five minute act. Rooney then was the top box office star in the nation; Garland's popularity would soon equal his. The opportunity to see them in performance turned midtown Manhattan into a madhouse and gave *Oz* the sendoff M-G-M had envisioned. Judy was later presented with a scrapbook to commemorate the experience; the cover was emblazoned with Loew's declaration that she and Mickey had received "the greatest New York demonstration ever accorded a stage or screen celebrity."

STUDIO NEWS

'Wizard of Oz' Greeted With Record Ovation By Fans At Sneak Preview

The largest number of returned preview cards in the history of motion pictures was received at the Metro-Goldwyn-Mayer studios last week following the final sneak preview of "The Wizard of Oz" at Pomona, Calif. A total of 951 cards, all of them lauding the spectacular musical produced by Mervyn LeRoy and directed by Victor Fleming, poured into the studio after the showing.

An ovation which continued until the story portion of the picture started greeted the opening title "The Wizard of Oz" which flashed on the screen, proving the tremendous all-age appeal of this picture.

Return cards heaped high praise upon every feature of the picture. Every member of the cast was singled out for praise, including Judy Garland as Dorothy, Frank Morgan as the Wizard, Ray Bolger as the Scarecrow, Bert Lahr as the Cowardly Lion, Jack Haley as the Tin Woodman, Billie Burke as Glinda the Good Witch, and Margaret Hamilton as the Wicked Witch.

Particularly appealing to the audience, the cards show, were the 120 Munchkins, played by midgets in fanciful garb. Returns indicate that the Technicolor photography is the best in film history while the musical numbers came in for outstanding applause. Practically every card commented on the amazing effects which are found in the picture from the realistic cyclone to the final illusion which brings Dorothy home to her Kansas farm.

METRO-GOLDWYN-MAYER
STUDIO NEWS
Published In the Interests of Metro-Goldwyn-Mayer Pictures Studios
VOL. VI—CULVER CITY, CALIFORNIA, FRIDAY, JUNE 30, 1939—No. 20

LEFT: In-house informational organs like *The M-G-M Studio News* heralded a nonstop flow of films, shorts, and trailers from Culver City and other production centers. **RIGHT:** As far as the eye can see, they waited outside The Capitol Theatre for the New York engagement of *Oz* and its accompanying live show starring Judy Garland and Mickey Rooney. The patient, cross-generational crowd extended around the entire city block like a moat.

Events at The Capitol were also described in a contemporary Hugh Martin/Ralph Blane newsletter. The two young musicians would later write songs for Garland's 1944 *Meet Me in St. Louis*, but in 1939, they were two of "The Martins." Blane exulted, "When we met Mickey and Judy, I can't tell you the thrill at discovering they were two of the nicest kids you'd ever care to know. They weren't scared and bratty like so many stories you hear about the child film stars. They were perfect. A lady and a gentleman. I think the most fun I had was sitting in the dressing room with them, eating hamburgers, and having a jam session with a bunch of Mickey's hot records. The engagement made me realize what a great talent they have. . . . I think we had just as much fun onstage watching these brilliant performers as the audiences did. Throngs of people waited all day long outside the stage door (even in the pouring rain), just for a glimpse of the two most famous kids in the world."

Oz went on to excellent box office everywhere, aided by reviews that could have been written by M-G-M itself. In recent years, it's become important to stress this; the film has had to combat an inaccurate legend about its notices ever since Aljean Harmetz published *The Making of The Wizard of Oz* (1977). Her gleefully sour summation pointedly emphasized the handful of negative comments that *Oz* received from perhaps a half-dozen critics in 1939. She quoted at length from the two worst of these, implying that general reaction to *Oz* was mixed at best. For the record, the two reviews appeared in *The New Yorker* ("*Oz* . . . displays no trace of imagination, good taste, or ingenuity . . . I say it's a stinkeroo") and *The New Republic* ("Any kid tall enough to reach up to a ticket window will be found at the Tarzan film down the street"). Such selective reportage on Harmetz's part has been magnified to the extent that many histories repeat the "fact" that *Oz* was critically rejected in 1939.

It's true there were qualifications in some critiques. An occasional journalist felt the film should have been pure fantasy. A few didn't like the songs or musicomedy approach to story or characters. But such observations were comparatively minor. In magazines and newspapers everywhere, the jubilant professional response demonstrated much the same rapture *Oz* has amassed ever since. Prophetically, The Los Angeles *Herald-Examiner* declaimed, "[The film] should be revived every year for the benefit of the rising generations." *Motion Picture Daily* classified *Oz* as "of the essence of screen entertainment that lives for a long time," and *Newsweek* declared, "The average moviegoer—adult or adolescent—

LEFT: Holdover business was far and away the exception in 1939, but *Oz* warranted it in many venues. *Variety,* the major show-business trade paper, trumpeted the box office take as "socko," "great," "terrific," "outstanding," "mighty," "nifty," "hefty," and "chipper."

will find it novel and richly satisfying to the eye." The Los Angeles *Times* broke out all the adjectives: "Something new, daring, and genuinely path-breaking in the cinema . . . a pioneering step and an artistic realization at once." Finally, *Variety* summarized the situation by stating, "There's an audience for *Oz* wherever there's a projection machine and a screen." (It's worth noting that both The New York *Times* and New York *Post*—among others—publicly railed against the two or three "chip-on-the-shoulder critics" who dismissed *Oz* in their notices.)

When *Film Daily* conducted its poll of 450 journalists at the end of 1939, *The Wizard of Oz* was named one of the ten best films of the year. It also placed at number eight on *The Showman's Trade Review* of the top ten grossing films of 1939. (The Garland/Rooney *Babes in Arms* was number seven.) *Oz* went on to score five Academy Award nominations, including best picture, best art direction, and best special effects. It lost in the first two categories to *Gone With the Wind* and to *The Rains Came* in the third. But it won Oscars for best song ("Rainbow") and best original score; it also garnered a special award for Judy Garland.

In first release, *Oz* grossed just over three million dollars. Given production, promotion, and print costs, this meant a loss of three-quarters of a million dollars, and an odd combination of factors was responsible for the deficit. Though theaters enjoyed turn-away business, more than two-thirds of the *Oz* audience consisted of children who paid substantially less admission than did adults. A glut of pre-booked movies often meant that *Oz* couldn't be held over in many cities, even though attendance warranted extended engagements. Most detrimental, however, was the loss of much of the potential foreign market. World War II began in Europe in September, thus cutting off extensive venues for the picture. Where the film *could* be seen, the M-G-M drumbeating and public response was much the same as it had been in the United States. *Oz* triumphed in Great Britain, Mexico, and South America. In Canada, *Oz* anticipation was so strong that the government overturned an eight-year-old law that barred those under the age of sixteen from attending a movie unless accompanied by an adult.

Despite the financial loss, there's no question that Metro-Goldwyn-Mayer felt pride in their accomplishment. With *Oz,* they were able to demonstrate the perfection of creation and craft that placed them at the pinnacle of motion picture production at that time. Hal Millar of the prop shop later summed up the emotion felt by virtually every employee: "Other studios . . . made good pictures. We worked for M-G-M. We made better ones."

But even Metro was surprised at the hold on public affection that *Oz* continued to manifest, long after it completed its cinema circuit. Perhaps it was the underlying "no place like home" attitude attendant to the war; Judy found that "Rainbow" quickly became

ABOVE: The *Oz* premiere program, August 15, 1939.

BELOW: M-G-M's trade ad shows an animated box office window, drunkenly overwhelmed by *Oz* receipts. The "S.R.Oz" placard takes off on the S.R.O. (i.e., standing room only) sign employed by theaters when all seats were taken.

OZIFIED!

ABOVE: Aware that *Oz* would take many months to play the national cinema circuit, M-G-M posed Judy for 1939 Thanksgiving art. Her outfit should look familiar. **ABOVE RIGHT:** During the 1930s and 1940s, Jacques Kapralik created much in-house M-G-M promotional art, often in collage format. When designing a Garland paper doll for a 1941 fan magazine, he included a variation of her most famous costume to that date.

her most requested song, especially in countless appearances she made across America for the armed forces. During the mid-1940s, there was an increasing proliferation of *Oz* stage plays, and with M-G-M's cooperation and orchestrations, the shows were often augmented with the happily anticipated music and lyrics from the film. Meanwhile, the Oz book series—though interrupted by the war—enjoyed five more additions between 1940 and 1949. By decade's end, the omnipresence of Oz in popular culture was such that Metro found it had more requests for a reissue of that movie than for any of its other "older" motion pictures.

To test box office potential, *Oz* was booked into a few theaters in spring 1949. When the accolades and financial returns began, M-G-M quickly moved to cash in, and the film was put into widespread rerelease. A happy test case, *Oz* proved there was an audience for reissued "classics." It brought in over one-and-a-half million dollars in 1949; in the process, the picture both renewed its audience and moved into the profit column for its studio.

Five years later, Judy Garland regained her own box office hold on motion picture audiences with *A Star is Born* (1954). Capitalizing on this, M-G-M decided to send *Oz* around again. It may have been too soon; the 1955 reappearance enjoyed a promising debut but then fell victim to the times. A new breed of theater managers had grown less adept at programming, especially in competition with television. M-G-M itself, suffering under a different kind of hierarchy, wasn't able to marshal its promotion with the power or sweep of the past. As a result, *Oz* was often screened with inferior or inappropriate second features or relegated to second-run houses.

Still, the film added another $465,000 to its gross earnings and, as it turned out, was gathering momentum for a second career. In 1956, *The Wizard of Oz* began its gradual elevation to a plateau of fame and familiarity unique to any motion picture in history.

OZ

FLASH! TERRIFIC OPENINGS NATION-WIDE!

READY! SET! GO!—This industry is talking about nothing else but the greatness of M-G-M's "THE WIZARD OF OZ". The preview confirmed advance reports that it is one of the biggest box-office sensations of all time. 400 happy theatres are about to play it in the largest simultaneous booking of film history. M-G-M has set the stage. The American public is waiting!

$250,000 CAMPAIGN!

NATIONAL MAGAZINES

Full-page, full color ads

MAGAZINE	ON SALE	MAGAZINE	ON SALE
WOMAN'S HOME COMPANION	Aug. 5	GOOD HOUSEKEEPING	Aug. 20
LADIES' HOME JOURNAL	Aug. 9	PARENTS'	Aug. 15
McCALL'S	Aug 10	LIFE	Aug. 25
AMERICAN	Aug. 5	SATURDAY EVENING POST	Aug. 23
REDBOOK	Aug. 5	LIBERTY	Aug. 16
COSMOPOLITAN	Aug. 1		

JUVENILE MAGAZINES

Full-page, 2-color ads

AMERICAN BOY	Aug. 20	AMERICAN GIRL	Aug. 28
BOYS' LIFE	Aug. 20	OPEN ROAD FOR BOYS	Aug. 20

FAN MAGAZINES

2-color, 2-page spreads

SCREEN BOOK	Aug. 1	MODERN SCREEN	Aug. 1	SCREEN GUIDE	Aug. 1
HOLLYWOOD	Aug. 10	MODERN ROMANCES	Aug. 1	SCREENLAND	Aug. 3
MOTION PICTURE	July 25	MOVIE MIRROR	July 25	SILVER SCREEN	Aug. 12
MOVIE STORY	Aug. 1	PHOTOPLAY	Aug. 10	MODERN MOVIE	Aug. 1

2-page spread, 1-color

PICTURE PLAY	Aug. 1	SCREEN ROMANCES	Aug. 1	MOVIE LIFE	Aug. 5

THIS PAGE: M-G-M formulated this trade ad to tell the industry just how much space they'd taken or achieved to herald *Oz*. It's an extraordinary summation of the studio system at its promotional peak.

COMIC SUPPLEMENT ADS

Full-page 4-color ads (just like the funnies) in 29 newspaper in 21 cities!

CITY	NEWSPAPER		CITY	NEWSPAPER		CITY	NEWSPAPER	
ALBANY	Times-Union	Aug. 20	DETROIT	Times	Aug. 20	PROVIDENCE	Journal Bulletin	Aug. 20
ATLANTA	American	Aug. 20		News	Aug. 27	ROCHESTER	Dem.-Chronicle	Aug. 20
BALTIMORE	American	Aug. 20	LOS ANGELES	Examiner	Aug. 20	SAN ANTONIO	Light	Aug. 20
	Sun	Aug. 27	MILWAUKEE	Journal	Aug. 27	SAN FRANCISCO	Examiner	Aug. 20
BOSTON	Advertiser	Aug. 20		News Sentinel	Aug. 20	SEATTLE	Post Intelligencer	Aug. 20
	Globe	Aug. 27	NEW YORK CITY	Journal-Amer.	Aug. 20	ST. LOUIS	Post Dispatch	Aug. 20
BUFFALO	Courier Express	Aug. 20		News	Aug. 27	SYRACUSE	American	Aug. 20
CHICAGO	Herald Examiner	Aug. 20	PHILADELPHIA	Inquirer	Aug. 20	WASHINGTON	Star	Aug. 27
	Tribune	Aug. 27	PITTSBURGH	Press	Aug. 27		Times Herald	Aug. 20
CLEVELAND	Plain Dealer	Aug. 20		Sun Telegraph	Aug. 20			

NATION-WIDE TEASER ADS

100-line insertions have been running for months in 99 newspapers in 43 cities radiating national coverage

ALBANY · ATLANTA · BALTIMORE
BOSTON · BRIDGEPORT · BUFFALO
CHARLOTTE · CINCINNATI · COLUMBUS
DALLAS · DAYTON · DENVER
DES MOINES · EVANSVILLE
HARRISBURG · HARTFORD · HOUSTON
INDIANAPOLIS · MILWAUKEE
MINNEAPOLIS · NASHVILLE
NEW HAVEN · OAKLAND · OMAHA
OKLAHOMA CITY · PHILADELPHIA
PITTSBURGH · PORTLAND
PROVIDENCE · ROCHESTER · ST. LOUIS
ST. PAUL · SALT LAKE CITY
SAN ANTONIO · SEATTLE
SPRINGFIELD · SYRACUSE · TULSA
WASHINGTON, D. C. · WATERBURY
WILMINGTON · WORCESTER

RECORD PUBLICITY RESULTS

Never such a barrage of pre-release publicity as that which greets "The Wizard of Oz"! Just a fraction of it listed below!

Most of publications mentioned hereunder will be on sale during July, August or September. List incomplete

COSMOPOLITAN: Story in the August issue, entitled "Hollywood Discovers We Never Grow Up," by Florence Ryerson and Edgar Allan Woolf; illustrated by stills from the production.

GOOD HOUSEKEEPING: General production story by Jane Hall, illustrated by production stills. "The Wizard of Oz."

LIFE: Two-page spread in color, using our kodachrome production stills, in issue dated July 17th. "Dazzling Brilliance Marks M-G-M's Color Version of 'The Wizard of Oz'."

VOGUE: Full color page, using one of our kodachromes.

RED BOOK: Has selected THE WIZARD OF OZ as "Picture of the Month"; will use a layout of kodachromes from the production.

AMERICAN: Using our kodachromes.

COUNTRY GENTLEMAN: Stills of Judy Garland and Billie Burke from the production.

LOOK: Layout.

GLAMOUR: Layout and stills.

McCALL'S: Layout

TOWN AND COUNTRY: Layout.

NEWSPAPERS, out of town, which use ROTOGRAVURE: Full page layouts.

TRIBUNAL, OPEN ROAD FOR BOYS, INSTRUCTOR, GRADE TEACHER, SCHOLASTIC, BOYS' LIFE, AMERICAN BOY, YOUNG AMERICA, CATHOLIC BOY, PARENTS': Story material and layouts for August and September breaks.

NORTH AMERICAN NEWSPAPER ALLIANCE (serving 100 newspapers, including 50 large metropolitan dailies); Victor Fleming life story installment with art, to break simultaneously with our play dates.

BOYS' LIFE: Layout "Movies of the Month."

FAWCETT PUBLICATIONS, including HOLLYWOOD, MOTION PICTURE, SCREEN BOOK, MOVIE STORY: Layouts and production stories.

PHOTOPLAY: Several pages of layout and a production story by Dixie Willson. "The Wizardry of Oz."

PICTURE PLAY: Double-page layout.

MOVIE MIRROR: "It's All a Dream!"

SCREEN GUIDE: Double-page layout in color, using our kodachromes.

MODERN SCREEN: Layout.

SCREEN ROMANCES: August cover and fictionization. "Wizard of Oz."

SCREENLAND: Layouts. "Judy's Crushes" by May Mann

SILVER SCREEN: Layouts. "Marvels of Make-up."

MODERN MOVIES: Production story and layouts.

MOVIE LIFE: Cover and life story of Judy Garland. "Movie Life of Judy Garland."

PIC: Layout. "The Top Ten—Why."

HOLLYWOOD: On "The Wizard of Oz" set.

SCREEN BOOK: "This Dream Cost $3,000,000."

FAMILY CIRCLE: "The Wizard of Oz"—Dudley Early.

MOVIES: "Hollywood finds the Wizard."

SUNDAY MIRROR (N. Y.): Magazine Section. Front Cover, August 20, 1939.

M-G-M's Technicolor Wonder Show "THE WIZARD OF OZ" with Judy Garland · Frank Morgan · Ray Bolger Bert Lahr · Jack Haley · Billie Burke · Margaret Hamilton · Charley Grapewin and The Munchkins A VICTOR FLEMING Production · Screen Play by Noel Langley, Florence Ryerson and Edgar Allan Woolf · Music and Lyrics by Harold Arlen and E. Y. Harburg · From the Book by L. Frank Baum · Directed by Victor Fleming · Produced by MERVYN LeROY

BELOW/RIGHT: M-G-M sent postcards to answer fan mail and also distributed them to visitors to the lot. It was a quick and easy way of trumpeting a film like *Oz*, and the studio encouraged guests to address cards on the spot; Metro then paid postage and did the mailing.

Only Metro-Goldwyn-Mayer, with its 117-acre studio, its thirty huge sound stages and 4000 employees representing 150 different arts and sciences, could have made "The Wizard of Oz" as all-age entertainment. On the front of this card you see Judy Garland as Dorothy, Ray Bolger as the Scarecrow, Jack Haley as the Tin Woodman, Frank Morgan as the Wizard and Bert Lahr as the Cowardly Lion. And there is Toto, the dog, the most important animal role a super-picture ever had. Eight thousand other actors appear amid startling photographic effects, accompanied by melodic tunes and catchy lyrics. The film was directed by Victor Fleming and produced by Mervyn LeRoy.

THIS SPACE FOR MESSAGE

We will be seeing you soon
Judy Garland

THE TALK OF HOLLYWOOD

In the world's motion picture capital "The Wizard of Oz" is being heralded as Movieland's triumph of 1939. Filmed in Technicolor, set entirely to music and given realism throughout, it faithfully tells the story which has sold nine million copies since it was written by L. Frank Baum in 1900.

"Result of discussions on *Oz* campaigns: New York is to plant all national and fan magazine art, color and black and white, including covers and any special layout material. Coast is to plant all rotogravure and newspaper art, color and black and white, as well as all special out-of-town material. We have agreed . . . to fix publication release date July 1 which covers July and August magazines. Same applies to roto sections. . . . Believe this date for simultaneous national break will also obviate complications with *Life*, which is putting on pressure for pre-release break. On newspapers, apart from roto sections, think best to withhold all art until later date as publication in dailies likewise would affect importance of national breaks. Newspaper campaign would be handled entirely through Coast plantings in accordance with actual release date of picture."

— Ralph Wheelwright, M-G-M publicist, *April 7, 1939*

RIGHT: The studio supplied theater owners with different "teaser" ads, designed for advance placement in local newspapers.

ABOVE: Artwork from the souvenir program. **RIGHT:** *Oz* was shown to the press on both Coasts in special screenings on August 9. Reaction was overwhelming; one reporter publicly noted that "many critics still had tears in their eyes" when the lights went up in the projection room at the end of the picture. *Oz* was described as "an inexhaustibly entertaining and great motion picture." This page of excerpts from a handful of preliminary reviews was assembled for *The M-G-M Studio News* for the week of August 14. The next night, many of the same Los Angeles journalists attended the Grauman's premiere and again wrote and raved.

PRESS LAUDS "WIZARD" AS MIRACLE PICTURE!

LOUELLA O. PARSONS, UNIVERSAL SERVICE: "A flesh and blood successor to 'Snow White' has been achieved in 'The Wizard of Oz.' In many ways this reviewer liked 'The Wizard' better than 'Snow White' because it has human actors and for that reason is more believable and less juvenile in its conception.

"I didn't see how it was possible to photograph Dorothy's trip to the land of the Munchkins, her visit to the Emerald City to find the Wizard of Oz, or any of the weird happenings that befell her after she left Kansas. All of this has been done on a magnificent scale, with settings that are breath-taking.

"Mervyn LeRoy, the producer, can easily put this down as his ultimate achievement. As for Victor Fleming, he must have loved the Oz stories to have given the movie version such creative and appreciative direction. The extremely difficult task of adapting the Oz books and combining them with the musical comedy was entrusted to Noel Langley, Florence Ryerson and Edgar Allan Woolf.

"The music is no small part of the success of 'The Wizard of Oz' and to Herbert Stothart goes credit for the musical direction, to E. Y. Harburg for the charming lyrics and to Harold Arlen for the catchy music. Bobby Connolly staged the musical numbers. Adrian designed the original costumes and Hal Rosson was responsible for the beautiful photography."

JACK MOFFIT, KANSAS CITY STAR: "Three generations will see their gayest dreams come true in 'The Wizard of Oz.'"

HARRISON CARROLL, L. A. HERALD-EXPRESS: "If Hollywood's human actors have been smarting under the supremacy of animated cartoons they can sit back and relax. M-G-M's 'Wizard of Oz' is an amazing adventure in the world of fairy tales. None will deny that 'The Wizard of Oz' is one of the greatest novelties ever offered on the screen. When you consider this and the tremendous ready-made audience of Baum readers, it is hard to see how the picture can fail to be a box-office hit."

EDWIN SCHALLERT, L. A. TIMES: "Fantasy is at last brought to the screen in full-fledged form and a victory to compare with the time when Metro-Goldwyn-Mayer brought the musical feature lustrously to the screen with its first 'Broadway Melody' is achieved in 'The Wizard of Oz,' which may well be described as epochal. It will in the future be regarded as one of the most truly important contributions to the motion picture. 'The Wizard' is a picture worthy of road show exploitation and rebounds to the credit of Mervyn LeRoy as producer, Victor Fleming as director, all the cast members, art director, photographers and everybody."

HOLLYWOOD REPORTER: "'The Wizard of Oz' will, beyond question, be accorded recognition as a milestone in motion picture history. It scintillates with artistry, yet it possesses such an abundance of qualities which predict broad audience success that there can be no question of its being headed for spectacular playing time and grosses.

"The M-G-M picture will undoubtedly reflect great credit to the motion picture industry at large. It is a creation entirely out of the usual order, brilliantly inventive and arrestingly beautiful and dramatically compelling to the eye, the ear, and the emotions. Somehow in its lavish creation, producer Mervyn LeRoy has captured a spirit of earthy drama of a strong moral flavor, and combined this with outright fantasy and with striking effect.

"The production is remarkable in every department. Its cast is superb, its music delightfully tuneful, its settings as remarkably effective as they are unusual. Victor Fleming's direction is amazingly sensitive, yet graphic."

HEDDA HOPPER, ESQUIRE SYNDICATE: "Metro has finally accomplished the impossible. In 'The Wizard of Oz' they have done with humans what Disney so successfully achieved with his cartoon characters in 'Snow White.' 'The Wizard' is truly a great picture."

FRED OTHMAN, UNITED PRESS: "The best picture that Metro has turned out in many a day."

JAMES FRANCIS CROW, HOLLYWOOD CITIZEN-NEWS: "It isn't often that Hollywood preview critics admit their enthusiasms among themselves. It was different when 'The Wizard of Oz' was shown to the press in an M-G-M projection room yesterday. The reviewers expressed their opinions to one another freely, and the opinions all amounted to the same thing: 'The Wizard of Oz' is a great motion picture. It is not only a magnificent, history-making technical achievement, it is a warmly human, deeply emotional photoplay, too."

DAILY VARIETY: "An amazing achievement in entertainment as well as technical wizardry is this elaborate, magnificent and thoroughly beguiling screen treatment of 'The Wizard of Oz!' Occasionally a film rates the designation 'great' and this is such an occasion. It outshines any fantasy heretofore attempted, the only comparable picture in its class being 'Snow White,' with which it will compete for world grosses, critical and popular applause.

"Picture cost around $3,000,000 and shows its colossal budget in every foot of its opulent Technicolor grandeur. Sold on its merits and its flash and exploitable elements the picture should pay handsomely on its heavy investment and may very well prove to be one of Metro's all-time top money offerings.

"The musical program is exceptionally fine and in itself recites a complementary melodic fantasy, adaptations having been made by Herbert Stothart, with lyrics by E. Y. Harburg and music by Harold Arlen. George Stoll acted as associate conductor. Orchestral and vocal arrangements are splendidly done by George Bassman, Murray Cutter, Paul Marquardt and Ken Darby, and the musical numbers are staged by Bobby Connolly."

VIRGINIA WRIGHT, LOS ANGELES EVENING NEWS: "Jam-packed with entertainment for the entire family, 'The Wizard of Oz' should be required show-going for every member of the industry. A good picture, handled so neatly as to make reviewing a pleasure."

HARRY MINES, L. A. ILLUSTRATED DAILY NEWS: "If you're off 'To See the Wizard,' then you're off to see the best picture of this year. 'The Wizard of Oz' is this critic's idea of the perfect piece of entertainment."

CLARK WALES, SCREEN AND RADIO WEEKLY: "A great adventure in the world of make-believe. Metro has made a charming, exciting and beautiful picture from one of the best-loved books of all time, 'The Wizard of Oz.'"

PAUL HARRISON, NEA: "An exciting flesh and blood fantasy. Will probably play for the next five years."

THIS PAGE: M-G-M designed many different *Oz* newspaper ads. Once circulated via studio press and exploitation books, such artwork was adapted by local entrepreneurs for the presentation they felt would best solicit and seduce their audiences.

IS ONE OF THE GREAT PICTURES OF ALL TIME, PERHAPS THE GREATEST PICTURE EVER MADE! BEYOND YOUR WILDEST DREAMS ARE ITS TECHNICOLOR WONDERS, AS THOUSANDS OF LIVING ACTORS CREATE SCREEN MAGIC TO THRILL THE WORLD!

Preview-
PREMIERE
TOMORROW NIGHT at 8:30
TUESDAY, AUGUST 15
GRAUMAN'S
CHINESE

M•G•M'S Wonder Show "THE WIZARD OF OZ" with Judy Garland • Frank Morgan • Ray Bolger • Bert Lahr • Jack Haley Billie Burke • Margaret Hamilton Charley Grapewin and The Munchkins • A VICTOR FLEMING Production • Screen Play by Noel Langley, Florence Ryerson and Edgar Allan Woolf • From the Book by L. Frank Baum Directed by Victor Fleming Produced by MERVYN LeROY

SEATS Now
THEATRE BOX OFFICE
ALL AGENCIES...Or CALL ASHLEY 43311
EXTENSION 396 • ALL SEATS $2.20

REGULAR ENGAGEMENT at LOEW'S STATE and GRAUMAN'S CHINESE Starts WEDNESDAY

ABOVE: Trumpeted as the greatest opening in five years, the official premiere took place in Hollywood on Tuesday, August 15, drawing 10,000 gawkers and participants. But *Oz* launched its first engagements in major and minor vacation or "lake" spots: Cape Cod, Massachusetts and Kenosha, Wisconsin (Friday, August 11), and Oconomowoc, Wisconsin (August 12). Positive reaction to such "test bookings" made for good word-of-mouth and, in *Variety* parlance, offered "key to *Oz* possibilities" with family audiences anywhere.

ABOVE: A happy reunion—and reminiscence of the 1902 *Oz* musical play—was enjoyed by Maud Baum and Fred Stone. On that earlier occasion, he'd won acclaim as The Scarecrow, and Mrs. Baum's husband made a speech of gratitude from the stage in response to audience demands for "author! author!" **BELOW:** For *Oz*, Grauman's forecourt was augmented by a studio-designed cornfield, scarecrow, and Yellow Brick Road. Uncle Henry (Charley Grapewin) kibitzed with a tin man on his way into the theater.

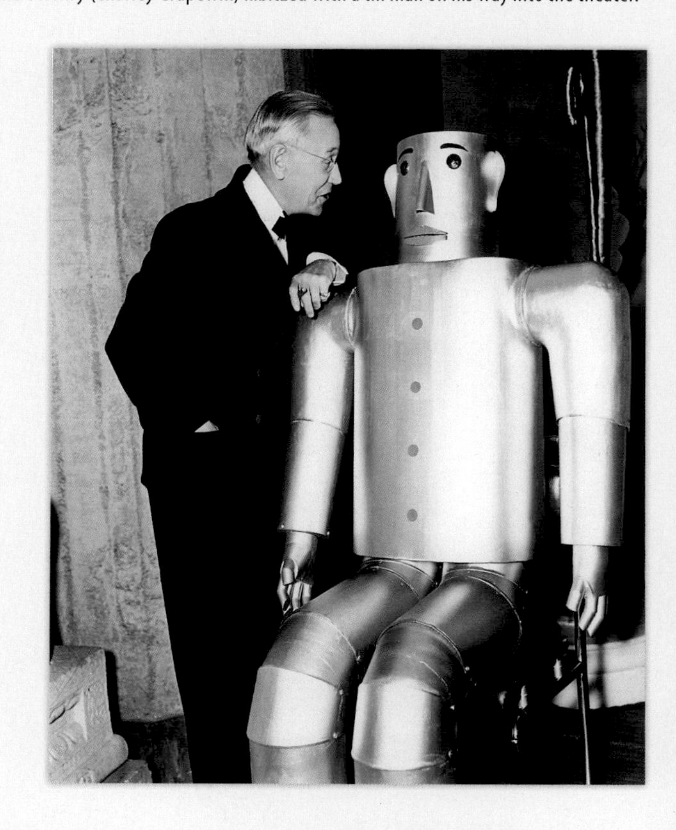

ABOVE: Adding to the atmosphere, several Munchkins were recalled and re-outfitted for the event. Billie Burke greets coworkers Tommy Cottonaro, Jerry Maren (forsaking The Lollipop Guild to pose as The Mayor), Nona Cooper, and Victor Wetter.

ABOVE: M-G-M provided bleachers, an orchestra, and a radio hookup for local listeners. On air, Maud Baum offered, "One of the greatest thrills of my life will be to see the Land of Oz, with all of its queer people that Mr. Baum created, come to life under the magic of Metro-Goldwyn-Mayer in their marvelous production of *The Wizard of Oz*." She later exulted, "I was well satisfied; the film was grand! But I would have liked more singing and dancing and less of the witch. Frank wouldn't have liked the witch part [either]. He never wrote anything that might frighten children."

ABOVE: With wife Lu, Victor Fleming celebrated both the early raves for *Oz* and the fact that—except for retakes—he'd finished *Gone With the Wind*. **ABOVE RIGHT:** Mervyn LeRoy attended with his wife, flanked by Mrs. Darryl Zanuck, director Ernest Lubitsch, and an "extra" wearing a Frank Morgan costume. The eighteen months it took to realize *Oz* had damaged LeRoy's reputation. But the morning after the premiere, it was restored in a front-page Hollywood *Reporter* editorial: "The big chunk [of credit for *Oz*] must justly go to pint-sized LeRoy, who engineered a whale of a job in maneuvering all forces to such a happy conclusion."

ABOVE: Beaming over advance praise he'd won as The Lion, Bert Lahr arrived with his stunning fiancée, Mildred Schroeder.

RIGHT: A front office memo "formalizes" the Garland/Rooney trip back East. **FAR RIGHT:** A studio photographer captured their departure. They were the first teen team of superstars, long before such a noun was imagined—or could be media-manipulated on the basis of fame rather than talent. Both were genuine, legitimate entertainers; Garland, seventeen, and Rooney, one month from nineteen, had already clocked thirty-three years of performing experience.

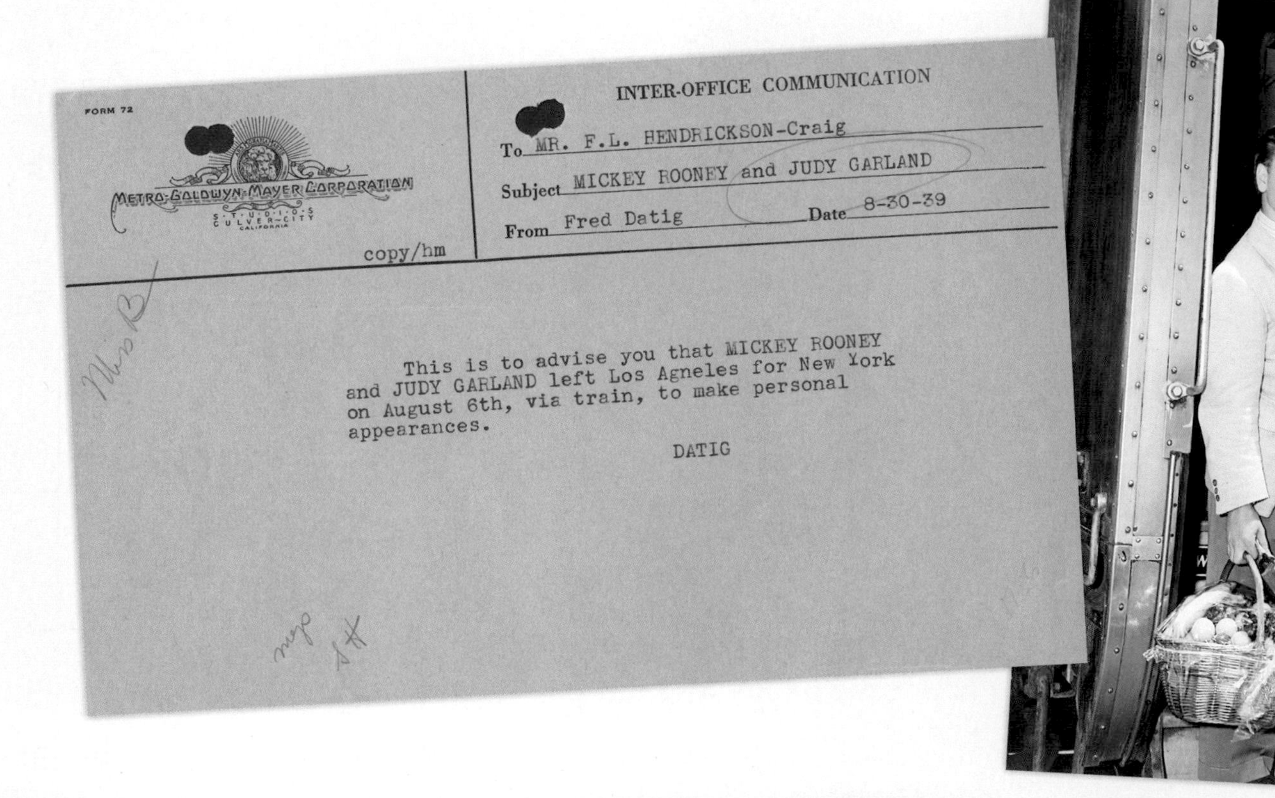

FORM 72

METRO-GOLDWYN-MAYER CORPORATION
STUDIOS
CULVER CITY
CALIFORNIA

INTER-OFFICE COMMUNICATION

To MR. F.L. HENDRICKSON-Craig

Subject MICKEY ROONEY and JUDY GARLAND

From Fred Datig Date 8-30-39

copy/hm

This is to advise you that MICKEY ROONEY and JUDY GARLAND left Los Agneles for New York on August 6th, via train, to make personal appearances.

DATIG

BOTTOM ROW: Prior to their Broadway debut, Judy and Mickey played Washington, D.C., and Bridgeport, New Haven, and Hartford. They participated in luncheons, press conferences, interviews, and meet-and-greet poses with local celebrities and teens. The main thrust of each stop was the thirty-minute song-and-dance act they performed multiple times daily at a local Loew's theater. Here, they're feted at a Taft Hotel brunch (left); surrounded on arrival at New Haven station (center); and proclaimed from atop a local landmark (right).

"The Capitol Theatre will present its greatest show of many years on Thursday, August 17, in conjunction with the eagerly awaited Broadway premiere of M-G-M's Technicolor production, *Wizard of Oz.* The Capitol will present in person in a stage act Judy Garland, one of the stars of *Oz*, together with Mickey Rooney, who was selected by the M-G-M Studios to be her escort on the trip East. These two popular players will leave their current work in *Babes in Arms* at the West Coast studios to take part in this gala premiere."

— Loew's, Inc. press release, heralding the New York City Oz launch

LEFT: Winners met the Garland/Rooney train from Connecticut on August 14; six of the 150 (plus police and press) served as the stars' "honor guard" from the platform into the Grand Central Station waiting room.

Would You Like to Have Lunch With Mickey Rooney and Judy Garland

And Serve on the Official Reception Committee?

One young man and one young woman of high school age will be selected from among the patrons of Yonkers Loew's Theatre to serve on the official committee to welcome Mickey Rooney and Judy Garland to New York for their personal appearance at the Capitol Theatre starting August 17th. They will appear with M-G-M's "The Wizard of Oz."

Members of the Committee selected will be the guests of Judy and Mickey at a special luncheon on Aug. 16 at a leading hotel (no cost to you whatever).

If you are of high school age, fill out the coupon below and drop in the box provided in the lobby of Loew's. On FRIDAY NIGHT, August 11th, the name of one boy and girl will be drawn upon our stage. To be eligible you must be in the theatre that night. Names will be drawn until an applicant, who is present, responds.

P. S. — When you see Mickey Rooney in "Andy Hardy Gets Spring Fever" at Loew's how proud you'll be to have chatted with him in person.

I want to be on the MICKEY-JUDY COMMITTEE!

Name ....

Address .... Apt. ....

High School I Attend Is .... Age ....

ABOVE: M-G-M arranged a promotional contest to select 150 youngsters as New York's "official welcoming committee" for the teens. **RIGHT:** As souvenirs, the ballot for the competition and the subsequent press outpouring were mounted for Judy in an oversized scrapbook under the aegis of Loew's publicity executive Oscar A. Doob. (For the duration, he signed his name as "Ozcar.") The huge volume was embossed "Judy Garland Takes New York!"

PICKED TO GREET STARS

Mildred Lorenz, 111 Garrison Av., Jersey City, 16-year-old Dickinson High School student, and Richard Corless, 1099 East Boulevard, West New York, age 16, of Memorial High School, pose with life-size photographs of Mickey Rooney and Judy Garland, after winning the honor of representing Loew's Jersey City Theatre on the official welcoming committee organized by Loew's metropolitan theatres.

The youngsters will meet and have lunch with Mickey and Judy at a New York hotel Wednesday, together with 150 other high school boys and girls on the committee. The reception will be held in honor of the Hollywood stars' personal appearance engagement at a New York theatre, starting Thursday.

Friday announcement -- WHN

Tonight's the big night at Loew's ! In every Loew's Theatre from Westchester to Coney Island, from Newark to Jamaica, thousands of girls and boys are eagerly awaiting the announcements that will bring one hundred and fifty of them into the limelight. In each theatre, one girl and one boy will be chosen to serve on the official committee to welcome Mickey Rooney and Judy Garland to New York for their personal appearance engagemant at the Capitol Theatre with "The Wizard of Oz".

The lucky group will be the happiest, most envied lotof kids in town. They will be a true cross-section of New York's greathhigh school population.

The committee will greet Mickey and Judy at the train when they arrive, but that's only the beginning. Next Wednesday the youngsters will actually have lunch with Mickey and Judy at the Waldorf-Astoria Hotel in one of those gorgeous dining rooms. That'll be another thrill ! We're hoping that Mickey and Judy will feel like shagging, because Guy Lombardo and his band will be there to swing a few hot numbers. WHN will broadcast this happy affair.

We urge every boy and girl who has made application to serve on this committee to be at their Loew's Theatre tonight. To be eligible, they must be in the theatre when their names are called. Announcements will be made, in most theatres, between 8.30 and 9 P.M.

ABOVE: Loew's bought time on local radio stations to play up Manhattan's *Oz*/Mickey/Judy triumvirate. This is the original copy for one such announcement.

LEFT: Both stars and their anticipatory audience of 15,000 braved mid-August heat and humidity in those pre-air conditioning days. A percentage of the bedlam came courtesy of Loew's prearrangement; the majority was a spontaneous surge of affection for the two teens. But all were caught off guard by the crowd; twenty-five detectives and 250 patrolmen were hastily summoned to Grand Central.

THRONGS JAM STATION TO SAY "HELLO" TO MICKEY AND JUDY !

The Loew-Down
TO KEEP LOEW on HIGH!

CROWDS ECLIPSE THOSE WHICH GREETED PRESIDENT !

No. 1744 August 14, 1939

NEW YORK GREETS MICKEY AND JUDY

Terrific and colossal aren't big enough words to describe Gotham's enthusiastic welcome to Mickey Rooney and Judy Garland when they stepped off the train in Grand Central this morning. Over 10,000 people packed the huge rotunda; another 3,000 brought traffic to a standstill at Vanderbilt Ave. and 42nd St. Capt. Hogan of the station police claimed a greater outpouring than that which greeted the President. 250 city police headed by the Chief Inspector; 25 city detectives and 25 station police were pressed into service to handle the crowds. The 140 girls and boys who formed the Official Reception Committee met at 42nd and Lexington and paraded to the station headed by Loew's Cadet Band. There was 100% coverage by the N.Y. dailies, the photo-services and the syndicates. (Watch for those clippings -- we want 5 copies of each). The reception was orderly and beautifully handled. After Mickey and Judy were whisked to their hotel, the committee paraded in taxicabs and Crosley midget cars. So -- today's orchid to Eddie Dowden of Loew's, Mel Heymann of MGM and the Loew publicity staff, for a tremendous job that worked with unbelievable precision.

RIGHT: Loew's in-house newsletter took pride in noting their achievement. But this paragraph was nothing compared to the front-page headlines, column inches, and photography provided by New York and wire service media. **FAR RIGHT:** The New York *Sun* was particularly declarative, yet typical of the coverage.

"Our first appearance was in Washington, D.C. From the station, we went to a press reception in our honor. At the White House, they permitted us to enter President Roosevelt's and the First Lady's private chambers; Mickey even sat in the President's chair! Then, before we tackled New York, we had a two-day rest. When we arrived at Grand Central Terminal, fifteen thousand people were waiting . . . Mickey and I didn't say a word; we just looked at each other. When we went to the show for our first performance, we started at 11 in the morning and ended at about 8:30 at night. Curfew was 10:30, so there wasn't all that much time to sight-see, [but] we did manage to spend one evening at The Rainbow Room. We wanted to know how it felt to dance 'on top of the world.'"

— Judy Garland

NO, IT WASN'T JULIUS CÆSAR

Nor One-way Corrigan, Nor Napoleon, Nor Lindbergh.

GARLAND AND ROONEY ARRIVE

Or, More Specifically, Judy and Mickey—Ask the Police.

BIG DOINGS AT GRAND CENTRAL

Judy Garland and Mickey Rooney come to town.

Grand Central looked today as though Lindbergh, Corrigan, Julius Cæsar and Napoleon had come to town. At the terminal there was standing room only (and not much of that) as crowds packed together, policemen swarmed about, bands blared, confetti flew, flash bulbs snapped and Kleig lights blazed to welcome Judy Garland and the screen's representative of Young America, Mickey Rooney.

Obviously sweltering, the irrepressible Mickey grinned and swaggered throughout the tumult and, when a Sun reporter yelled into his ear: "How do you like it?" he yelled back: "Swell."

When last seen, hopping into a taxi for the Waldorf, he let out an Apache-like shriek that sounded like: "Whoooo, wooooooo!"

Several thousand people gathered in the terminal more than an ohur before the train was to bring the two young stars from Bridgeport at 11:30 A. M., where they last appeared on their personal appearance tour.

Hundred Policemen There.

About 100 policemen under Inspector George Heitman held the crowds well back from the gates. Inspectors, captains, sergeants and plain clothes men milled about.

Some 150 high-school-age boys and girls who were picked by ballot in Loew theaters (and who were played up by press agents from three different organizations) were allowed into the usually forbidden territory between the big gates and the ramps leading to trains. The girls wore buttons and ribbons marked "Mickey Rooney" and the boys wore paper high hats and similar buttons and ribbons marked "Judy Garland."

Only newspaper men and women, press agents' representatives (including a couple of outsiders who tried to crash the publicity) and policemen and detectives were allowed on the platform where the train was to arrive.

Three young girls of the reception committee were allowed on the platform, too, with bouquets and three young men. They were Louise Levy, 16 years old, a Negro, of 72 West Ninety-ninth street; Lucille Gerstenfeld, 16, of 854 East Twenty-fourth street, Brooklyn; Dorothy Chung, 16, a Chinese, of 41 Mott street; Robert Mannheimer, 15, of 46 Linden Boulevard, Brooklyn; George Wong, 16, a Chinese, of 63 Bayard street, and Sylvester Conyers, 17, a Negro, of 302 West 119th street. (Mickey has a colored valet named Sylvester, too.)

The train arrived at 12:10 P. M. and police officials yelled instructions and scrambling newspaper photographers muttered curses.

Passengers First.

All the passengers were let out before Mickey and Judy alighted. Mickey's wild reddish-blond hair could be seen in the center of the pushing mob of photographers. He posed with his bow-tie untied and his jacket off, with Miss Garland fanning him with her big red hat and purse. Mickey's face was almost as red as Miss Garland's lipstick.

Mickey and Judy stepped back on the train a moment, then began the long walk along the platform to the crowds outside.

"Notify the band! Notify the band!" screamed a frantic publicity man. Several of his agents ran to notify the band.

Dozens of train employees stood in car doors and yelled to the young stars.

Just inside the outside gates Mickey and Judy walked between two lines of the 150 reception committee members. The lines didn't last long. Kleig lights blared down on Mickey and Judy. People were crushed against doors. People climbed up on doors. Then the gates were opened and Mickey and Judy escorted by a big flying squad, went out into the terminal into a gale of confetti, cheers, whistles and music.

While being rushed upstairs to Vanderbilt avenue, Mickey answered a reporter's yelled question about how he liked it all with a yelled, "Swell!"

He and Judy were hustled into a taxi and sped for the Waldorf. The two young stars, who have just finished "Babes in Arms," will appear at the Capitol Theater, beginning next Thursday, where Miss Garland will be in "The Wizard of Oz."

Andy Hardy rode high today.

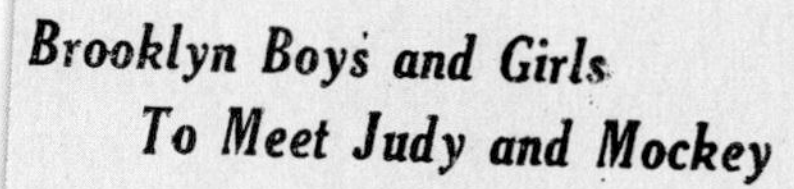

Brooklyn Boys and Girls To Meet Judy and Mockey

Brooklyn youngsters are all agog at the plans made by the Loew's Theatres for welcoming Mickey Rooney and Judy Garland to the city when they arrive from the coast on Monday, Aug. 14.

A welcoming commitee of 150 boys and girls is being organized. Each one of the seventy-one Loew Theatres in New York, New Jersey and Westchester will be representd on th committee by a girl and boy of high school age The theatre representatives will be selected on Friday evening. Ballot boxes, for the girls and boys who wish to represent their neighborhood on the committee are now in the lobbies of all Loew Theatres.

After the youngsters have greeted the two stars at the train, they will be guests at a luncheon to be held at a leading hotel. This will probably be the first and only cocktail party to honor movie stars at which there will be NO cocktails or anything near it!

Mickey and Judy, who are scheduled to make a personad appearance o nthe stage of the Capitol Theatre beginning Thursday, Aug. 17, wil present a special comedy sketch in conjunction with the premiere of "Wizard of Oz," in which Judy is starred.

THIS PAGE: Grandly described as "the first cocktail-less cocktail party for movie stars," The Waldorf-Astoria luncheon on August 16 featured lamb chops and milk; Tin Man Jack Haley as emcee; Guy Lombardo, His Royal Canadians, and Louis Prima for live music; the teen winners of the earlier Garland/Rooney balloting; and Judy and Mickey themselves, offering a grateful welcome and then dancing—first with each other and then with fortunate guests.

LEFT: Thirty-seven thousand cash customers jammed The Capitol Theatre on opening day alone. The crowd, four-deep, was estimated at somewhere between 10,000 and 15,000.

To celebrate the Fall opening

IN PERSON
Mickey (himself) ROONEY
Judy (herself) GARLAND
(with Georgie Stoll and his orchestra)
in a marvelous specially created act
5 performances daily

Air-Conditioned
CAPITOL
BROADWAY & 51st STREET
Major Edward Bowes, Mng. Dir.

Gala New Season
Premiere TOMORROW
DOORS OPEN 8:45 A. M.
NO ADVANCE IN PRICES

The Wizard of Oz
by L. Frank Baum

For you . . . and you . . . and you

At last it's here—M-G-M's Technicolorful production after 2 years of painstaking creation. Greatest sensation since "Snow White". A cast of 9200 living actors, including Judy Garland as Dorothy, Frank Morgan as The Wizard, Ray Bolger as the Scarecrow, Bert Lahr as the Cowardly Lion, Jack Haley as the Tin Woodman, also Billie Burke as the Good Witch, Margaret Hamilton as the Bad Witch, Charley Grapewin as Uncle Henry, Toto as himself, The Munchkins.

Screen Play by Noel Langley, Florence Ryerson & Edgar Allan Woolf. From the book by L. Frank Baum. A VICTOR FLEMING Production. Produced by MERVYN LeROY. Directed by VICTOR FLEMING. Lyrics by E. Y. Harburg. Music by Harold Arlen

A METRO-GOLDWYN-MAYER PICTURE IN TECHNICOLOR

Last Times Today—"FOUR FEATHERS" *In Technicolor*

15,000 in Broadway Jam To See Mickey and Judy

Rooney and Garland Pack 'Em Outside as Well as Inside (Including 60 Cops)

LEFT/ABOVE: Judy and Mickey remained headline fodder for the entire two weeks' engagement. According to The Hollywood *Reporter*, any excess audience unable to squeeze into The Capitol "filled almost all the other Broadway houses, jammed the restaurants, soft drink parlors, and candy stores." In their act, Garland sang two solos; Rooney played drums and did impersonations of Clark Gable and Lionel Barrymore. Together, they plugged the forthcoming *Babes in Arms* with two duets; as an encore, Judy crooned Mickey's composition, "Oceans Apart."

"Between shows, we went to luncheons, dinners, broadcasts. Crowds turned out like we'd never seen before; the mounted police came out to keep order. We felt like Latin American dictators inching along in our limo to the stage door. Were we bored by all this? No, we were show business kids. This is what we'd been working for all our lives. [But] we were stretched pretty thin from the pace. One day, I heard commotion in one wing. Judy was out flat, a mob of nervous fumblers trying to help her. 'Ladies and gentlemen,' I said, 'my partner has just been taken ill.' I wasn't sure what to do next; we were halfway through the show. 'She'll be all right!' somebody shouted from backstage. 'Stall 'em, Mickey!' In four or five minutes, Judy was back on stage with me, and I realized that if I hadn't mentioned her collapse, no one in the audience would have known. That's the sort of trouper Judy was and is. That's one reason why I, like so many others, love the lady."

— Mickey Rooney

LEFT/BELOW: Along with *Oz*, Judy and Mickey also served as a wholesome sales force for local goods, goodies, and emporiums. Whelan's "double rich chocolate malted" indicates one such tie-in.

LEFT/RIGHT: The Capitol kept *Oz* for a third week, but Mickey was due back in California for his next film. So two costars were brought in to work with Judy, and the trio clowned backstage in an "Off to See the Wizard" pose. Onstage, they sang "The Jitterbug," explaining its deletion from the movie; Bolger also did a comedy routine and eccentric dance, and Lahr performed his signature "Song of the Woodman," written for him by Arlen and Harburg for *The Show Is On* (1936).

NEXT PAGE: An artist-enhanced frame enlargement recaptures the scene that awed audiences in 1939. Then "open the door" to the Technicolor wonders of Oz and see Dorothy in Munchkinland and The Poppy Field as first encountered by "the famous five."

ABOVE: October 10, 1939: Back in Hollywood, Judy's star status was confirmed when she became the seventy-fourth actor to put hand and footprints into the Grauman's cement. Mickey assisted; the movie that premiered that night was *Babes in Arms*. (*Babes* also launched Arthur Freed as the producer of what was later declared "the most outstanding series of musicals in motion picture history." Between 1940-48, thirteen of his productions would star Garland.)

"Judy had played minor roles, two of them with Mickey, when *Oz* came along. With *that,* her billing grew like a mushroom. It jumped above the picture's title, making her technically a star. Metro smelled gold in billing Mickey and Judy together for *Babes in Arms*. . . . The two of them sat together in the darkened theater. On one side was Irene Dunne; on the other, Sonja Henie; behind them, Cary Grant. When the house lights came on, Judy was crying through the applause. 'I know what you're thinking,' Mickey said. 'We're two kids from vaudeville, and we didn't mean a damn thing for so long, and now it's happened to both of us.'"

— Hollywood columnist Hedda Hopper

RIGHT: Having survived the cutting room, "Over the Rainbow" won 1939's "Best Song" Oscar from the Academy of Motion Picture Arts and Sciences. **LEFT:** Composer Arlen is shown with announcer Gene Buck; lyricist Harburg was not in California on that occasion. **ABOVE:** Another *Oz* Oscar was presented to Herbert Stothart for Best Original Score. The conductor/orchestrator and his coworkers made masterful use of Arlen's melodies for the underscoring, also incorporating everything from Mendelssohn to Mussorgsky.

THE OUTSTANDING
1939
ORIGINAL SONG

Gratefully

Music
HAROLD ARLEN

Lyric
E. Y. HARBURG

"OVER THE RAINBOW"

from Metro-Goldwyn-Mayer's
"WIZARD OF OZ"

LEO FEIST PUBLISHING CO.
HARRY LINK, Gen. Mgr.

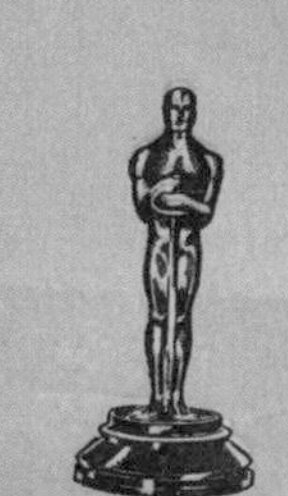

TWELFTH ANNUAL AWARDS OF MERIT BY THE ACADEMY OF MOTION PICTURE ARTS AND SCIENCES

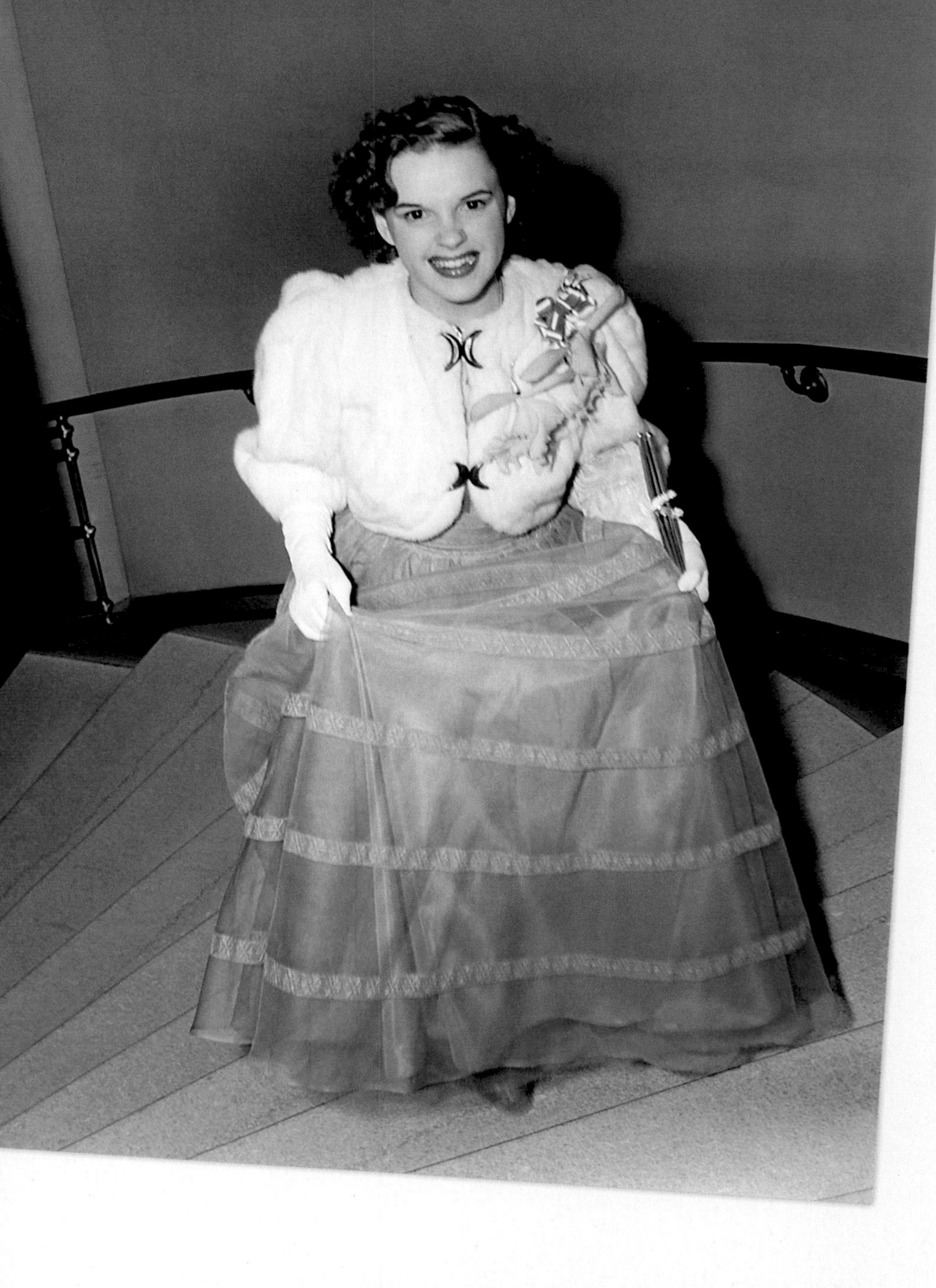

THIS PAGE: The February 29, 1940 "Oscars" were especially memorable for Judy. She wasn't in competition, but she received a special award for "outstanding performance" as a screen juvenile. (The three earlier recipients had been Rooney, Deanna Durbin, and Shirley Temple.) Mickey made the presentation, and Guy Lombardo's orchestra accompanied her rendition of "Rainbow" in response. Garland cherished the recognition although, with typical humor, she later dubbed her miniature statuette "The Munchkin Award."

ABOVE/OPPOSITE: Thanks to Loew's licensing efforts, there was a brief spate of *Oz*-related merchandise in 1939-41. Five "Par-T Masks" came with a flyer offering "8 Ways to Have Fun at a Hallowe'en Party with *Wizard of Oz* Masks."

LEFT/ABOVE/OPPOSITE: The American Colortype Company issued valentines for 1940 and 1941; the dozen different designs were credited as "from the Motion Picture—*Wizard of Oz*." They depicted a cross-section of Ozzy characters, although what appears to be a ruby slipper variation was not part of the original group.

ABOVE: In 1939, Bobbs Merrill published the only full-length version of *The Wizard of Oz* on the market. (The rest of the Oz series was under the Reilly & Lee imprint.) So Whitman Publishing Company worked with Bobbs or Loew's to create story-or-film-related products: picture puzzles, children's stationery, a game, a paint book, a picture book, and a storybook. The latter is shown here in a promotional edition for Cocomalt food powder.

Come with me down the yellow brick road
and be my
VALENTINE

LEFT: In addition to "The Strawman by Ray Bolger" rag doll in two sizes, The Ideal Novelty & Toy Company also manufactured an all-wood composition "Judy Garland as Dorothy in *The Wizard of Oz*" in three sizes. Sculpted by Bernard Lipfert, the Dorothy doll boasted either human hair or mohair wig and (in most cases) a blue-and-white checked dress.

KINEMATOGRAPH WEEKLY, FEBRUARY 1, 1940.

Vol. 276. No. 1711. FEBRUARY 1, 1940 Regd. at G.P.O. as a Newspaper.

Kinematograph WEEKLY

WORKERS' WAR BONUS DEMAND

See page 3

Price 1/- PER ANNUM 30/- POST FREE IN U.K. & CANADA U.S.A. $12 OTHER COUNTRIES 50/-

"A GREAT ACHIEVEMENT—MOST GORGEOUS TECHNICOLOR I HAVE YET SEEN—SOMETHING REVOLUTIONARY IN SCREEN FARE" Daily Mirror . . . "IT'S CINEMAGIC!—EXQUISITE—IMPOSSIBLE TO COMPARE IT WITH ANYTHING ELSE" Daily Herald . . . "A FILM WHICH JUST ABOUT JUSTIFIES THE USE OF THAT WORD—STUPENDOUS" Daily Sketch . . . . "A BEAUTIFUL, MIGHTILY ENTERTAINING SHOW—WILL BE REMEMBERED IN THE ANNALS OF THE SCREEN" Evening News . . . "A DELIRIUM OF DELIGHT—A PAGEANT OF MAGIC AND SURPRISE" The Star . . . "ALL THE WIZARDRY ANYONE COULD WISH—A FILM OF IRRESISTIBLE CHARM" Daily Mail . . . "AN IMPORTANT STEP IN THE PROGRESS OF FILM ART—INGENIOUS, BEAUTIFUL AND AMUSING" Sunday Dispatch . . . "A DAZZLING WIZARD DISPLAY OF SPECTACLE—A REMARKABLE FILM" Sunday Express . . . "I AM UNDER THE SPELL OF OZ" Evening Standard.

OZ IS A BOX-OFFICE WIZARD

2nd RECORD-OZZIFYING WEEK FOR LEO'S TECHNICOLOR WONDER AT THE EMPIRE!

RIGHT: Despite (or perhaps because of) the onset of World War II four months earlier, Great Britain embraced *Oz*. It played to nearly 40,000 customers in first-run at the London Empire, M-G-M's Leicester Square flagship theater. It also seemed to strike an emotional chord with the populace; Garland's "Rainbow" was second only to "God Save the King" in its transmission of faith and hope for the country.

Fifth Page

ARS GRATIA ARTIS

THE LION'S ROAR

(A column of gossip devoted to the finest motion pictures)

Australasia, meet Dorothy! Dorothy is the little girl in *M-G-M's* gay and glorious *Technicolor* production, "THE WIZARD OF OZ", who runs away from home, gets lost, and goes to see if the Wizard will help her get home again!

★ ★ ★

Played wonderfully by bright little *Judy Garland*, Dorothy is told to *Follow the Yellow Brick Road*. She does, and has more adventures than Alice in Wonderland. And she sings—*"Over the Rainbow"* and . . .

"We're off to see the Wizard,
The Wonderful Wizard of Oz.
We hear he is a Whiz of a Wiz
If ever a Wiz there was.
If ever, if ever a Wiz there was
The Wizard of Oz is one becoz
Of all of the wonderful things he doz!
We're off to see the Wizard,
The Wonderful
WIZARD OF OZ!"

★ ★ ★

On her way to see the Wizard, Dorothy meets *the Scarecrow* (played by *Ray Bolger*), and he joins her in hopes that the Wizard will give him a *Brain!*

★ ★ ★

There are other marvellous people in *"THE WIZARD OF OZ"* and we'll tell you about more of them later. Meanwhile, *watch for it*. It's the *biggest* sensation since "Snow White".

★ ★ ★

Your Wizard of the *best* in entertainment,

LEO, of M-G-M.

LEFT: "The Lion's Roar" ads were regular features in North American publications, and two variations of *Oz* text were published in 1939. When the film debuted "Down Under," additional copy was developed for the Australia column.

ARS GRATIA ARTIS

MGM PRESS BOOK

ADVERTISING - PUBLICITY - SHOWMANSHIP - ACCESSORIES

"THE WIZARD" MUSICAL RETURNS BY UNPRECEDENTED DEMAND!

M-G-M's THE WIZARD OF OZ

Ⓤ

JUDY GARLAND ★ FRANK MORGAN

RAY BOLGER ★ BERT LAHR ★ JACK HALEY

BILLIE BURKE • MARGARET HAMILTON

CHARLIE GRAPEWIN and THE MUNCHKINS

A VICTOR FLEMING Production. From the book by L. Frank Baum. Screenplay by Noel Langley, Florence Ryerson and Edgar Allan Woolf. Directed by VICTOR FLEMING. Produced by MERVYN LeROY. An M-G-M picture. Cert. U.

COLOUR BY TECHNICOLOR

IN GORGEOUS COLOUR METROSCOPE

This Cover, suitable for Programmes, Hanging Cards, Heralds, Direct Mail, etc., is available to Exhibitors in two colours at a hire fee of 37/6 and in one colour at a hire fee of £1. When ordering, please quote "The Wizard of Oz" Cover, one or two colours.

ABOVE: At war's end, *Oz* was revived for the United Kingdom cinema circuit on a semi-steady basis. In 1975, it also began a series of showings on British television, much as it had nineteen years earlier in the United States.

"The film was passed by the British Board of Film Censors in November 1939 with an adult permit, 'because the Witch and grotesque moving trees and various hideous figures would undoubtedly frighten children.' Some shots were deleted for showings in Denmark, and in Sweden, the censors 'deleted the alleged terrifying shots of the Wizard in the throne room. Also shots of the Witch and flying monkeys, and Miss Gulch's disagreeable face in the crystal.'"

— *The American Film Institute Catalog*, 1993

¡EL MAS ESPLENDOROSO ESPECTACULO DEL MUNDO DESDE "BLANCA NIEVES"!

EL MAGO DE OZ

En Technicolor

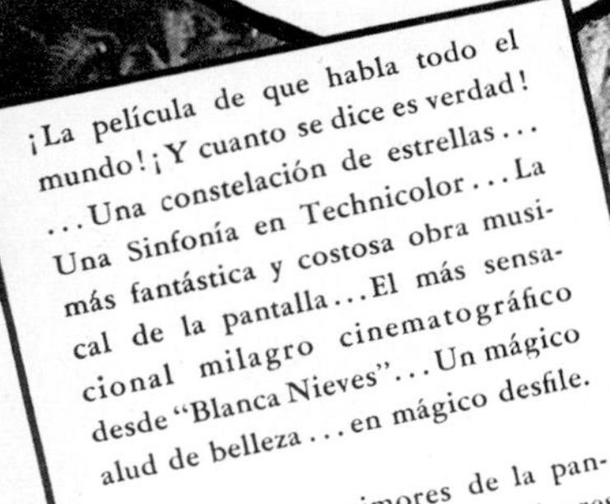

¡La película de que habla todo el mundo! ¡Y cuanto se dice es verdad! ...Una constelación de estrellas... La Una Sinfonía en Technicolor... La más fantástica y costosa obra musical de la pantalla... El más sensacional milagro cinematográfico desde "Blanca Nieves"... Un mágico alud de belleza... en mágico desfile.

Junto con los primores de la pantalla... canciones sencillas, alegres y de indecible hechizo, que quedarán vibrando dulcemente en la memoria y en el corazón...

¡EN EL AIRE EL 16 DE NOVIEMBRE! No pierda el emocionante programa de "EL MAGO DE OZ". ¡Cantará Judy Garland! También Frank Morgan, Romualdo Tirado y otros. ¡Media hora de Hollywood! ¡Música, risas y alegría!

JUDY GARLAND | FRANK MORGAN | RAY BOLGER | JACK HALEY | BERT LAHR

con Billie Burke, Margaret Hamilton, Charley Grapewin y los Munchkins. Versión cinematográfica de Noel Langley, Florence Ryerson y Edgar Allan Woolf. Tomada de la obra de L. Frank Baum. Producción de Victor Fleming. Productor Mervyn LeRoy.

Pelicula Metro-Goldwyn-Mayer. Director Victor Fleming.

ABOVE: World War II didn't keep *Oz* from thriving "south of the border." In late 1939, Argentina not only heralded the film release but served notice of a special radio show on the "16 de noviembre!" M-G-M and The General Electric Company assembled two thirty-minute programs, one in Portuguese and one in Spanish, to promote the Latin *Oz* in Rio de Janeiro and Buenos Aires; the film premiered the following day. Their ad twice (and joyously) compares *Oz* to Disney's international triumph, *Blanca Nieves*.

ABOVE: This hand-colored scene still was part of the South Africa *Oz* promotion. **BELOW:** After the war, *El Mago de Oz* was seen in Spain.

RIGHT: The popularity of the picture sometimes led to book publication of the Oz screen story, the original Oz title, or some of Baum's sequels. *Il Mago di Oz* was one of many Italian variations.

ABOVE/RIGHT: Foreign bookings were scattered in the 1940s. Some countries saw *Oz* at the onset of the decade; in others, the film didn't begin to proliferate until post-1945. These ads and flyers celebrate the appearance of *Oz* in Japan, Austria, and Italy. For such engagements, dialogue was generally dubbed in the local language, while the songs remained in English.

THIS PAGE: Wherever and whenever M-G-M was able to internationally launch *Oz*, its score remained a selling point. Metro-associated music publishers quickly adapted stills and sketches to promote the familiar (or quick-to-become-familiar) songs—including, in the case of the British "Selection," the long-gone "Jitterbug." These visuals display enthusiasm for *Oz* in English in Great Britain, as well as in French, Spanish, and Swedish.

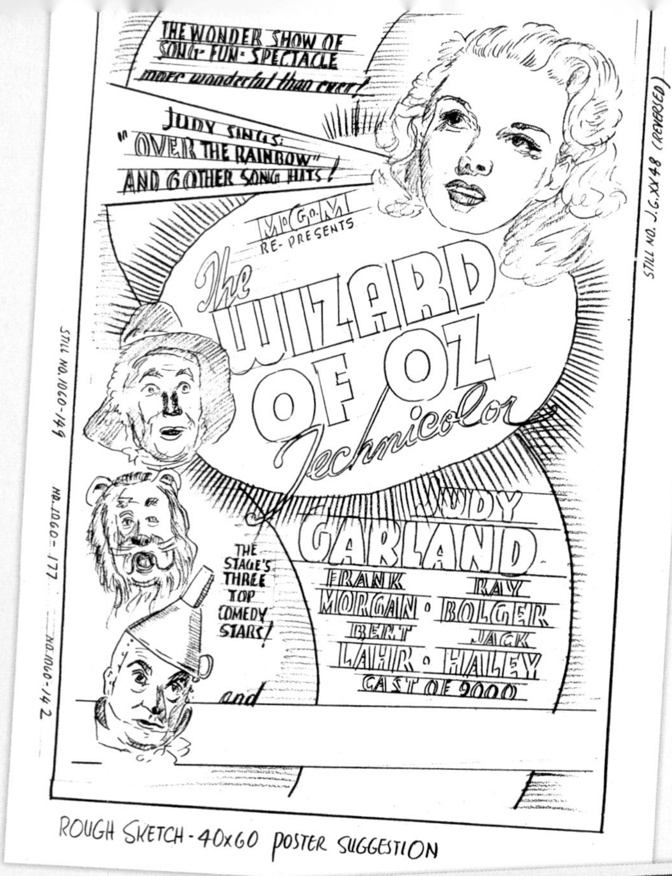

LEFT: M-G-M used images of Judy as Dorothy on some 1949 ad art but hedged their bets by featuring the adult Judy on the rest. The later Garland "look" was more familiar to moviegoers who had come of age since the war. A number of ads emphasized as well the current Broadway and theater hits of Bolger, Lahr, and Haley.

ABOVE: Easter 1949: *Oz* reopened at New York's Mayfair Theatre. Whatever the weather, this test engagement was a smash, and the film was held over for five weeks. By summer, the picture had become a key element in M-G-M's twenty-fifth anniversary season. **BELOW:** If I Only Had an "F": one actor's name seems to have been suffering a gross indignity—or at least a temporary omission—at the moment this photograph was taken.

ABOVE: Once they began earnest 1949 reissue plans, M-G-M increased the size and prominence of Garland's billing. She had starred in two of the top-grossing films of the preceding year and was considered in a "draw class" of her own: Metro's greatest asset.

ABOVE: The 1955 reissue followed Garland's Oscar nomination as Best Actress for Warner Bros. *A Star is Born*. She had requested her *Oz* team, Arlen and Harburg, as songwriters for that project; the infamous Hollywood blacklist precluded Yip's participation, and Ira Gershwin came onboard instead. But Arlen and Harburg would twice more work with Judy: on the score for the cartoon feature, *Gay Purr-ee* (1962) and on the title song for her final picture, *I Could Go On Singing* (1963).

ABOVE/LEFT: The second reissue of *Oz* got off to an excellent start, although it didn't achieve the box office of 1949. New promotional catch-phrases centered on Garland's celebrity and signature song: "Judy and Joy!" or "Let's Go 'Over the Rainbow' with Judy in her Greatest Hit!"

THE ODDITIES OF OZ

Even in 1939, *The Wizard of Oz* was a unique motion picture—innovative in its Technicolor and integrated songs; its combination of children's fantasy and musical comedy scripting; its prolonged shooting schedule and astounding final cost. But one thing it had in common with other films of the day was transience. Movies then came and (almost as quickly) went, whether in city cinemas or on village screens. Pending population, a picture would play for a week, split week, or weekend; in rare cases, it might be held over for—in trade terms—a second "stanza." But the next day, it would be followed by another film. This was the pattern, in metropolis or hamlet, starting in the 1920s and continuing for decades.

After making such a circuit, many film prints were worn and subsequently destroyed. Those in relatively good condition might be preserved in the odd event of a future booking. But major reappearances were comparatively unusual. (So was home-viewing; until the late 1940s, television was a dream delayed, thanks to World War II. Accessible video machines and cable TV were virtually unimagined until the 1970s.) When *Oz* was first produced, few realized that Hollywood product—whether mediocre or prized—could be recycled for ongoing profit and, in some cases, renewed or eternal popularity.

ABOVE: *Oz* editor Blanche Sewell was photographed as she worked on the final assemblage of the film on the M-G-M lot in Culver City. Many *Oz* oddities resulted from the deletions, tightening, and trimming that occurred between the rough cut, the sneak previews, and the premiere.

Via national telecast, home recorders, and commercial tape and disc, *Oz* has now been available for at-will screening for thirty years. There are youngsters who have seen the movie hundreds of times; they've been joined in their passion by adults who love to examine the film almost frame-by-frame. As such, it's possible to note some random idiosyncrasies that no one in 1939 could have imagined would be discovered. "Eccentricities," of course, are indigenous to every film, but when a picture is as well known as *Oz*, the discoveries are fun to share. The magic somehow remains undiluted, and lessons can be learned about the movie-making process, the mind-workings of the rabid, and the hyper-imagination and (ir)rationalization that is sometimes put forth in the guise of authority!

Here are some "oddities of *Oz*," presented for enjoyment, pleasure, and trivia and fact-sharing purposes. One caution: don't use them as a spoiler—and don't be an interrupter. Share them only with those who know the movie well and are ready for (and request) minutia.

OPENING CREDITS AND KANSAS

- The film musically opens and closes with the six-note "Glinda motif"; it's not unlike the five-note quaver used for communication between representatives of earth and the mother ship from outer space at the conclusion of *Close Encounters of the Third Kind* (1977).
- The clouds that accompany the main title remain the film's only "location" footage; everything else was shot on soundstages. (Many concepts were considered for the opening, including that of showing M-G-M's "Leo the Lion" in black and white, changing to color for the movie title, and then reverting to black and white for the rest of the credits.)
- The Kansas scenes were photographed in black and white, and the film then was bathed in a sepia wash to achieve the amber tones seen in the original release prints and in the recent restored editions.
- In early scripts, Miss Gulch's profession is given as schoolteacher; such designation remains in contemporary press releases about her character.

ABOVE: Dorothy meets Professor Marvel; the latter wears the coat that supposedly belonged to L. Frank Baum.

- In a deleted scene, farmhand Jack Haley complained that his joints felt rusted. Then he demonstrated for Dorothy "something that really has a heart": his invention designed "to break up winds, so we don't have no more dust storms." (This foreshadows Aunt Em's complaint, "I saw you tinkering with that contraption, Hickory!")
- It's Judy's double who falls into the pigpen, but Garland herself is carried out by Bert Lahr.
- The entire Miss Gulch sequence was orchestrally underscored, but most of the music was dropped when it was decided the parlor scene played better with just dialogue. The deletion also provided more aural accent for Margaret Hamilton's bicycle entrance/exit to her theme, "Miss Gul[t]ch/The Ultimate Witch." According to orchestrator Bob Stringer, this composition was derived by distorting and repeating the initial melody of "We're Off to See the Wizard." (Underscoring also was recorded for—and cut from—a number of other scenes, including the farmhand/wagon sequence and Dorothy's first confrontation with The Lion.)
- When Dorothy cries in her bedroom, both Toto's doghouse and her photo with Aunt Em can be seen as décor.
- The gully set wherein Dorothy meets Professor Marvel was later adapted and used for the paddock scene in *Gone With the Wind* (1939), as played by Vivien Leigh and Leslie Howard.
- An announcement painted on the side of Marvel's wagon notes that he is a "Balloon Exhibitionist."
- The coat worn by Marvel is that touted by M-G-M publicity as having been discovered among secondhand clothes and originally the property of L. Frank Baum—with the author's name sewn into the lining.
- Deleted dialogue between Dorothy and Marvel referenced "poppies on the wallpaper" of the girl's bedroom, another presage of Oz-to-come. (In discarded scripting, Marvel traveled with—alternately—a dwarf assistant, a moth-eaten old lion in a cage, or a timorous sidekick, the latter to be played by Lahr.)
- What is the name of Marvel's horse? Listen closely; it's Sylvester.
- Additional footage of the Oz tornado was utilized in M-G-M's *Cabin in the Sky* (1943) and *High Barbaree* (1947).
- An excised scene showed Hickory trying to get his wind machine up and running to combat the approaching twister.
- The rough cut edit featured an extraordinary shot of the tornado enveloping the farm in clouds of dust; this was the first scene of Dorothy's delirium, after she was hit by the imploding window. Perhaps the visual was deemed too disturbing; it was dropped from the picture prior to release.
- An experts' debate: During her ride past Dorothy's window, does Hamilton morph into The Witch of the West? Or is she the ruby slipper-wearing Witch of the East, about to be squelched by the farmhouse?

MUNCHKINLAND

- Judy's double opens the door to Munchkinland; the "real" Dorothy walks out onto the set.
- The 1933 Oz cartoon illustrated its opening scenes in shades of dark blue and white; the animated Dorothy and Toto became Technicolored as they toppled from the farmhouse aloft and fell into Oz.
- "Toto . . . I've a feeling we're not in Kansas anymore" is #4 on the list of the most famous motion picture dialogue, compiled by The American Film Institute as "100 Years/100 Movie Quotes." ("I'll get you, my pretty, and your little dog, too" is #99. "There's no place like home" is #23.)
- The manhole utilized for Munchkin Harry Doll's entrance was quickly covered, but (according to townsperson Betty Tanner) not before Mervyn LeRoy inadvertently toppled into it between takes.

ABOVE: "Toto, I've a feeling we're not in Kansas anymore. . . ."

- Meinhardt Raabe's coroner scroll gives the death date for The Witch as May 6, 1938—nineteen years to the day after Frank Baum passed away.
- The sidelong glance Garland gives Raabe after his speech is a touch of humor she repeats moments later, looking down at Mayor Charley Becker when she sees The Lollipop Guild dance into view.
- When Oz premiered in Los Angeles, the Lollipop trio won appreciative applause from first-nighters for the unexpected "Dead End Kids of Oz" interpretation of their couplet.
- During the fracas involving The Witch of the West, Dorothy holds onto her bouquet, but her lollipop vanishes.
- When The Witch appears, Lollipop Guild member Jerry Maren runs across the upstage set from right to left and dives into a cottage window; for the rest of her visit, his legs protrude whenever the hut is visible.
- Purists point out (as a flaw) the visible smoke vent in The Yellow Brick Road as The Witch is about to disappear. Others interpret this as a story point, in which The Witch merely descends to one of her hellish realms.

THE CORNFIELD AND ORCHARD/FOREST

- When Dorothy Met Scarecrow: This is a favorite spot-the-changes segment, as the girl's braids waft back and forth between long/tousled and shorter/kempt. The former moments were photographed in November 1938; continuity went amiss when portions of the scene were redone five months later, and Ray Bolger performed a new version of "If I Only Had A Brain."
- When the Dorothy/Scarecrow dialogue was first filmed, the cord that attached the leg of Jim the Raven to his off-camera trainer snapped as the bird flew away. The unit shut down until the raven could be coaxed from the eaves.
- Several Munchkins, including Karl Slover, were taken on a tour of the orchard prior to its use. In astonishment, Slover turned to his roommate: "That durn tree just made a face at me!" His statement was dismissed, until his compatriot saw the same thing. A technician then explained there were men encased in the rubber trunks, rehearsing branch and knothole movement.
- An apocryphal Oz anecdote involves a less-than-adept actor who implored M-G-M to use him in any film at all. The studio finally cast him, totally unseen, as one of the trees.
- As the branches throw their fruit, a full-length Garland can be glimpsed at screen right. Her feet weren't supposed to be in the shot, but there's a split-second flash of comfortable black shoes—not the appropriate (if more unwieldy) ruby slippers.
- Disney's *Snow White and the Seven Dwarfs* vocalist Adriana Caselotti was paid $100 to prerecord "Wherefore art thou, Romeo?" for the soundtrack of "If I Only Had a Heart."

ABOVE: Dorothy and The Scarecrow take cover in the deleted "bee" sequence.

- When Dorothy follows The Tin Man as he topples up-screen right at the end of his dance, his oil can falls out of her basket. It's back for use in the next shot.
- A segment in which The Tin Man becomes a beehive (with animated insects emerging from sleeve, collar, and funnel) was deleted from this sequence. His subsequent sorrow at accidentally killing one of them was adapted from Baum's book—proof positive that he (like Dorothy's other companions) already possessed what he felt was needed from The Wizard.
- When the bee scenes were dropped, it was necessary to "flop" the preceding shot to maintain continuity with the placement of Dorothy and her friends in their ensuing dialogue. This explains a momentary fuzzy film quality, and the fact that the trio is suddenly gazing up and off-camera-right at the cottage roof, rather than to the left, where it had been moments before.
- As the travelers depart up The Yellow Brick Road, a large crane can be seen in the background, shuffling its wings in reaction to the singing/dancing aggregation. This is the moment and movement that have passed into urban legend, wherein a stagehand is supposed to have been caught in the scene—or another M-G-M employee or lovelorn Munchkin (wrapped in aluminum foil) is supposed to have hung himself in the glade.

THE LION'S FOREST

- Judy's sense of humor created havoc here; she kept breaking up at Lahr's comical hysterics. Director Victor Fleming finally had to administer a sharp facial slap to get her settled down, and she managed the next take—but barely. (Her brief near-smile as Lahr wails on remains totally in character for Dorothy, who'd have to be bemused by her latest Oz encounter.) When the scene was finished, Fleming confessed to on-set writer John Lee Mahin that he felt like a monster for reprimanding the child. Seeking retribution, he grumbled, "I wish you'd hit me in the nose and break it again." Unbeknownst to Fleming, Garland had come up behind him, overheard his comment, and smiled, "Well, I won't do that, but I'll kiss you on the nose." Up on tiptoes, she went—and did.
- *Oz* scrupulously divides the on-screen time of the male principals. Bolger appears first and sings a full song. Haley enters later, but gets a full song and dance. Lahr arrives last and only has a half-chorus of "If I Only Had the Nerve," but he does "If I Were King of the Forest" later in the picture.

THE POPPY FIELD AND EMERALD CITY, PART ONE

- Hamilton lost screen-time and dialogue in Poppy Field deletions. When The Scarecrow screams for help for Dorothy, the early edit of the film showed The Witch cackling, "Call away! Call away! She won't hear *any* of you again. And there's *nothing* you can do about it, either. . . . It worked very smoothly!" As in Baum's book, she next planned to use the golden "wishing cap," which gave her control over The Winged Monkeys: "I'll call [them] to fetch me those slippers."

ABOVE: Even in a posed publicity still, Judy seems poised on the verge of laughter as she looks at Bert Lahr.

- Thanks to the edit, Nikko is never shown as he retrieves the cap. But after Glinda rescues Dorothy from the flowers in the finished film, the monkey offers the unexplained prop to Hamilton, who hurls it away in anger.
- After the snowstorm, Lahr contributed the ad lib, "Unusual weather we're having, ain't it?" ("Fleming couldn't see it. I said, 'Vic, I'm sure it's a laugh.' He trusted me. . . . I was right. It was a big laugh.")
- As the quartet departs the snow-soaked poppies, Judy stumbles en route and almost falls down.
- Memories are divided as to the coloring process used for the "Horse(s) of a Different Color." Contemporary reports credit a gelatin powder (like Jell-O), while a more recent account cites vegetable dye. Whatever the substance, it must have been palatable; the purple horse spends much on-camera time trying to eat itself.
- "The Merry Old Land of Oz" supplanted working titles for other songs: "Horse of a Different Color" and "Laugh a Day Away." During Dorothy's hairdressing, a bit of "Over the Rainbow" can be heard in orchestral counterpoint as underscoring to the vocal.

- The group's encounter with The Soldier was also edited, which explains why the ends of Frank Morgan's moustache point up when they meet him but down a moment later. (During the deletion, he excused himself for "the changing of the guard": a brief exit and the turn-down of the tips of his facial hair.)
- In "If I Were King of the Forest," Dorothy catches a slipper on the edge of carpet laid for Lahr's procession; she steps over it and keeps going.
- Alternate flowerpot "crowns"—one that breaks and one that bounces—were used during the course of that number.
- Filming in The Throne Room was interrupted when special effects got out of control and the set caught on fire.
- The procession of the four principals throughout *Oz* was echoed by George Lucas in groupings of his *Star Wars* actors (1977). Such homage was then parodied by Mel Brooks's *Space Balls* (1987), when his protagonists encountered the giant head of The Great Schwartz.
- It's Lahr's double who dashes down the corridor and jumps through a picture window to conclude the sequence.

THE HAUNTED FOREST AND WITCH'S CASTLE

- Moments later, Tin Man Haley gets hoisted into the air by unseen "spooks," but it's his double who crashes down to earth.
- As The Witch dispatches The Winged Monkeys to The Haunted Forest, she makes a totally inexplicable statement about Dorothy & Company: "They'll give you no trouble, I promise you that. I've sent a little insect on ahead to take the fight out of them." This references the deleted "Jitterbug," but Hamilton's set-up line was too intrinsic to the scene to eliminate.
- Over the years, the chant of The Winkie Guards has been inventively translated by some eager listeners as "All we are, we owe her" or "Oh, we owe The Old One." The *Oz* conductor's score indicates that The Guards are merely uttering the nonsense syllables, "O-Ee-Yah! Eoh-Ah!"
- When our heroes make hash of three marauding Winkies and change into their wardrobe, Toto gets into the act by carrying one of the Adrian-designed tassels in his mouth.
- During The Lion's walk into The Witch's Castle, his tail is manipulated from the catwalks above the set by a stagehand holding a fishing rod and line. This trick was used several times in *Oz*; occasionally, the line unintentionally flashes in the background.
- When Dorothy is released from The Tower Room, she embraces her friends and murmurs, "Lion, darling." It's the same affectionate term she employs when Toto returns to her in Kansas, indicating that at least one Midwestern twelve-year-old of 1939 possessed a fairly sophisticated vocabulary.

ABOVE: Whenever it seemed appropriate to add a quip to the *Oz* script, scenarist John Lee Mahin would work on-set with the three vaudevillians to couch the phrase in language and humor he felt Baum would have approved. In this scene, it was The Lion's speech that culminated with "There's only one thing I want you fellahs to do . . . Talk me out of it!"

- The wooden casement of The Witch's Hourglass is highlighted by carvings of mystical gryphons.
- As The Witch sinks on her elevator platform, Hamilton wears a larger hat than she sports elsewhere in the film. This adds to the visual illusion of her melting.
- In Baum's book, Dorothy angrily throws a bucket of water at The Witch because the woman stole one of her slippers. In the film, M-G-M maintains the girl's essential purity and has her accidentally melt The Witch in an attempt to douse the burning Scarecrow.

EMERALD CITY, PART TWO

- When Dorothy presents the broomstick to Oz, it's been considerably trimmed and neatened since it was used to torch The Scarecrow in the preceding scene.
- In Baum's book, Toto unmasks The Wizard by knocking over a screen. At M-G-M, the hem of the concealing curtain was conveniently attached to the dog's collar, and he blithely trots aside the drapery.
- As the characters threaten the humbug, there's a bunch of artificial flowers on his console

counter in the background. These were brandished by The Wizard as a carnival trick to distract their anger in a moment edited from the film.

- Error-spotters take glee in noting that The Scarecrow's proof-of-brain is an inaccurately summarized Pythagorean Theorem. This may well be a sly joke from scenarists Langley or Harburg; it would be their conceit that if you sound like you know what you're talking about, people will buy into your statements.
- As he explains courage to The Lion, The Wizard stumbles over the noun "philanthropists"—hereinafter known as "good-deed doers."
- The Tin Man's preoccupied action while peering after Dorothy and Toto in the crowd is frequently misinterpreted. He thinks he's securing the balloon; instead, he unintentionally releases it.
- Dorothy's heartfelt adieu to her companions is underscored by counterpoint renditions of "If I Only Had a Brain," "There's No Place Like Home," and "Over the Rainbow."
- The entire farewell sequence is somewhat reenacted in the closing moments of Steven Spielberg's *E.T.* (1982), as that title character bids goodbye to the three friends who helped him during his stay on earth. (In case the parallels aren't obvious enough in both dialogue and emotional execution, E.T.'s departing spaceship leaves a rainbow trail in its wake.)
- Dorothy's statement to The Scarecrow—"I think I'll miss you most of all"—is the only remaining reference from an early script in which her character was sixteen years old and on the brink of romance with farmhand Buddy Ebsen, who was to depart for agricultural college at the end of the picture (!).

ABOVE: The farewell sequence ranged in emotion from Morgan's pontifical humor to such genuine sentiment that its dialogue has been adapted for countless other television and film scripts.

- In the film, Glinda directs Dorothy to "tap her heels together three times." In Baum's book, The Good Witch tells the girl to "knock the heels together," and Dorothy obeys by "clapping" them the requisite number. Oddly, the universal impression is that the heroine is told to "click" her heels three times.

RETURN TO KANSAS

- Dorothy's journey home was originally a much longer montage. Accompanied by musical themes from the film, the transition included glimpses of The Munchkins waving, The Wicked Witch laughing, The Wizard at his console, Glinda leading The Munchkins in a dance, The Lion growling, The Tin Man chopping through the tower door, Hickory's wind machine, a horse in a stall, a flock of chickens, and Aunt Em with a pan of crullers. All of this was replaced by brief views of the ruby slippers, Dorothy's face, and the farmhouse crashing to earth.
- The film ends without resolving the problem of Toto and Miss Gulch, although a bit of footage that conveyed a semi-solution actually landed on the cutting room floor. Early on, when Dorothy decides to leave Professor Marvel and return to the farm to care for the supposedly ailing Aunt Em, the girl declares (about and to Toto), "I know what I'll do! I'll give you to Hunk! He'll watch out for you!"
- Finally, for the few naysayers who rail against the "no place like home" finale (claiming accurately that one can't hide forever "at home"), it should be added that such an attitude basically misses the point of the story. This was probably best explained by Ray Bolger, who summarized the Oz books as possessing a "great [but] very simple philosophy—that everybody had a heart, that everybody had a brain, that everybody had courage. These were the gifts that were given to people on this earth, and if you used them properly, you reached the pot of gold at the end of the rainbow. And that pot of gold was a home. And a home isn't just a house or an abode . . . it's people. People who love you—and that you love. That's a home."

• • •

The late Rob Roy MacVeigh was an exemplary artist, animator, and Oz historian. Thirty years ago, he wrote the first scene-by-scene examination of the film, noting it was billed in its 1955 reissue as "M-G-M's Entertainment of 1000 Delights!" MacVeigh summarized, "Taken literally, that works out to about ten delights for each of the picture's 101 minutes—or approximately one delight every six seconds. No wonder it can be run again and again to an always welcoming audience."

Hopefully, this annotation of the film's delights and "oddities" will add even more entertainment and enjoyment to the pleasures of Oz.

Designed to embrace art, fashion, and film, "The Inspirations of Oz Fine Art Collection" was established by Warner Bros. Consumer Products as a seventieth anniversary exhibition and unveiled at Art Basel Miami in December 2008. Fifteen contemporary artists created Oz-related images for a 2009 tour and charity auction of select pieces. The art offered here presents two portraits and one nontraditional approach to the greater Oz legend; the contributing artists are **ABOVE:** Glen Orbik; **RIGHT TOP:** William Joyce; **RIGHT BOTTOM:** Alex Ross. (Additional "Inspirations" artists: Angelo Aversa, Romero Britto, Ragnar, Phillip Graffham, Gris Grimly, Marcus Antonius Jansen, Johnny Johns, Joel Nakamura, Nelson De La Nuez, Todd White, Yakovetic, and Gentle Giant Studios.) Limited Editions created by the "Inspirations of Oz" artists will be sold internationally through fine art galleries.

THE MERRY OLD LAND OF OZ

Best-Loved Motion Picture of All Time

CBS presented *The Wizard of Oz* on television for the first time on November 3, 1956. The network's contract with M-G-M included "additional showing" options, but it's doubtful that either corporation thought they would be implemented; movies were not then a coast-to-coast programming staple. Yet even though few households had a color set on which to maximally enjoy the film, the initial colorcast was a ratings smash. The network waited three years to repeat the picture, but from then on, *Oz* was an annual TV event. In its first dozen telecasts, it never placed lower than number four in the weekly ratings. In its first twenty-seven, it was only once out of the top twenty.

If the audience seldom varied, the network did. When the CBS contract expired, NBC won *Oz* rights for 1968-1975 by tripling the monetary figure M-G-M had been receiving. Realizing what it had relinquished, CBS reclaimed the picture in 1976, retaining it until 1999. Eventually, *Oz* brought M-G-M more than one million dollars per telecast, and a TV executive noted, "That picture is better than a gushing oil well."

Financial and contractual facts are one aspect of the story; its miracle is the emotional impact the film never ceased to deliver. By the time of its seventh showing, *Oz* was defined by *Time* as "a modern institution and a red-letter event in the calendar of childhood." In those pre-home video days, the movie was a once-a-year celebration, important as the December holidays or a youngster's birthday. It was anticipated, discussed, and relived, with family, at school, and with friends. Since 1980, *Oz* has been available on home video. Since 1999, it has been shown on multiple cable channels, sometimes with four or five airings in a single weekend. But even with that multiplicity, the pleasure for new or old audiences doesn't abate. Thanks to television, *Oz* has become a happy, at-home, family friend. Meanwhile, the familiarity bred by such exposure has long since created its own Ozian subculture; virtually everyone recognizes and can appreciate allusions to the picture. For thirty years or more, it has been possible to find (at least) weekly *Oz* references in comic strips, editorial cartoons, television programs, commercials, newspaper and magazine articles, or other motion pictures.

TONIGHT AT 8

Let the kids stay up with the entire family to watch the first television broadcast of the brilliant musical fairy tale set in the enchanted Land of Oz.

Ford Star Jubilee presents

THE WIZARD OF OZ

starring

JUDY GARLAND

FRANK MORGAN, RAY BOLGER, BERT LAHR, JACK HALEY

Billie Burke, Margaret Hamilton, Charley Grapewin and The Munchkins

Photographed in Technicolor
Victor Fleming Production
Directed by Victor Fleming, Produced by Mervyn LeRoy
A Metro-Goldwyn-Mayer Picture

IN COLOR AND BLACK AND WHITE ON

CHANNEL 2

CBS TELEVISION

LEFT: The first *Oz* telecast was hosted by Bert Lahr and ten-year-old Liza Minnelli. "Mama" Judy watched on a backstage TV at The Palace Theatre, midway in the run of her second record-breaking engagement. Thirteen-year-old Justin Schiller was a silent presence on TV, invited to appear because he provided a special "prop": a first edition of *The Wonderful Wizard of Oz*.

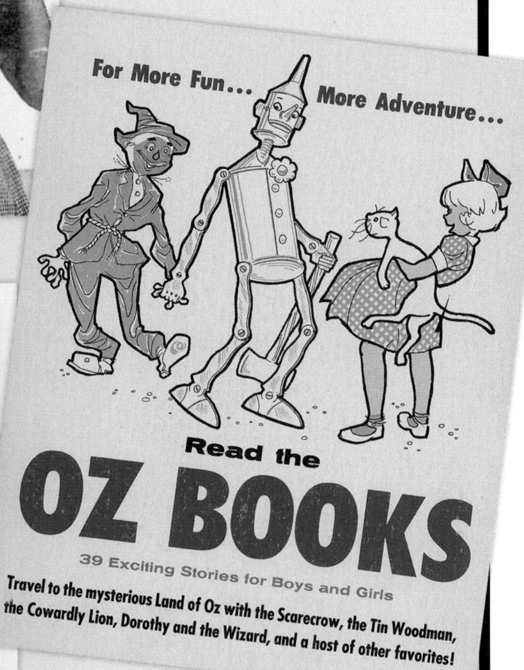

ABOVE: For decades, *Oz* fought condemnation from librarians and literature "specialists." But by 1963, there were forty official books in print, and a full-swing resurgence in effect for Baum, Denslow, Thompson, Neill, and the later authors and illustrators: Jack Snow, Frank Kramer, Rachel Cosgrove, Dirk Gringhuis, Eloise Jarvis McGraw, Lauren McGraw Wagner, and Dick Martin.

ABOVE: In 1970, M-G-M sold their real estate, junked their files, and auctioned their costumes and props. This Dorothy ensemble mingled a Garland test blouse with a jumper worn in the film, but the top price at the May sale was $15,000, bid for a pair of ruby slippers.

By coincidence, the film's 1956 TV debut coincided with the copyright expiration of *The Wizard of Oz* book. M-G-M's script, songs, and concepts remained (and remain) protected, but Baum's basic tale and his characterizations suddenly were open to any republication, interpretation, or performance. The ongoing television popularity of the film further increased public enthusiasm for Oz-related entertainment; by the 1960s and '70s, the earlier snowball of Ozzy products and productions was well on its rolling progression to a freefall avalanche.

Since then, Oz books have ranged from paperback reprints to full-color facsimiles of first editions issued by Books of Wonder/HarperCollins. *Ages of Oz*, a new history vastly expanded from Baum's writings, will appear via Scholastic in 2010, while Oz fans themselves have been authoring and publishing their own original stories since the 1920s. Novels capitalizing on adult fascination with the 1939 movie include Stuart Kaminsky's *Murder on the Yellow Brick Road* (1977); his fictional detective of 1940 is summoned to M-G-M because "Someone had murdered a Munchkin . . . " Geoffrey Ryman's *Was* (1992) mingled improbable episodes imposed on the lives of Baum and Garland with the horrors experienced by a gay Oz fan dying of AIDS. Most pejorative of the novels were *Wicked* (1995) and its sequels, complexly written by Gregory Maguire but dismissing the genuine, joyous Oz spirit.

Much of *Wicked*'s fame derived from its lighter, immeasurably successful Broadway musicalization; its continuing popularity has much to do with public knowledge of and affection for the M-G-M film. Ironically, similar emotions have spelled failure for almost every other Oz theater, movie, and television endeavor. The only triumphant adaptations have come with the all-black stage musical *The Wiz* (1975) and London's Royal Shakespeare Company version of *The Wizard of Oz* (1987), which has toured worldwide with the film script and songs.

Such en-masse devotion to the movie has turned its memorabilia into an almost untouchable feature of present-day auctions. Premium prices have been commanded for Garland's ruby slippers, her Dorothy "jumpers" and blouses, the Cowardly Lion costume, the Wicked Witch's hourglass and hat, random Munchkin and Winkie wardrobe, and the "Witch Remover" spray can. Those thousands of adulators who can't afford original collectibles have found solace in the floodtide of commercial product, now proudly inspired, honed, and monitored for quality by Warner Bros. Keeping pace with technological advances, the film currently is available in Blu-ray Disc format, providing an almost three-dimensional viewing experience. According to one critic, "There are moments when you feel you're standing on the set, next to the camera, watching the action happen in front of you." Fandom also finds its release in the Oz festivals that have occurred with increasing regularity over the last thirty years. Crowds ranging from several hundred to seventy-five thousand have taken part in celebrations throughout the country, drawn by the chance to meet M-G-M Munchkin cast members.

It would now take a multivolume encyclopedia to chronicle the Oz events, merchandise, projects, auction prices, and pop culture references that stretch back to 1900. But one organization has successfully traced the majority of Oz news for over fifty years.

From its charter roster of sixteen, The International Wizard of Oz Club has grown until its membership topped out in the thousands. Their *Baum Bugle* magazine has collated Oz history, past and present, in over 150 issues since 1957; members have convened at national conferences since 1961.

As can be seen, enthusiasm for Oz has never wavered, despite ever-changing tastes in popular entertainment, entertainers, and music. The film itself continues to win respect and recognition. In 1989, it was one of the first motion pictures termed "culturally significant" by the Library of Congress, thereby marked for inclusion on the National Film Registry for preservation and protection. It placed in the top ten "greatest American movies" listings in both the 1998 and 2007 polls of The American Film Institute (AFI). Additionally, it ranks as AFI's number one "best fantasy" and number three "best musical." The United Nations Educational, Scientific, and Cultural Organization (UNESCO) further insured the longevity of *Oz* by adding the movie to its "Memory of the World Register" in 2007. Meanwhile, *Oz* has appeared on the "best" film lists of (among others) *The Village Voice, Entertainment Weekly, Rolling Stone,* and *Sight and Sound.*

ABOVE: In 1957, Justin Schiller organized The International Wizard of Oz Club; his *Baum Bugle* newsletter soon became a deluxe journal. This issue (Spring 1993) shows two of "The Oz Kids," animated offspring of Baum characters. Hyperion Entertainment conceived and produced these cartoons in a savvy circumvention of audience expectation attendant to the famous M-G-M prototypes. "The Oz Kids" were especially enjoyed in Japan; the programs appeared on video in the United States.

Further accolades have been accorded "Over the Rainbow." In 2004, the AFI voted it the number one film song of all time. Three years earlier, the Arlen/Harburg theme was categorized as the number one "Song of the [Twentieth] Century" in a poll conducted by The National Endowment for the Arts and The Recording Industry Association of America. Both Garland's original recording of "Rainbow" (1939) and the first *Oz* soundtrack album (1956) have been elected to The Grammy Hall of Fame.

Of course, such attainment also has left Baum and M-G-M's *Oz* incarnation open to the extremes of gushy or bitter analysis and interpretation. His books are praised or damned for their feminist leanings; the central (or controlling) figures are almost always female. The movie has been the victim of everything from sodden, hypothetical musings by Salman Rushdie to objections from the Christian right. (Per their interpretation of the Bible, there can be no such thing as a good witch.) Dorothy's ruby slippers have been deified as the symbol of her physical passage from young girl to womanhood. Perhaps not surprisingly, both movie and story have withstood and risen above such angst. The Oz series has sold countless millions of copies, and M-G-M's *Oz* has been seen, remembered, and revisited by more people than any other entertainment. If the Wizard's scripted declaration about the human heart is true, it can be paraphrased to sum up the status of both book and motion picture: *Oz* is now judged "by how much it is loved by others."

M-G-M gets a portion of the credit, of course. In the mid-twentieth century, no other motion picture studio was so efficient at producing effective, cross-generational entertainment. It was their business, to be sure; profit was their goal. But there was an undeniable artistry that often accompanied the product, born of an extraordinary cabal of talent. *Oz*, in its quality and reception, stands as the perfect example of their capacity to entertain.

In addition to the monolithic structure that was M-G-M, the specific staying power of *Oz* can be credited to two individuals. The film found its emotional center in possibly the greatest communicative entertainer of recorded time; Judy Garland pulls every audience into the movie's storyline within moments of her first line of dialogue. It doesn't matter if one is girl or boy; everyone can identify with the concept of trouble "after school," the threat of losing a pet, the impulse to run away, or the terror that comes from being lost. Garland is Every Child, with the added boost of being Dorothy herself: a Midwestern girl, swept up by the tornado of her talent and dropped into the good/bad fantasy life of show business. Any who see and hear her become boon companions, sharing the complex and satisfying adventure.

L. Frank Baum and his capacity to entertain win the final credit. He once acknowledged the onset of his most famous work: "*The Wizard of Oz* was pure inspiration. It came to me right out of the blue. I think that sometimes the Great Author has a message to get across, and He has to use the instrument at hand. I happened to be that medium, and I believe the magic key was given me to open the doors to sympathy and understanding, joy, peace, and happiness. That is why I've always felt there should never be anything except sweetness and happiness in the Oz books, never a hint of tragedy or horror. They were intended to reflect the world as it appears to the eyes and imagination of a child."

Add M-G-M's prevailing potency and Garland's joyous charisma to Baum's avowed intent, and it seems that *The Wizard of Oz* will only endure—and entertain—as long as there are children.

Or people who used to be children.

"Judy seemed in fine spirits and engaged in easy-going camaraderie with the cast. But when airtime came, she was the consummate professional and never fluffed a line. Dorothy was played with conviction and charm; it was impressive to see Judy achieve this while speaking into a microphone and reading from sheets of script. It was also interesting to note how the adult Judy could create the impression of a young Dorothy vocally—save for portions of "Rainbow" for which she pulled out several stops! Four-year-old Liza was in the audience and she, too, was properly impressed by her mother's performance."

— Charlotte Stevenson, in the "Lux Radio Theatre" audience, December 25, 1950

LEFT: Only once after 1939 did Judy "play" Dorothy, in a 1950 broadcast of the "Lux Radio Theatre." She later offered, "[*Oz*] covers all ages—little children, people my own age, and older people. It pleases them. And I think Dorothy is a darling character. Just darling." In 1963, singer Mel Torme thoughtlessly suggested that Garland parody "Rainbow" on her TV series. Incredulously, she responded, "You've got to be kidding. There will be no jokes of any kind about 'Over the Rainbow.' It's kind of . . . sacred. I don't want anybody, anywhere, to lose the thing they have about Dorothy and that song."

RIGHT: "The Scarecrow" proudly wore his original costume on TV's *The Ray Bolger Show*, Christmas Eve 1954. He later presented it to The Smithsonian Institution where it joined a Noel Langley *Oz* script and a pair of ruby slippers.

ABOVE: Dorothy and The Scarecrow reminisced on *The Judy Garland Show*, October 1963. They sang three *Oz* songs (including "The Jitterbug"), and Judy quoted the Metro executives who wanted to cut "Rainbow" from the film in 1939: "They thought it would 'take up too much time with this little fat girl singing'!"

ABOVE: Margaret Hamilton made a brief visit when Garland hosted *The Merv Griffin Show*, December 1968. "You're my favorite witch!" exclaimed Dorothy, to which Maggie riposted, "I'd better be!" Then Judy implored, "Laugh! Just do that wicked, mean laugh." Hamilton obliged, brought down the house, and took off for rehearsals for the Broadway musical, *Come Summer*, starring Ray Bolger.

LEFT: Garland's death on June 22, 1969, was worldwide front-page news; Jack Jurden's cartoon graced The Wilmington *Evening Journal* two days later. Among other laudatory journalism, there was a quote from a Broadway stage manager who'd attended Judy's 1951 Palace opening but "really couldn't see her" because of the tears in his eyes. The editorial concluded, "The rest of us loved Judy, sang with her, stood with her, wished her all the best, and even now, some of us are having trouble seeing."

RIGHT: In 1970, NBC reunited the surviving principal cast, who appropriated minor props and major attitude to strike their pose. (Frank Morgan had died in 1949, Charley Grapewin in 1956, Clara Blandick in 1962, Bert Lahr in 1967, and Billie Burke in 1970.) Haley would pass away in 1979, Hamilton in 1985; in every obituary, *Oz* was the first credit mentioned. Maggie had already accurately forecast her headline: "Ding-dong, the witch is *really* dead!"

ABOVE: "The last to go will see the first three go before" him, and Stuart Carlson's cartoon in The Milwaukee *Sentinel* reflects that dialogue as The Scarecrow scurries to rejoin his compatriots.

LEFT: September 1993: "Taking the Bus to Oz [Fest]" meant The Munchkins were met at O'Hare Airport and transported en masse to Chesterton, Indiana. From left: Karl Slover, Margaret Pellegrini, Betty Tanner, Marcella Kranzler, Anna Mitchell Cucksey, Olive Wayne, Marie and Meinhardt Raabe, Myrna Swensen, Lewis Croft (at rear), Jerry Maren, Clarence Swensen, Elizabeth Maren, and Nels Nelson. (The Mrs. Kranzler, Cucksey, Wayne, Raabe, Swensen, and Maren were "Munchkins by Marriage.")

ABOVE: "Dorothy lookalikes" compete at several annual, national festivals. These began in 1978 in Chittenango, NY (Baum's birthplace) and have since sprung up in Chesterton, IN; Grand Rapids, MN (Garland's birthplace); Liberal, KS; Aberdeen, SD; Fayetteville, NY (home of Baum's mother-in-law, Matilda Joslyn Gage); Banner Elk, NC; and Wamego, KS. The latter boasts a delightful, year-round, all-encompassing Oz Museum.

ABOVE: (top, left to right) On the festival circuit: Margaret Pellegrini (flowerpot dancer and sleepyhead) and Karl Slover (first trumpeter/herald, soldier, townsman, townswoman). Clarence and Myrna Swensen (he was a soldier, but appendicitis kept her out of the cast); they married in 1945. Jerry Maren (The Lollipop Guild) and Elizabeth Barrington; they married in 1975. (bottom, left to right) Meinhardt Raabe (coroner) with wife Marie; she died in an automobile accident in 1997, the year after their fiftieth wedding anniversary. Baum's great-grandson Robert and wife Clare present family history dressed as Frank and Maud Baum; with Caren Marsh-Doll, Judy's *Oz* stand-in. Baum's great-grandson Roger and wife Charlene; he's authored a dozen new Oz books, with *Lion of Oz* and *Dorothy of Oz* sold for feature animation.

> **"I think making this picture was one of the greatest things ever, because it makes us—the little people—feel great, because we're noticed. When I was in eighth grade, I was smaller than girls in first grade; I was always the smallest. I wasn't noticed then . . . but today, I'm noticed. Great! Good feeling!"**
>
> — Betty Tanner, Munchkin Townswoman.

ABOVE: After two years of campaigning by Ted Bulthaup, president of the Hollywood Blvd. Cinema in Woodridge, IL, The Munchkins received their star on The Hollywood (CA) Walk of Fame, November 20, 2007. From left: Mickey Carroll, Clarence Swensen, Jerry Maren, Karl Slover, Ruth Duccini, Margaret Pellegrini, and Meinhardt Raabe. ("Soldier" Lewis Croft and "Lullaby League" dancer Olga Nardone were not present; Croft has since passed away, as has Swensen.) Other surviving Munchkins include four women who, as children, filled in the ranks during 1938 filming: Betty Ann Bruno, Priscilla Montgomery, Joan Kenmore, and Ardith Dondanville.

ABOVE: The Land of Oz Theme Park, Banner Elk, NC, opened in 1970 with a combination of live tour and stage show. Vandalism and a fire closed the attraction in 1980, but current owner Cindy Potter now reopens the grounds for a "return to Oz" weekend every October. **LEFT:** A new generation of fans joins in; in 2008, Sean Barrett played The Scarecrow, in company with Jana Prather (Dorothy), Nolan McKew (The Tin Man), and Billy Potvin (The Lion). For the families who throng the mountain for the two-day event, such characterizations are a visual dream-come-true.

ABOVE: M-G-M's 1939 entry in the Tournament of Roses Parade provided a preview of the forthcoming *Oz*. Several film Munchkins were joined by star doubles: Pat Moran (The Lion), Harry Master (The Tin Man), Stafford Campbell (The Scarecrow), and Bobbie Koshay (Dorothy).

ABOVE: For the film's 2009 anniversary, Warner Bros.' marketing efforts included the creation of this logo.

RIGHT: Seven decades later, Bayer Advanced of Research Triangle Park, NC, won the Fantasy Trophy for their *Garden of Oz*, the most outstanding display of fantasy and imagination in the 2009 parade. Bayer makes consumer rose care products, and their float was created in conjunction with the Pasadena-based Phoenix Decorating, whose Michelle Lofthouse provided the design. Mark Schneid, head of Bayer marketing, was jubilant about the firm's association with the film and stated, "The *Garden of Oz* is symbolic of the type of wishes [we] grant: Rose Parade—quality roses in your own backyard."

LEFT: According to a posting at The Oz Museum in Wamego, Kansas, at least six pairs of ruby slippers were made for *Oz*; five survive. Pair One was sold at the 1970 M-G-M auction and eventually donated to The Smithsonian Institution. Pair Two was won by Roberta Jeffries Bauman in a 1940 contest and auctioned to Anthony Landini in 1988 for $165,000, who then re-auctioned them in May 2000 for $666,000 to David Elkouby. Pair Three was privately owned by Michael Shaw and stolen from Minnesota's Judy Garland Museum in 2005. It has not been recovered. Pair Four has been privately held since 1970, auctioned in 1981 for $12,000, and resold in 1988 for $165,000. It is now part of Philip Samuels' Americana collection in St. Louis. Pair Five, the "Arabian" set worn only in tests, is owned by Debbie Reynolds. Pair Six, covered in bugle beads, was worn by Judy during filming under Richard Thorpe; it was thereafter abandoned and is not known to exist.

LEFT/ABOVE: To further celebrate the film's 70th anniversary, Warner Bros. partnered with CRYSTALLIZED™ - *Swarovski Elements* and invited nineteen of the world's top shoe designers to reinterpret Dorothy's iconic footwear for *The Wizard of Oz Ruby Slipper Collection.* Following their September 2008 launch at New York's Saks Fifth Avenue and a nationwide tour, the one-of-a-kind shoes were destined for auction, with proceeds benefitting the Elizabeth Glaser Pediatric AIDS Foundation. Shown here are designs by (from left) Moschino, Jimmy Choo, and Betsey Johnson.

"Many times have people stopped me on the street and said, 'You must have made a fortune out of *Oz*.' As a matter of fact, we get nothing, not one penny. I think my wife has the best reply to that statement. When asked does Ray get any residuals from *The Wizard of Oz*, she says no: 'No residuals, just immortality.' I'll settle for that."

— Ray Bolger

"WE THANK YOU VERY SWEETLY . . ."

BIBLIOGRAPHY

The following books aided in the assemblage of this project and can be recommended to anyone with an interest in Oz, L. Frank Baum, Judy Garland, or general entertainment history. Some are wonderful; some are infinitely more accurate than others.

Baum, L. Frank: *The Wonderful Wizard of Oz* (Chicago: The George M. Hill Co., 1900)
Burke, Billie: *With A Feather On My Nose* (New York: Appleton-Century Crofts, Inc., 1949)
Carroll, Willard: *I, Toto* (New York: Harry N. Abrams, 2001)
Cox, Stephen: *The Munchkins of Oz* (Nashville: Cumberland House, 2002)
Ebsen, Buddy: *The Other Side of Oz* (Donovan, 1994)
Finch, Christopher: *Rainbow* (New York: Grosset & Dunlap, 1975)
Fordin, Hugh: *The World of Entertainment* (New York: Doubleday and Company, Inc., 1975)
Fricke, John: *Judy Garland: A Portrait in Art and Anecdote* (New York: Bullfinch Press, 2003)
Fricke, John: *Judy Garland: World's Greatest Entertainer* (New York: Henry Holt, 1992)
Fricke, John: *100 Years of Oz* (New York: Stewart, Tabori & Chang, 1999)
Fricke, John, with Jay Scarfone, William Stillman: *The Wizard of Oz: The Official 50th Anniversary Pictorial History* (New York: Warner Books, 1989)
Geist, Kenneth L.: *Pictures Will Talk* (New York: De Capo Press, 1983)
Haley, Jack: *Heart of the Tin Man* (Tinman Publishing, 2001)
Harmetz, Aljean: *The Making of The Wizard of Oz* (New York: Alfred A. Knopf, 1977)
Hearn, Michael Patrick: *The Annotated Wizard of Oz* (New York: W. W. Norton & Co., 2000)
Hopper, Hedda: *The Whole Truth and Nothing But* (New York: Doubleday, 1963)
Jablonski, Edward: *Rhythm, Rainbows & Blues* (Boston: Northeastern Press, 1996)
Lahr, John: *Notes On a Cowardly Lion* (New York: Alfred A. Knopf, 1969)
LeRoy, Mervyn: *Take Two* (New York: Hawthorn Books, 1974)
MacFall, Russell, with Frank Joslyn Baum: *To Please A Child* (Chicago: Reilly & Lee Co., 1961)
Maren, Jerry: *Short and Sweet* (Nashville: Cumberland House, 2006)
Marsh-Doll, Caren: *Hollywood's Babe/Dancing Through Oz* (Albany, GA: BearManor Media, 2006)
McClelland, Doug: *Down the Yellow Brick Road* (New York: Pyramid Press, 1976)
Meyerson, Harold, with Ernie Harburg: *Who Put the Rainbow in The Wizard of Oz?* (Ann Arbor: University of Michigan Press, 1995)
Monush, Barry: *The Encyclopedia of Hollywood Film Actors* (Milwaukee: Hal Leonard Corp., 2003)
Raabe, Meinhardt, with Lt. Daniel Kinske, U.S.N.: *Memories of a Munchkin* (New York: Backstage Books, 2005)
Rooney, Mickey: *i.e.* (New York: G. P. Putnam's Sons, 1965)
Rooney, Mickey: *Life is Too Short* (New York: Villard, 1991)
Scarfone, Jay, with William Stillman: *The Wizardry of Oz* (New York: Applause Books, 2004)
Schickel, Richard: *The Men Who Made the Movies* (Chicago: Ivan R. Dee, 2001)
Steen, Michael: *Hollywood Speaks* (New York: Putnam, 1974)
Stone, Fred: *Rolling Stone* (New York: Whittlesey House, 1945)
Swartz, Marc Evan: *Oz Before the Rainbow* (Baltimore: The Johns Hopkins University Press, 2000)
Torme, Mel: *The Other Side of the Rainbow* (New York: William Morrow and Company, Inc., 1970)
University of California Press: *The American Film Institute Catalog/Feature Films, 1931-1940* (1993)
Wilk, Max: *They're Playing Our Song* (New York: Atheneum, 1973)

PHOTO, ARCHIVAL, AND RESEARCH CREDITS

Unless otherwise noted, all illustrations are from the authors' collections.

As ever, books such as this one are glorified by materials held by The Academy of Motion Picture Arts and Sciences/The Margaret Herrick Library: *The Tom Tarr Technicolor Collection*: 31 right center, 41 right bottom, 45 left top, 46 center bottom, 48, right bottom, 50 left center, 51 left bottom, 65 right, 66 left column, 67 left bottom, 69 right top/center, 75 right bottom, 79 right bottom, 80 right top, 84 right center, 86 left top/bottom, 87 right top, 89 left bottom, 90 left/center bottom, 92 left top/center, 93 right, 94 left bottom, 96 left top/center bottom, 97 center/left bottom, 99 left top/center,101 left bottom, 104 left top/bottom, 105 left/center/right bottom, 106 left bottom, 107 left bottom. *The Victor Fleming Scrapbook*: 7 right top, 40 left bottom, 65 left, 73 right bottom, 74 left bottom, 93 left bottom, 101 right bottom, 124 left. *The A. Arnold Gillespie Collection*: worksheets on 110, 111; *The M-G-M Collection*: 124 right bottom, 125 left/right top, 134 center, 144. *The John Truwe Collection*: 36, 37 left/center, 39 top three, 40 center top, 43 left top, 45 center/right top, left bottom, 47 left top two, 51 left/center.

Additionally, we wish to acknowledge the splendid cooperation of Warner Bros. Consumer Products: 150, with special thanks to Glen Orbik, William Joyce, and Alex Ross; 158 bottom, with special thanks to Bayer Advanced and Brian R. Pia; 158 right top; 159 center left/center/right, with special thanks to Moschino, Jimmy Choo, Betsey Johnson, Jorg Wallrabe, Lauren E. Miller, and Branding Iron Worldwide (photography by Mike Rosenthal); and Warner Home Video 157 left top.

Also: The Neal Peters Collection: Chadwick Pictures—15 left center, 22 left top; 155 right bottom; The Kobal Collection: Chadwick Pictures—15 left top; David Maxine: 18 left, 19 all but "Woggle Bug Parade"; The Oz Museum (Wamego, KS), Jim Ginavan and Tim Akers: 64 and 71; Everett Collection: 75, right top; The Woolsey Ackerman Collection: 137 center bottom, photographed by Pete Struve; The Wilmington *News Journal*: 155 right top; The Milwaukee *Journal Sentinel*: 155 right bottom; Carla Sellers: 156; Sean Barrett and Cindy Keller Potter: 157 right top; James T. Josephs: 157 bottom. (Additional appreciation to David, Carla, Jim, Tim, and documentarian extraordinaire Sean for answering the S.O.S. that went out to each of them.)

Others wished their contributions to be cited generally. Fred McFadden once again demonstrated customary selflessness and hospitality in opening his unparalleled Garland files. His love for the topic continues to enrich and enliven so many products, and his generosity benefits any and all who revel in such glowing history. Willard Carroll has offered boundless friendship, professional counsel, and limitless cooperation for nearly two decades. His devotion to (and collection of) all-things-Oz is world-class—as are his honesty, candor, and kindness. The International Wizard of Oz Club, Inc. (ozclub.org) and *The Baum Bugle* garner the warmest possible affection. For over fifty years, their publications and members have informed virtually any Oz or Baum project of merit; their contribution herein is immeasurable. Robert and Clare Baum have provided savvy and sustenance (Ozzy and otherwise) through a long and happy acquaintance. They're living proof that "Baum bonding" can expand to embrace general, genial, mutual pleasures all over the map. Woolsey Ackerman is ever-ready to jump into the fray in terms of sharing any and all helpful intelligence. He defines dedication—and support. Darkroom Unlimited (Rome, NY) provided expert scanning and photographic service at a moment's notice and with excellent professionalism and results.

We happily recognize the mother load of diverse information and material provided by *Variety* and The Hollywood *Reporter*; by Ned Comstock and The University of Southern California Cinematic Arts Library/The Arthur Freed Collection, pages 34 (left) and 52, The M-G-M Collection, 60; and by such past and present Oz-associates as Jane Albright, Roxanne Allen, Zach Allen, John Anderson, Kim Anderson, Alan Artz, Clark Balderson, Roger and Charlene Baum, Susie Boyt, Marilee Bradford, Robert Butts, Angelica Carpenter, Gregory Catsos, Marc Charbonnet, Carlos Colon, Larry Costlow, Steve Cox, Scott Cummings, Eric Decker, Kathleen DiScenna, Joshua Dudley, Sean Duffley, Michael Feinstein, Allan Fisch, Peter Fitzgerald, Bradley Flanagan, Phil Flynn, David and Douglas Greene, Michael Patrick Hearn, Mac Hudson, Peter Jones, David Kempel, Lt. Daniel Kinske U.S.N., Kregg Klein, David Krauss, Miles Krueger, Jane Lahr, Tony and Ruth Landini, Allen Lawson, Marc Lewis, George Makrinos and the *Ages of Oz* team, Leonard Maltin, Hugh Martin, Dorothy Maryott, Gita Morena, David Moyer, Robert Osborne, Karen Owens, Al Poland, Bronson Pinchot, Max Preeo, Ned Price, Justin G. Schiller, Sandi Shane, Michael Siewert, Dan Smith, Josh Smith, Joe Soriero, Charlotte Stevenson, Anne Suter, Charles Triplett, John Walther, John Van Camp, Dr. Sally Roesch Wagner (MatildaJoslynGage.org), Jerry Waters, Elaine Willingham, and Danny Windsor. And those Ozian and Garland friends, fans, coworkers, and/or collectors now with us in spirit: Bill Chapman, Dana Correll Dial, Lois January, Rob Roy MacVeigh, Ozma Baum Mantele, Dona Massin, Colonel James and Dorothy Tuttle Nitch, Scott Perry, Chris Sterling, Donna Stewart-Hardway, Bill Tuttle, Betty Welch, Wallace Worsley, and especially Fred M. Meyer and Dick Martin.

As re: the all-important corporate factor, we're more grateful than space permits us to say to: Warner Bros. Consumer Products: Kathleen Wallis, Carmella Johns, Adam Bodenstein, Ariella Roberts. Warner Bros. Publishing: Melanie Swartz, Victoria Selover, Elaine Piechowski. Warner Home Video: Jeff Baker, Michael Crawford, Ronnee Sass, Alexis Hemphill, Thomas Lukas, Valerie Lukban, Kim King, Jason Medley, Christine Monticelli, Amy Keioglian, Janet Keller, Julie Kelley, Noelle Sukow. Carl Samrock Public Relations: Carl Samrock, Carol Samrock, Karen Penhale, Marie Remelius. becker&mayer!: Kristin Mehus-Roe, Amy Wideman, Chris Campbell, Todd Bates, Samantha Caplan, Diane Ross, Josh Anderson, Kelly Notter.

George Feltenstein of Warner Home Video gets his own line! After more than two decades, his professional and personal devotion to quality and caring need no touting—but they could never get enough recognition.

In addition to the aforementioned Wamego, KS—and their "Oztoberfest" and exciting Oz Museum—we want to thank the other Oz festivals and their representatives or founders: Barbara Evans and Colleen Zimmer and their families ("OZ-Stravaganza!," Chittenango, NY); Jean Nelson ("Oz Fest," Chesterton, Indiana); and John Kelsch and Polly Edington ("Judy Garland Festival," Grand Rapids, Minnesota).

. . .

Ranse Ransone has proved to be friend in need and in deed throughout this arduous process. His tangible, physical presence and aid were equaled by his customary bazazz and energy; no one "knows his stuff" better than Ranse.

We offer joyous gratitude to Margaret Pellegrini for her jubilant company, wonderful memories, and instant willingness to contribute to this book. And we extend affection and appreciation to all the "little people" of Oz, who have been exemplary, trusting companions across many years. Some have gone on ahead; some continue to excite and enthrall all who meet them. In either category, here's to Munchkins (and Munchkins-by-Marriage) Mickey Carroll, Elizabeth Cottonaro, Anna Mitchell Cucksey, Lewis Croft, Ruth Duccini, Fern Formica, Nita Krebs, Emil and Marcella Kranzler, Jeane LeBarbera, Jerry and Elizabeth Maren, Nels Nelson, Olga Nardone, Meinhardt and Marie Raabe, Karl Slover, Mary Ellen St. Aubin, Clarence and Myrna Swensen, Betty Tanner, and Gus and Olive Wayne.

In terms of acquiring and sharing Oz and Garland-related information, fans should investigate the Oz Club, as mentioned above, as well as The Judy Garland Club (recognized and appreciated at its inception by "Dorothy" herself): judygarlandclub.org. For online gatherings of the enthusiastic, one can also revel in everythingoz@yahoo.com, Friends_In_OZ@yahoogroups.com, The Judy Garland Database: jgdb.com, thejudygarlandexperience@yahoogroups.com, thejudylist@googlegroups.com,and thejudyroom.com.

SPECIAL THANKS

From Jonathan Shirshekan: My specific appreciation to Rebecca Swift, for her help in obtaining previously unpublished production photography; to Jaclyn Arnold, Colby Linebarger, and Dawn Dyle, for defining "friendship" and for being cheerleaders throughout this project; to J--, for all the love and support; to Shelley Boren and Maria, Jessica, and Mark Shirshekan for the joy they bring into my life; and a very special thanks to Janet Pigioli, who first introduced to me the wonderful land of Oz.

From John Fricke: First gratitude to Jonathan Shirshekan—the next generation of Oz!—whose well-founded passion and indefatigable collecting and capacity to share made possible this book. It wouldn't have happened without him; he deserves maximum credit. Additional gratitude (for too many specifics to list): Russell Adams, John Burke, Dennis Cleveland, Rick Coombs, Eric Decker, Frank Degregorio, Denis Ferrara, Dan Fortune, Richard and Jan Glazier, Sam Gratton, Howard Hirsch, Jim Jensen, Richard Jordan, Ken Kleiber, Michael Kocher, Paul Larson, Joseph Luft, Lorna Luft (Colin Freeman and Jesse and Vanessa Richards), Kim Lundgreen, Peter Mac, Christian Matzanke, Patrick McCarty, Frank McCullough, Erick Neher, Sue LeBeau Parry and family, Les Perkins, The Reverend Dave Peters, Dave Rebella and Jim Downs, Josh Reynolds, Scott Roberts, Steve Sanders, John Schaefer, Mark Sendroff, Eric Shanower, Rick Skye, Donald F. Smith, Lynne Smith, James H. Spearo, Martha Wade Steketee, Ryan Sucher, John Walther, Ben Wetchler, Tom Wilhite, The Reverend Raymond Wood—and Barry, Marc, Marty, Gregg, and Scott. Especially: to Brent Phillips—"just (*just?!*) a perfect blendship"; and to family—my ever-encouraging, ebullient mom, Dottie; my copyeditor/ proofreader and cherished sister, Patty; my stagnastic brother and incomparable sister-in-law, Michael and Linda; and my extraordinary nieces, Erin, Noel, and Haley. Finally, with love—always to Christopher O'Brien, intermediary over the rainbow—and always and again to Kellen Lindblad . . . with heartfelt thanks to him for everything.

MGM
CHILDREN'S MATINEES
The Wizard of Oz
MGM's MIRACLE MUSICAL SHOW OF SHOWS!
COLOR BY TECHNICOLOR
Starring JUDY GARLAND · FRANK MORGAN · RAY BOLGER · BERT LAHR · JACK HALEY · BILLIE BURKE · MARGARET HAMILTON · CHARLEY GRAPEWIN and the MUNCHKINS · A VICTOR FLEMING PRODUCTION
Screen Play by NOEL LANGLEY, FLORENCE RYERSON and EDGAR ALLAN WOOLF · From the book by L. FRANK BAUM · Lyrics by E. Y. HARBURG · Music by HAROLD ARLEN · Directed by VICTOR FLEMING · Produced by MERVYN LeROY From MGM